MURDER ON THE ISLAND

DAISY WHITE

To Mum,

Happy Birthday!

hope you'll enjoy the
book,

Love from

Daisy xxx

02/06/2023

BLOODHOUND
— BOOKS —

Print ISBN 978-1-913942-27-4

For Rob, James and Ollie x

'You can go to heaven if you want to. I'd rather stay in Bermuda.'
Mark Twain (1910)

1

As the plane dropped a few feet, the ceiling creaked alarmingly. Chloe fixed her eyes firmly on the back of the seat in front, staring fixedly and slightly manically at the safety card poking out of the blue pocket.

The jolting and plunging continued for another thirty-five minutes, until they reached a blessedly calm stretch of air, and the seat belt sign pinged off. The captain announced they would be landing in approximately one hour.

Chloe staggered up the aisle to the toilets, tidying her long blonde hair as best she could in the smeared mirror. Her round, pale, still-slightly-terrified face stared back. In the harsh lighting of the aircraft toilet she looked much older than her fifty years. Wrinkles that she had always laughingly called smile lines had etched deeper in the last few months, and that was definitely a triple chin lurking.

The big birthday had been celebrated with both divorce and redundancy. Not a great way to start what she had told herself firmly were her middle years. There had been too much sadness, too much loss recently, and the desire to escape had been overwhelming.

Which was why, although she was desperately sad to hear her grandmother had passed away, the unexpected inheritance felt like a gift from the heavens.

Although not blood relatives, her grandfather's second wife, Dre, had raised her on the island of Bermuda until she was seven. Chloe's mother, Natalia, by then working in London for a multi-national real estate company, had remarried and sent for her daughter. Busy with her career, and a string of lovers as well as a new husband, Natalia had promptly dispatched her only daughter to boarding school.

Return visits to the island had been few, and by the time Chloe was old enough to travel on her own, she felt awkward about contacting Dre. Her grandfather had moved on to his fourth wife. Too much time seemed to have passed, and they weren't really even relatives anymore... So she left it at cards on birthdays and Christmas.

But now it was different. Hair now neatly plaited (the grey strands mingling with the blonde of her younger years), lipstick applied, Chloe returned to her seat and ordered a Bloody Mary. She had made the momentous decision to return to the island. There was nothing for her in the UK. Her mother was herself twice divorced, retired and living in the US. She was still as unmaternal as ever. Chloe had no children of her own. It hadn't really ever factored into her life. Mark, her ex-husband, hadn't wanted children, and although Chloe was a godmother three times over, and adored her friends' babies, she had never felt her own biological clock ticking.

Her friends, the few that were left after her marriage breakdown, would definitely come and visit. Her godchildren, growing up fast, were delighted she was moving to such an auspicious destination. She loved them dearly, and was amused and pleased that they regarded her new adventure with such enthusiasm.

She smiled, recalling her best friend, Alexa's reaction to the news. '*Hell, Chlo, you try and stop me coming to that paradise island! I might come and live permanently in your spare room.*'

As the plane finally touched down, Chloe felt a surge of excitement override her fears. She was coming home, and she was shocked at how right it suddenly felt. Perhaps this was what had been missing for all these years. Her childhood had set her on a different course, dictated by her mother, then by her career, and later by Mark. But perhaps now she could take control, change her life and start over.

The other passengers were already searching for their belongings, opening the overhead lockers, and passing heavier bags. The chatter of tourists, business travellers and those returning home, mixed with the wail of a baby.

After queuing impatiently, Chloe stepped out of the plane and the hot air swirled around her. The deep blue of the sky, the turquoise water beyond the runway, the smells of salt, spice and aircraft fuel stirred her memory. After the faded grey skies and icy rain of London this was incredible. Intoxicating. She almost laughed out loud.

The small airport wasn't crowded and Chloe managed to pass through immigration without any problems. It was strange joining the Bermuda resident's line, rather than going through the tourist channel. She still didn't feel she had a right to do that, but her papers now stated otherwise.

She pushed her trolley, loaded with cases, hesitantly out of the glass doors, welcoming another blast of warm air, tasting salt on her lips.

The taxi driver beamed at her, his hat pushed back on top of his head, face full of wrinkles with shrewd brown eyes that sparkled with interest. 'Where do you want to go?'

'Beachside Riding Stables? It's off the South Road, in Warwick?' She spoke quickly, nervously, but was reassured by his friendly response.

'I know it! That Dre's old place, and you must be her granddaughter. She used to talk about you a lot. Welcome to Bermuda. I'm Peter.'

'You know about me? I mean... Sorry, I'm Chloe.' She belatedly remembered her manners, as he gathered her cases and threw them single-handedly into the boot. In London, taxi drivers didn't know your name, and nobody hailed you in the street. Even eye contact marked you out as a weirdo. This would take some getting used to, she thought.

But it fanned the warm spark of happiness that was already burning merrily in her chest. Her caring, busy nature had been flattened over the years; by a disappointing marriage, by lack of direction. Yet here in the warmth, enjoying Peter's friendly conversation, she found herself responding in kind. 'How lovely to meet you!' Her mouth stretched into a grin. Home, she was home. She hadn't expected to feel quite so emotional. Quite so happy.

'Of course I know about you... I remember you from when you were a kid too, but I bet it's too far back for you to recognise me. Dre and I have been friends for years. I was sad to see her go.' His expression changed, and he shrugged. 'Antoine's been looking after the place since your grandmother died. He's a good boy.'

Chloe slipped into the passenger seat, winding down the window, unable to take her eyes off the tantalising gleam of the sea. There was a slash of white sand curving around the volcanic rock of a little bay. 'Yes, the lawyers mentioned she had someone working for her.'

'You haven't been to visit for a while, have you? I remember Dre always said her family was all busy working in London and the US... What are you going to do with the place? You like horses?' He turned the radio down, and drove slowly across the causeway, joining the queue of vehicles at the roundabout.

Chloe was so busy absorbing the hit of colour, the smells of dust and spice, she found the conversation hard to follow. 'I lived here until I was seven, as you know, and I visited a couple of times as a teenager.' Even as she said the words, regret and a fair bit of guilt wormed up inside her stomach. Her family situation had always been odd, distant even, but she should have come back sooner, should have re-established her relationship with Dre in her later years. She changed the subject quickly. 'Do you live locally?'

'Seventy-two years I've lived on this island, and for almost all of them I've had a house in Devonshire Parish.'

Chloe smiled at him. She remembered that Bermuda was divided into nine parishes, stretching across the island from St George's in the east, to Sandys right down on the west end.

As a child she had learned about the history of Bermuda, chanting the names of each parish in a sun-drenched classroom. History had always been a bit of a secret passion in her adult years. She was fascinated by ancient buildings, imagining the people who had built them, fought for them, lived and died in them...

Alexa loved to tell the tale of how she and Chloe went to a revival festival, where the tea dance was held in a historic building, and halfway through the dancing Chloe went missing. The lure of the ancient cobweb-encrusted rooms meant she had wandered off to explore, oblivious to the free cocktails and the colourful whirl of dancers.

Chloe grinned to herself. She thought there might be quite a lot of scope to explore this secret passion of hers in Bermuda; an island with a fascinating history and so many ancient buildings.

The taxi driver continued to fill her in on local gossip, mentioning a diner for breakfast if she got bored of home-cooking, a few pubs, and the upcoming Kite Festival ahead of Easter weekend. '...And you've got a good market and petrol station within walking distance. Not to mention Stefan's garden centre. He's doing some lovely spring freesias at the moment. Dre was a regular. Tell him who you are and he'll probably give you a discount!'

Chloe half-listened, allowing his pleasant chat to wash over her, but her attention was now focused on the scenes from her window. She drank them in almost greedily.

The pastel-coloured houses were set neatly alongside the road, climbing up the terraces. Occasionally she caught a quick glimpse of occupants going about their business, hurrying along the pavements with bags of shopping, or pausing to chat at the roadside. It made Chloe wonder what colour her new home would be. Each building had the obligatory white roof, where rainwater was caught and used for everything from washing to drinking.

She had never lived at Beachside Stables, having spent her early Bermudian childhood in an apartment in the city of Hamilton. Dre had still been living in Hamilton when Chloe visited at thirteen and fifteen. There had been no photographs exchanged in those Christmas and birthday cards and Dre didn't do email or social media.

Each side of the road was now crammed with lush green plants, bell-shaped flowers in dark purple and scarlet, a sky-blue church high on a hill. A field made a splash of brown, with lines of pale green indicating a crop. And everywhere, the vibrant glimpses of that turquoise sea, with strips of white sand gently cupping the water.

The taxi passed through Paget and entered Warwick Parish. Chloe had caught sight of signs to Elbow Beach and Warwick Long Bay and was almost shivering with excitement and anticipation. She thought Peter might find it weird if she bounced up and down on her seat like a kid on a seaside trip, but that was exactly what she felt like doing.

'It's just along this track,' the taxi driver announced at last, bumping over potholes and up a steep hill.

Chloe leaned forward eagerly, excitement making her feel distinctly nauseous, and nerves jangling at the first sight of her new home. A large white-painted sign announced Beachside Stables, and as they rounded a corner a tangerine-coloured house appeared behind the shrubs.

She climbed awkwardly out of the taxi, breathing in great lungfuls of sea air, and nearly fell over a cockerel that strutted out of the hedge. It gave a squawk of annoyance, and rushed off up the dusty path.

Peter unloaded her cases, and pressed his business card into her hand. 'Don't forget, you call me if you need any help. One of my boys runs a delivery service so if you need any help when your bigger stuff gets shipped out, he can bring it down to you.' He beamed at Chloe again. 'And welcome home to Bermuda.'

2

After a couple of days of complete confusion, Chloe began to settle into her new home. Although the outside was neat, with the orange paint fresh on the walls, and the white roof clean and free from lichens, the inside had been a shock; sad and dusty with a few dead houseplants decorating the window ledges.

Chloe began to get used to shooing a few hens and the ever-present cockerel from the path before she could get into her front door, and to waking up to blue skies and a stiff Atlantic breeze. She woke up with the birds, instead of jerking into consciousness at the bleep of her alarm clock, and went to sleep when the velvety darkness crept across the sea.

One of her new neighbours, she thought it was Ailsa, but she was having trouble keeping track of all their names, had left her a parcel of home-made Bermudian fishcakes yesterday, a delicacy she remembered from childhood.

The kindness and welcome had reduced her to tears on a number of occasions but she was careful to keep her sadness indoors. Having not seen Dre for years, it was strange and lovely to find her everywhere in this neglected, dusty house. In those first few days, Chloe spent time with her grandmother, allowing her childhood memories to swirl around her mind, finally acknowledging the wonderful days as a carefree kid on the island.

There was still a lot of guilt that she hadn't managed to come back whilst Dre was still alive, ailing and possibly in need of family, but her father had discouraged any contact, and her mother, Natalia, didn't like to be reminded of her ex-spouse's 'other family members' as she called them disdainfully.

Chloe thought, with hindsight, that although her mother had never displayed any affection towards her daughter, she had always been jealous of anyone else who did. She had come to terms with this long ago, but that didn't mean it didn't still sting occasionally.

Tucked away, but niggling at her conscience, was the thought that she should visit her grandmother's grave, to pay her respects, but something in her shied away from this. She didn't want to see a gravestone on a hill, she wanted to keep Dre with her in this house and garden. Her grandmother had no other family on the island, so there would be nobody to offend if she didn't take this, to her mind, very final step.

In a box under the dressing table, Chloe discovered Dre's old perfume bottles, a collection of antique wooden tobacco boxes she remembered from the Hamilton apartment, and a precious book of handwritten recipes. She cleaned the whole house, leaving beautiful framed prints of Bermuda, but carefully packing away delicate china ornaments that weren't to her taste.

One wonderful find was a complete set of Bermuda postage stamps featuring the nine parishes and their coats of arms. The set was dated 1985, and slipped inside a plastic wallet. Chloe, lost in the beauty of the artwork, spent a long time studying them, and finally decided to frame the whole set and hang the result in her kitchen.

Now, four days after she had arrived, sparkling white blinds, and white cotton curtains framed the shining window glass, and the furniture was cleared down to Chloe's preferred minimalistic state. Heirlooms such as the spectacular cedarwood chest, the shell collection nestling on the bathroom window ledge, a large scrubbed kitchen table, and an ornate wrought-iron bed in the spare room, would fit beautifully with her own treasured pieces from London.

Chloe had so far only explored the immediate perimeter of her land, and was slightly overwhelmed. In fact, she secretly wondered how on earth she was going to manage. It was like acquiring a whole new family, she thought. Outdoors, the efficient and stunningly-attractive Antoine, kept an immaculate stable yard. It was home to six horses, a couple of goats and a whole load more chickens.

There was a small, untidy square of back garden, two steeply sloping green paddocks for the animals, a big storage shed and the tack room, not to mention a patch of scrubby grass outside her front door which was littered with fragments of broken flowerpots.

It was a shocking contrast to her small London flat, where the only greenery had been several pot plants on the balcony. After the initial burst of energy, the colours and heat made her want to laze around, and do nothing but walk from her little garden to the beach and back, so Chloe indulged herself as she hadn't done for years.

She found stacks of old photograph albums inside the sweet-smelling cedar chest, and spent an evening reminiscing, smiling through her tears at old family pictures, of Dre riding, her mum sailing, of herself in her Bermudian school uniform. For the first time in ages, the emptiness inside seemed to be filled, and the guilt receded slightly.

If a dark thought, or flicker of sadness entered her mind, she only had to look out of her window at the blue sky, or wander out into the night and hear the soft crash of waves on the beach below.

The warmth encouraged her to ditch her usual jumpers and heavy cord trousers, and she found herself picking out colourful shirts, cotton shorts and pretty flowery summer dresses. Instead of worrying about her weight and the rolls around her middle, she enjoyed the sun's warmth on her bare skin, and celebrated the fact she was both healthy, and finally something approaching happy.

The mirror, previously a dreaded instrument of torture, now showed her a pretty woman; round, soft and smiling, her blue eyes sparkling with life and interest. Maybe, Chloe thought, as she hummed to herself, picking up discarded clothes ready to donate to a charity shop, maybe the woman in the mirror had been there all along, she just hadn't recognised her.

After successfully sorting out the house and arranging her newly arrived possessions, it was time to tackle the mound of paperwork, which was growing at an alarming rate on her new office desk.

There were big decisions to be made regarding the riding stables, the animals, and another pile of legal papers, this time regarding her new residency and her divorce, which were stacked on one corner of the kitchen table.

Vowing to attack both piles later today, she sorted the paperwork neatly in order of priority. Clearly, she needed to provide herself with some sort of income, so the faded brown folders, labelled *Beachside Stables* in Dre's confident blue scrawl, would have to come first. Not only was there her own livelihood to consider, there was also Antoine, not to mention the animals, who would depend on her to get things sorted out.

Chloe wandered out of the back door, feeling the heat instantly, revelling in it, smiling at the vivid tangle of shrubs and flowers that lined her lawn. The grass was some sort of native large-leaved stuff, almost like plastic to touch and very bright green. It was neatly trimmed along the edges but the flower beds were a wild mix of little purple flowers she thought might be Bermudiana, and some huge red-and-yellow lilies.

A wrought-iron gate led out to the yard, where the white-painted stables were smothered in purple bougainvillea. She greeted each of the animals in turn, breaking up carrots for the horses and goats.

'Morning, Mrs C!' Antoine called from the water tap, where he was scrubbing buckets. 'Did you want me for something?'

'Morning, Antoine.' She smiled at him, squinting into the sun. She had asked him repeatedly to just call her Chloe, but he appeared to be more taken with Mrs C. It could be worse. 'I've finished sorting the house now, so I thought I'd spend a couple of weeks just... you know, sorting out all the paperwork and exploring the area. I might walk along the Railway Trail or something today.'

'You could take one of the horses out? Then you could go down the Railway Trail or just hack along one of the rides along the cliffs,' Antoine suggested, disappearing with a full water bucket and reappearing from behind the storage shed with a wheelbarrow load of fresh straw.

'I haven't ridden for years,' Chloe told him, laughing. 'Maybe I should just ease myself back into it gradually?'

He was a sweet boy, she thought, and from what she had seen obviously adored the horses. In his early twenties, he had already told her he lived in Somerset Parish, played for the

Somerset Trojans football team, and had a girlfriend, Louisa, who worked at Dockyard whilst she studied graphic design.

'Go on, you'll be fine! I'll tack up Goldie. She's so chilled out she should be drinking rum on the beach.' He smiled. 'Stay out as long as you want, we've only got one booking today.'

Accepting the challenge with some trepidation, she retraced her steps and went indoors to get changed. Twenty minutes later, Chloe, in jeans and pink shirt, climbed inelegantly aboard a chunky palomino mare. The saddle and bridle were Western style and she sank comfortably into the soft leather.

'Go along the lower trail, it eventually takes you across to Warwick Long Bay, and you can go as far as you like. You can't get lost on there and there's a decent track. Just make sure you stay off the public beaches at this time of day.'

The sun was hot, but further along the coastal path there was a strong breeze to keep horse and rider cool. Chloe meandered along, enjoying the gentle thump of Goldie's hooves on sand, the chirrup of a thousand unknown birds and insects, and the distant murmur of the sea. She could still ride! Well, sort of. Luckily there was nobody to see her firmly gripping Goldie's mane with one hand. She suspected anything faster than a trot might present problems until she got used to the exercise again, but this was heavenly.

Another little spark of happiness made her catch her breath. Her fiftieth birthday earlier this year, the muted celebration, the row at the restaurant, and Mark's declaration that he was moving out, all seemed far away. It was beginning to feel like all that had happened to another person, in another life. Her arms were already tanning a gentle golden brown, and her muscles, moving easily in time with the horse's stride, felt sure and strong.

What had Mark said? Oh yes, '*I do love you in a way, Chloe, but I feel like you've changed so much. You're tired all the time, and no fun to be around. I'm not being mean, but you've put on weight and you're just not the same woman I married. We never do anything exciting, and I feel like I'm wasting my life.'*

The cruelty of his words had taken her breath away and she had felt so wounded that for days after he packed up and left, she stayed in the flat alone, unable to function. But now, she was discovering perhaps she wasn't the burnt-out overweight wreck he had taken her for. Her new neighbours didn't care what she looked like, as long as she was friendly and up for a gossip, and she still had her friends back home, including darling Alexa, who constantly checked in via social media and email.

She had seen a flyer for a local history group, down in the supermarket, and another in the garden centre advertising a yoga class. That would have to wait until she was more organised, of course, but suddenly, to her quiet satisfaction, there were far more possibilities than she had previously hoped for.

What had Antoine said? Just one booking today. Surely with six horses to feed and care for, not to mention his wages, the stables should be buzzing with clients. She resolved to take a careful look at those brown folders. Could she run a riding stables? She certainly couldn't let everyone down when they had been so welcoming.

That was another thing. She could hardly stand and watch, like some kind of lady of the manor, while Antoine did all the hard work. As a teenager at boarding school, she had spent long holidays with pony-owning friends and could easily take on many of the associated tasks. Mucking out, tack cleaning and general looking after horses, she vaguely remembered, was very satisfying.

The horse's stride was soothing and the heat soporific. Chloe rode further along the trail, still lost in thought. The sandy trail took her along a clifftop path, before plunging down into tangled trees and dense shrubbery towards the beach.

There was a derelict building higher up on the trail to her right, and she tugged the horse to a halt, peering through the twisted trunks and vines. Yes, it was the remains of a long, low house set in an L shape. The front door was all peeling blue paint, and the roof looked like it had caved in on one side. But it had clearly been an impressive residence once.

Stone walls and a large mossy driveway surrounded the wreck, and although most of the windows were boarded up, it looked as though the three at the front of the house were clear.

Staring at the cracked windowpanes, she almost fancied she could see movement. A quick flit of passing shadows, maybe. She shivered.

Despite a frisson of fear, the familiar urge to explore was still there. She couldn't really explain it, except to say that she was very nosy, but it was more than that. The smell, the feel of old buildings, and the echoes of the people who had lived in them was just plain fascinating, touching her imagination, taking hold of her emotions. If time travel had been invented, Chloe would have been first in the queue. Just for little trips back and forth, though, she thought, amusement bubbling up until she laughed out loud.

It had driven Mark crazy when they took road trips. She would be twisting in her seat at the sight of derelict railway stations, warehouses, farm buildings, as well as the usual castles and historic houses. Chloe had soon learnt to keep her nosiness hidden from her husband.

He never saw anything but the obvious. To begin with she had fallen for his dynamic personality, his good looks and confidence. Now she saw he was just rude and arrogant. There wasn't anything deliberately nasty about him, it was just that he and Chloe had nothing in common. It was a miracle they had plodded on together for as long as they had.

Leaving the house, which looked a lot like a dreamy stage piece from *Sleeping Beauty*, in its tangle of intertwined tree trunks and silver vines, she kicked the mare onward. Now the trail descended steeply, and Chloe ducked under a low bough, her hair brushing the horse's neck. The overhanging branches grew more densely here, blocking out all but bars of flickering sunlight.

Goldie saw it before she did, propping to a halt, and nearly tumbling Chloe from the saddle. Jolted from her daydreams, she struggled back off the horse's neck where she had ended up, murmuring soothing words. But Goldie was trembling and staring at something lying in the bushes. Chloe could see what looked like a bundle of clothing. There were dark red-and-brown stains on the white sand.

She dismounted, her own legs trembling. Reluctantly, pulling the reins to make the horse follow her, she approached. Heart thumping, she could feel sweat dripping down her face. It wasn't a load of old clothes, it was a body.

One hand was outstretched, palm up as though pleading, the other hidden by the torso. He was on his side, legs carelessly crossed, face bare but bloody, and eyes mercifully shut. If it hadn't been for the blood, he might have been sleeping. The smell of sour blood and sense of violent death almost made her retch.

Chloe forced herself to bend down, touching his cheek, glancing hopefully at his chest for any breathing. There were no signs of life and although the skin was warm from the heat of the day, the hand she tentatively tugged was rigid. Half-hidden by the pose, giving no further doubt as to his condition, was a bloody wound. The man had been stabbed in the chest. There were slash marks on his hands and arms. Perhaps he had tried to defend himself?

As she looked more closely at his bloody face, she noticed something that made her freeze in horror. As if the violence wasn't bad enough, it was clear the killer had carved three very distinct shapes in the victim's forehead; a triangle and two squares.

What kind of crazed murderer would do that? Chloe blinked, half wondering if her imagination had traced the shapes from the bloodstains, but no, the lines were blurred but distinct.

As she looked more closely at the vegetation surrounding him she could see there was a lot of blood. Spatters across the silver tree trunks and a pool of dark, dried redness under the body. Goldie had pulled back to the far reach of her reins, nostrils wide, snorting in horror.

'Oh hell!' Chloe inched backwards, eyes darting around the jungle, back up the trail. Was the murderer still around? The blood wasn't fresh, but suddenly the shadows were threatening, and every twig crack was a footfall. She was shaking so much it took several attempts to mount the horse, but she finally managed it by clambering onto a fallen tree trunk.

Long-disused muscles aching, she pushed the horse into a trot, then canter, clinging half to her mane, half to the saddle, as they headed back to the stable yard at a brisk pace.

Antoine had taken the booked ride out as she arrived back, jumping off the sweating horse and struggling to stand up on shaking legs. She shoved Goldie into her stable and slammed the half-door shut. Rushing across the yard she caught her thumb on the iron gate, tore her nail and cursed. Nearing the house she ran straight into a tall man, who was rounding the corner. '*Oh!*'

'Sorry, I didn't mean to scare... Hey, are you okay?' The man steadied her by the elbows, peering at her obviously distraught face.

'I...' She was gasping for breath now. 'There's a dead body on the trail-path down towards the beach. A man. He's been murdered. I could see lots of blood and...'

'A body?' The man's face blanched and his eyes widened. But despite the obvious shock he was reaching for his mobile phone, punching out numbers. 'It's okay. I'll ring the police. I take it you haven't already done that?'

'No! I haven't organised a new phone yet. Mine died and I couldn't remember if it was 911 or 999... It doesn't matter.' Chloe was trying to get a hold of herself, to calm her racing heart and be sensible. She heard the man asking for the Bermuda Police Service, and clutched at the trunk of the spice tree, trying to steady her wobbly legs.

'Right, that's all done. They're on their way, and they'll come here first so you can give them directions.'

'Okay. Thank you.' Chloe was trying to gather her thoughts, still feeling her heart pounding, her palms sweaty. There was nothing more she could do for that poor, poor man but wait for the police. She leant against the wall, fighting the wave of dizziness that threatened to overwhelm her.

'Are you okay? Do you need to sit down?' The stranger watched anxiously as she struggled to compose herself.

The feeling passed, leaving her with wobbly legs but nothing worse. 'Sorry, I'm fine, honestly. It must be the shock or something... Thank you so much...'

'You look like you could do with an iced drink. Why don't we go inside and wait?' the man suggested, watching her carefully.

Perhaps he was still worried she was about to faint, Chloe thought. He had a slight accent; European, she thought, possibly Spanish? Normally she wouldn't have invited a stranger into her home, but under the circumstances, she supposed he seemed fairly trustworthy. Her city girl suspicion seemed at odds with the island friendliness she had met in Bermuda.

Her new friend was smiling now, and after that first initial shock, he had certainly been very helpful. Should she trust him? Chloe wondered, still dithering about letting a total stranger into her home. On the other hand, the police would be here soon, bright sunlight filled the garden, and she had neighbours within earshot. There was no reason to be so suspicious, she reasoned to herself.

He was tall and slim, with dark hair and olive skin, dressed in casual trousers and a green striped shirt. Was that some sort of military pin on his tie? Even in her shock she found herself noting it with interest. It looked like the insignia of the Royal Navy. 'We can go through the back door.' She ushered him down the path.

He trod carefully ahead of her towards her house, deck shoes crunching on the gravel. His accent was European, but his English was perfect. 'Sorry, I haven't introduced myself, have I? I'm Jonas Aliente, and you must be Chloe? I actually popped over to see if you would consider selling me your house.'

3

Jonas stayed with her, solicitously pouring iced orange juice from a jug in her fridge. As news spread, she felt glad of his calm presence, as he chatted to the neighbours who appeared at the door, occasionally shooting her a concerned glance.

The police inspector from the Serious Crimes Unit, tall and capable-looking, took a team of uniformed officers down the track to investigate the body, and Chloe sat huddled at her kitchen table, limp as a rag doll. She couldn't stop shaking, and felt freezing cold despite the fleece she had donned. The dead man's face was burned onto her memory, and she could still see in her mind's eye, his twisted body lying on the side of the track...

Ailsa, clearly sensing gossip, and aiming for the centre of the action, marched in the open back door, hugged Chloe and made her a cup of tea, 'Because you need something warm, darling,' then she settled down at the table, obviously intending to be right at the heart of the action.

Chloe cleared her throat, watching another police vehicle, blue lights flashing, jolting past on the track that led to the body.

'Jonas, you don't have to stay. It was very kind of you to call the police for me, and everything, but you don't need to babysit me.' She flushed, suddenly aware that her face was sweaty and her hair tangled from the wind. Not that anything should matter, she told herself sternly, compared to that poor man lying in the shrubs, but Jonas was so very sleek and unruffled, with his patrician good looks and immaculate clothing.

Jonas shrugged, sipping his own glass of juice. 'I'm happy to stay. I have already cancelled my next meeting. But if you would prefer, I can go?'

Ailsa was glaring at him, but Chloe sighed. 'It's just that you said something about buying my house, and I'm not really in any fit state to discuss anything at the moment. This is such a shock, and that poor, poor man. I wonder who he was and what happened?'

'Are you selling your place?' Ailsa asked Chloe quickly, sharp chin jutting out aggressively, ignoring Jonas.

'No...' Chloe rubbed a hand across her forehead. 'No, I'm not but...'

'Don't even think about it now.' Jonas smiled. 'I'm known for my bad timing, but this is crazy, even for me.' His expression changed and he frowned. 'It is a terrible thing, for you to find a dead man. Are you sure you didn't recognise him? I mean, he's not a neighbour or anything?'

'No, I don't think so, but then I haven't been living here long enough to get to know everyone in the area. I was horribly shocked and desperate to call the police so I didn't look to see if he had a wallet or anything...' Chloe liked him better now he was expressing more emotion. Of course it had been nice to have someone who was calm and cool to lean on for a while, but his icy control made her feel all the more inadequate as she struggled to get a hold of her emotions. Perhaps he was just one of those people who was terribly good in a crisis.

He smiled reassuringly at her. 'I feel like I might be able to help when the police get back to interview you, so I'm happy to stay.'

'Are you one of the Bartlett Apartments developers?' Ailsa asked him suddenly, her mouth pursed with apparent disapproval.

'In a way... I only joined recently, and as one of the investors, so not an actual developer myself,' Jonas said warily. 'I have a gallery in Dockyard, and I've been spending more time in Bermuda so...'

Ailsa cut across his explanations. 'Well you get back and tell them none of us want to sell, and they can stop bothering us or I'll be sending the police round to *them*, next.'

'I'm sorry, I had no idea...' Confusion flickered across Jonas' face. 'I had no idea you'd already been approached.'

'You want to get your facts straight,' Ailsa told him. 'We've been hassled for the last two years. Dre told them no, straight out, but they just kept upping the offer. Money isn't everything, and it isn't easy to get a place of your own round here.' She glared at him, eyes narrowed, lips still pursed with disapproval.

Jonas picked up his suit jacket and moved towards the door, briefly dropping a hand on Chloe's shoulder. 'I'm very sorry for what happened, Chloe, and Ailsa, I had no idea everyone had already been approached for land sales. Again, I apologise. I'll leave you in peace, but here's my card in case you need to contact me.'

Ailsa watched him walk out of the door, his demeanour still cool and calm. Turning back to her neighbour, her face was alive with emotion, she said fiercely, 'Another bloodsucker. Don't worry, Chloe, we've got your back. You let me know if he comes round again and I'll sort him out. We're not having any developers take our land!'

Her neighbour must be well into her seventies, and she was

barely five feet tall, but her black eyes were sharp and bright as a bird's. As an ally she was clearly formidable and Chloe thought she wouldn't like her as an enemy.

'It's true, and I'm sure Dre wouldn't have liked to see any of this line of coast developed either.' She pursed her lips, clearly inviting further comment.

But Chloe, unable to drag her mind away from the murdered man, merely smiled fondly at her. Her sudden defensiveness of their homes was somehow endearing, but she made a note to check on the development at a later date. She didn't want anything to potentially threaten her new-found home.

A clatter of hooves made her turn back to the window. Antoine arrived back with his ride. She was still struggling with that floating, nauseous feeling that goes with shock. That poor man with all the blood... She hardly noticed that Jonas had dropped his business card in the wooden box by her (currently disconnected) telephone. 'Sorry, Ailsa, but I need to go out and speak to Antoine... I've just remembered I left Goldie in her stable with her saddle and bridle still on.'

'Of course. You go and do what you need to. I'll see myself out later. I expect the police officers will want drinks when they come back up to interview you, so I'll get everything organised. There are all those constables, and the inspector from the Serious Crime Unit, not to mention those others that came with him...'

'Thank you but please don't worry. I can manage, honestly. Shall I pop over later and we can have a chat?' Chloe was exhausted suddenly, her nerves still jangling at the thought of speaking to the police. There was bound to be an interview, perhaps even down at the station. In Devonshire Parish maybe? She couldn't remember where the nearest police station was, but clearly a murder would be treated with the utmost importance.

'If you're sure...' Ailsa was transparently reluctant to leave such a prime spot, but good manners demanded it. 'I'll do some scones for later then – proper ones with some early raspberries in.'

Chloe was already halfway up the garden path, pursued by half a dozen chickens. 'See you later, and thank you again, Ailsa.'

Antoine, his handsome face serious, was talking to a man in uniform next to the wooden gate that led to the trail. A blue minibus was waiting on the drive to ferry the guests back to their hotel.

'Chloe! Josonne says you found a dead man!' Antoine hurried towards her, his arms full of tack. The minibus driver was shepherding the guests back to his vehicle.

Obviously intrigued by the drama, the tourists weren't moving very fast. Several were taking photos of the police vehicles and the first responders. Bermuda Fire and Rescue had also sent a crew, and their truck was parked near the top of the sandy path.

'Who's Josonne?' she said vaguely. 'I did. Oh God, it was so awful, and Goldie was so good to bring me home, but then I left her in her stable with all her tack on and just ran. I realised I didn't have a phone and...' Tears threatened and Chloe, suddenly aware of her attentive audience, stopped talking.

'Hey, don't worry. Goldie's fine. I've rubbed her down and given her a drink. Are you okay? Why don't you go back inside?' Antoine suggested, peering anxiously at her. The other young man had followed him, and Chloe saw he wore the smart uniform of Bermuda Fire and Rescue.

She sniffed, and wiped her tears away with the back of her hand, while both men watched with concern. 'I'm fine, honestly. Probably just shock,' she managed, smiling weakly at them.

'So very lucky we didn't go down that way.' A tall athletic

woman dressed in what looked like pink beach pyjamas, patted Chloe's shoulder. 'Such a horrible thing to happen, sweetie, but don't worry, the police are here now. We saw another officer go down there just nearby, didn't we, Noah?' She nudged her husband.

Her soft American accent and genuine concern made Chloe tear up again, but she smiled awkwardly, managing to control her emotions.

Noah, who clearly hadn't applied enough sunscreen and was turning a raw red around his nose and cheekbones, patted Chloe on the arm. 'The main thing is to let the emergency services get on with their job.'

'Noah was with the NYPD before he retired,' the wife said, 'and once you've been in law enforcement, you stay part of the family.'

Chloe could certainly see the stocky man as part of the police force. He had a calmness that was totally different to Jonas' icy charm. This man had an air of having seen battle and dealt with the casualties. He was now quietly urging his fellow tourists towards the waiting bus.

'Bus is ready here, guys, if you want to move right along. Let's get ourselves out the way and let these people do their job.'

The bus driver was getting impatient, and waved his thanks to the retired cop. The door finally slammed behind them, and navigated round the emergency vehicles before bumping away down the drive.

'Josonne is my cousin. I told him all about you,' Antoine explained, finally introducing the man standing with him. 'He's with the Bermuda Fire and Rescue Service, as you can see.'

Josonne nodded and smiled at Chloe. Like his cousin, his good looks were further highlighted by a large dollop of genuine charm. 'The police will want to ask you some questions, I'm afraid, Mrs C. Do you feel up to talking now?'

Chloe glared at Antoine for passing on the '*Mrs C*' thing, but was feeling too weak and shaken to correct Josonne. 'Why are you here though? I mean, sorry but I thought the BFRS attended fires.'

'We do, but we also had a report come in that a vehicle had come off the road, and this address was given.'

Chloe stared at him, confused. 'But there hasn't been a traffic accident. I mean, I never saw anything...'

Josonne nodded. 'Well we responded to that call, and arrived around the same time as the police. All 911 calls go straight to police dispatch and they send out the appropriate service. Our call came in ten minutes before the report of a body found. BFRS provides emergency medical response as well, so we stuck around in case we could help.'

A crowd of onlookers followed the police inspector up the hill. He smiled at Chloe and exchanged a few quick words with Josonne, who nodded soberly, smile vanishing, his face now etched with worry.

'I'm Inspector Finn Harlow. You must be Mrs Canton. I'm sorry you haven't had a great welcome back to Bermuda. Can we go inside and have a chat?' He was a big man, with dark-brown eyes, and close-shaven grey hair. With his size and athleticism, he reminded Chloe of a rugby player. His dark skin showed a sheen of sweat from the climb up the trail.

But he had an easy, polite manner which subconsciously soothed her nerves. She was soon explaining how she came to find the body, and he was nodding and taking notes. From time to time his colleagues would peer around the door, and he would gently excuse himself, before returning to her interview.

'Did you see anyone else on the trail this morning? Any walkers, or vehicles at this end?' the Inspector prodded.

Chloe shook her head. 'No... I did stop to look at a derelict building on the trail just before I found... him. I thought I might have seen a shadow at the window, but it would have been impossible to say if it was actually a person, or just a trick of the light.'

'Ahh yes, Tranquility House. It used to be the home of a romance writer. Serena Gibbons?' He raised an eyebrow, but Chloe shook her head again. 'She achieved moderate fame, mostly in the US, I believe.'

'What happened to her?' Chloe asked, interested in spite of herself.

'Oh, she used the island as a writing retreat, but she died in 1993, and the estate has been derelict ever since. We'll take a look at the house all the same.'

Another officer, who took careful notes throughout, was politely introduced, but Chloe instantly forgot his name. She was very grateful that she hadn't been taken down to the police station, and was instead able to sit in her own kitchen and relay what had happened.

'Do you know who he was? The dead man, I mean,' Chloe asked finally, when she had contributed all she could.

'We do. His name was Matthew Georgias. He was twenty-four and worked as an artist. There are a great many creatives on the island, and many galleries. It seems to be something in the air. Anyway, Matthew was part of a selection of up-and-coming artists who are currently exhibiting at the new art gallery in Clocktower Mall.'

He gave her an enquiring look, and Chloe shook her head. 'I know the mall, but I haven't had a chance to get up to Dockyard yet. In fact, I'd just decided to spend a couple of weeks playing tourist and revisiting all the places I remember. Does Matthew have family?'

'His parents live in Minnesota and have been notified. This is not the sort of thing that happens regularly in Bermuda. Of course there is crime, as there is everywhere in the world, but this type of violent incident isn't common. In fact, last year we had no murders on the island at all.'

He was trying to reassure her, and she managed to smile back. 'Thank you. I... Can I ask you something about the body?'

'Of course.'

'I thought... and I may have been confused because I was pretty terrified... I thought he had shapes carved in his forehead. Is that correct?' She had been looking down at her hands, twisting the ring on her thumb, but she looked up now and met his steady gaze.

'It is correct. Again, I'm sorry you had to find him.'

'Is there a significance to the markings?' Chloe asked. She wasn't quite sure what she was pushing for, but her imagination was conjuring up ritual killings and nightmares at the moment.

He paused, clearly giving her question careful thought. 'Our team are down there now, and once the autopsy has been done we will know more. It may be that the markings are significant, or it may be an expression of the perpetrator's anger. At this stage, we are just gathering as much evidence as possible.'

'Of course. Sorry.'

'Nothing to be sorry for. Now, I would definitely visit the art gallery. I'm not an art collector myself, but I can appreciate the talent exhibited there. The grand opening was only two months ago.' He sighed. 'The highlight of the night was the sale of Matthew Georgias' largest canvas. It was a stunning piece of work – a life-size figure merged into a beach and sea setting. I'm sure there's a technical way of describing it, but as I say, I wouldn't know. It was called *The Painted Lady* and it sold for twenty thousand dollars.'

Relieved at the change in subject, Chloe scuttled quickly down this new conversational path. 'Wow! Was he a well-known artist, then? Sorry, I'm afraid my own knowledge of the art world is a bit limited,' she added humbly.

Finn smiled. 'So is mine, to be honest. I think he has a following in the US, and his style is very distinctive. Jonas, that's the owner of the gallery, will be devastated to have his best talent snatched away from him.'

Chloe blinked, her eyes going to the wooden box and the business card. 'That wouldn't be Jonas Aliente would it?'

4

'Yes, do you know him?'

'I bumped into him this morning. He was coming to visit, and I came tearing up from the stables in a total panic. He was very good, and called 911 for me.'

'Did he?' The inspector sent her an unreadable look, his thick brows drawn for a moment. Then his eyes wandered towards her framed photographs and he grinned. 'Merry Bay Primary. How old were you in that picture?'

'I would have been around six,' she told him, grateful for the continued change in subject, but slightly puzzled.

He stood up and made his way over, examining the date on the print. 'No way, I bet we were in the same class, Mrs Canton!' he said.

'Make it Chloe. Really? You went there too?' she said, relaxing. He put his notebook away, still looking at her photos, and Chloe had the impression that his warm, genial persona disguised a rapier brain. She was good at reading people normally, and he seemed very genuine.

'Only if you call me Finn. Yes, and judging by the date we must be the same age. I knew Dre really well. My nieces and nephews all learnt to ride with her. She was a force of nature, and she talked about you a lot.' He put the photograph frame down and stood leaning against the table, broad shoulders blocking the light from the window. 'Do you think you'll keep the riding stables going?'

'I honestly don't know,' Chloe told him, 'I don't know anything about horses, and I haven't had a chance to look at the business paperwork yet. It was something I was going to settle down to this afternoon. I don't even know if the business makes any profit yet!'

'Plenty of time. I'd just settle in first. I'm really sorry again, that this had to happen. I know I said it before, but we really don't often have this kind of trouble on the island, so don't let this colour your first impressions of your new home.' Finn pressed his business card into her hand. 'If you need anything, please don't hesitate to call me, and we will be in touch with a few more questions as the investigation progresses, I'm afraid.'

Chloe thanked him, added his card to her growing collection, and watched him walk back through the garden, to the yard, the chickens misguidedly running behind him. Police and rescue vehicles were still much in evidence, and official blue tape now barred the entrance to the trail. She could just see a white tent erected further down the cliffside, and wondered if some vital piece of evidence had been discovered.

The crowd of onlookers had doubled, and many were taking photos, but all she wanted was a long hot shower.

The day dragged on, and Chloe's drive was patrolled by uniformed officers, who guarded the entrance to the trail from eager onlookers and a string of journalists.

She stayed indoors, making drinks and loading trays with biscuits for the emergency services workers. Antoine had turned the horses and goats out in the furthest paddock, to keep them away from the chaos. When she looked out of the window an hour later, three of the horses were lined up along the fence, watching the commotion, and the goats were back in the yard.

Finally, by six that evening, her home was quiet again. Antoine had done the evening stables routine and gone to play in a football match. The trail remained sealed off, but the police had gone.

Restless and troubled, Chloe sat down and opened her laptop, then closed it again. Part of her wanted to share the horrors of the day. But her best friend Alexa would be concerned for Chloe's safety, and many of her other friends would be eager for the gossip.

Now darkness had fallen she was jumping at every imagined footfall outside. Each gust of wind rattled the windows with invisible hands. Guilt niggled her as she pushed aside the paperwork she had intended to start on. Tomorrow. She would be more focused tomorrow. The murder, horrific as it was, clearly had nothing to do with her. But the shapes carved into the man's forehead bothered her. What kind of person did that?

Chloe picked up a bottle of Rescue Remedy from her kitchen counter and shook some drops into a glass of water. If this didn't work she figured a measure of rum would go down a treat.

A memory of Inspector Finn Harlow's massive, comforting presence and his professional manner further soothed her nerves.

Before she went to bed that night, she went around the whole house twice, locking and bolting everything, doors and windows. She even hauled a couple of chairs in front of both doors. From feeling confident and fearless this morning, she now felt like a snail creeping back into its shell, hiding from the world.

Luckily, she'd brought two huge boxes of books from her previous home, and Dre had left her a whole wall of shelving crammed with mysteries, romances, biographies and histories. Chloe selected a sizeable stack and went to bed with a black torch, which she felt was heavy enough to double as a weapon. She kept one wary eye on the front door.

She picked up and discarded a few books, lingering over two romance novels by Serena Gibbons; *His Last Lie* and *Second Chance for Love*. She wouldn't have pegged her grandmother as a romance fan, she thought, smiling at the thought of Dre sitting up in bed in this very room, flicking the pages, devouring the stories. The cover art was faded and very dated, with beautiful heroines and handsome beaus, but she wasn't in the mood for love and happy ever after.

Soon she was lost in Bermudian military history, having discovered an intriguing little paperback dedicated to Fort St Catherine. Constructed from stone in 1614, it had been upgraded throughout the years, and now boasted tunnels, ramparts and towers.

The paperback was smudged and the few photographs were black and white and of poor quality, but Chloe suddenly knew exactly why she had picked it out. She had visited the fort with Dre. Closing her eyes, she could see her thirteen-year-old self racing across the drawbridge, hair flying out in the wind. She could hear Dre adopting a stern, schoolteacher tone and telling her they were here to learn, not mess about. But later, her grandmother had delved in her bag and produced sandwiches and juices, which they had eaten on the beach below the fort.

She had found a dead fish washed up on the beach, she recalled. Flabby, grey and dull-eyed, it had laid on the rocks below the ramparts. Dre had been just as interested, prodding it with her foot, suggesting it might have died of natural causes, pondering on whether it was a grey snapper or some other type of fish.

Chloe's own mother wouldn't have gone within metres of a

dead fish. Or anywhere near a fort. But Dre's fierce interest in just about everything had spurred Chloe on, widened her horizons on those brief trips, and left her with memories to mull over. Dre had also taught her respect for culture and the people who had lived long ago.

When Chloe woke the next morning, she was lying on her back, clutching the paperback, her bed strewn with books, and the torch, having inched its way into the bed covers, was digging into her back.

~

Ailsa, clearly desperate for the gossip, came round first thing, with a home-made rum cake, which she informed Chloe was 'the real thing'.

It smelled heavenly. 'I'm so sorry I didn't get back to you yesterday. It was chaotic all day, and I just wanted to get to bed early,' Chloe told her, accepting the gift graciously and providing a few titbits of gossip in exchange for the cake. 'I'm just going out to check on the yard. Antoine should be here by now, but I can't hear him.'

'You don't look like you slept well either,' Ailsa said beadily, her black eyes raking Chloe's crumpled face and messy hair. 'That's all right, I've got Cheryl and Jordan coming over today to do a few repairs to my roof. See you later!' Ailsa called, departing at speed.

Chloe made another cup of coffee, scraped her hair back into a ponytail, and went bleary-eyed out into the garden. She felt, despite her penchant for gossip, or maybe because she was so blatant about it, that Ailsa could be trusted. The woman had shown her nothing but kindness since she moved in.

Cheryl was Ailsa's daughter, who lived and worked in Hamilton, and Jordan was her seventeen-year-old grandson. His twin, Alfie, was at boarding school in the UK, having won a prestigious cricket scholarship at the age of fourteen. Chloe had already briefly met and liked Cheryl, and seen numerous photos of the two boys.

At least her new mobile phone had arrived, and she had set it up earlier, leaving it to charge. Now it beeped in her pockets and she glanced down and smiled at the text.

'Antoine! I didn't think you were here.' She leant against the gate in relief, not entirely sure why she had been so worried, except that she was still feeling her way through the ragged nightmares that had dogged her sleep. Too many dead bodies and the smell of stale blood, that she just couldn't forget, had resulted in her staying awake reading the history book until three in the morning.

'I'm fine, and the animals are all done now. You don't look so good today, Mrs C... I'm not being rude, but you had such a shock, maybe you should take it easy this morning. You know, chill with a coffee or something.'

He was so earnest and kind that she laughed. 'I'll be okay, but thank you. Did you win your football match?'

'Yeah, we thrashed them. Anyway, we've got two rides today,' Antoine informed her. He was grooming a leggy black horse with a pretty white stripe on its forehead. 'One was a last-minute booking, and I've had another three parties in for tomorrow. I hate to say it, but murder is good for business, Mrs C.'

'That's horrible,' Chloe told him. She leant on the stable door and stroked the horse's nose. 'This is Jupiter, isn't it? I must learn all their names properly. I was also thinking I might get a dog when I've settled in. Do you know if there's a local rescue centre near here?'

He sent her a piercing look. 'Yes, there's the SPCA on Valley Road in Paget... You mean like a guard dog? You worried about security after you found the body?'

'No. Well yes, it was awful and I feel so bad for that man. He was a talented artist apparently. The police inspector...'

'Finn. He's the Chief Inspector of the Serious Crime Unit. Really nice guy and very professional. I play football with a couple of his nephews.'

'Right, Finn.' Chloe wondered why he hadn't used his full title when he introduced himself. 'Well he seemed very professional. He sent me a text earlier to check everything was okay. Wasn't that kind of him?'

'Very. You made a good impression on someone, Mrs C?' His grin made his eyes sparkle and she pretended not to notice the mischief in his face. Matchmaking could definitely wait.

She was curious about Finn though. 'It turns out we went to school together.'

'You maybe remember his wife, Ellie, then? She would have been the same age.'

'No.' Chloe shook her head. 'I don't remember Finn either. It was only because he saw an old photo when he was here yesterday that we worked it out from the dates.'

Antoine bit his lip. 'His wife was really nice. It was so sad when she was killed. I mean, how do you deal with something like that?' He shook his head.

'You mean she was murdered?' Chloe was horrified.

'No! Of course not. She was run off the road, and went over the edge near Shelly Bay. It was an accident, but still, really bad.'

'That's awful. Was it recent?' Chloe was thinking of Finn's professional concern and his calm management of the first responders.

'Four years ago now. He just carried on working. Josonne says he's one of the best too. He's been on a few jobs where the inspector's been involved, and in joint training sessions. He said he never gets rattled, just gets the job done.'

'Thanks for letting me know. I mean, so I didn't put my foot in it asking after his family or anything,' Chloe told him. Antoine was so sweet, and clearly not enjoying relaying this kind of gossip. She found she was already thinking of him as a friend and not just an employee.

'It's fine. He's got a son, Daniel, but I think he works abroad. Really sad,' he repeated soberly.

'Yes.' Chloe went back inside, horrified by Finn's tragic story. She made another coffee and sat down at the kitchen table, laptop open, for a quick catch-up with her friends.

Alexa emailed back, and wanted to come straight over, but Chloe dissuaded her. Her friend had three kids and a husband who worked shifts. It would cause chaos to their family.

Maria, Chloe's other best friend, was a wedding planner and her email was littered with exclamation marks and her usual extravagant wording. Chloe smiled, replying and suggesting Maria and her wife, Mandy, might visit in the autumn, when she was more settled.

An email from Mark via his solicitors urged her to access the online portal and sign the last of the divorce paperwork. She ignored it. Later, maybe tomorrow she would make herself sit down and deal with her divorce, but not now. Not when she felt jittery and emotional.

She glanced through the online news pages relating to the murder, wincing at pictures of Matthew's parents, and trying to relate the dark, brooding publicity photos of the crumpled body she had discovered. Matthew had been a good-looking man, with intense green eyes and a bony, interesting face.

Pictures of his work showed that the intensity seemed to have translated itself onto canvas. They weren't to her taste, but there was obviously a huge amount of talent and skill that was now wasted.

Almost without thinking she googled the three shapes and

added Matthew's name. Nothing. She studied his work again. No triangles or squares.

She shut the computer with a snap, suddenly tired again and her head ached from staring at the screen. The sun was still shining, and she couldn't bring Matthew back to life or catch the perpetrator, so she might as well be thankful *she* was alive and get on with her day.

And that meant getting stuck into those brown folders piled high on her desk. Chloe poured herself some iced water, and carried her glass over to the desk.

Slightly nervously, she began to tackle the mountain of paperwork marked *Beachside Stables*. There were six faded, brown folders, with dog-eared invoices tumbling out of every one.

The first folder was stuffed full of old invoices, scraps of paper with handwritten notes, and scrawled pages of bookings. Most of the dates were from two years ago. Chloe flicked through, noting an abundance of trail-ride bookings, especially from the Royal Majestic Hotel.

By the time she arrived at the last file, which was also stuffed with invoices, the dates were more recent. Bookings had dropped right off, she noticed with alarm. Was that because Dre had been unable to keep up with the business, or because demand simply wasn't there anymore?

The most recent, coupled with the handwritten bookings log, showed that the stables had been only just breaking even for the last couple of years. Since January this year, the bookings were right down, and certainly not enough money was coming in to cover the invoices.

There was a red-stamped final demand from the feed merchant and it was a similar story for the farrier, and the vet. Perhaps Dre had simply not been able to cope in her final months, but these would need paying immediately.

Chloe carefully totted up the amount. It came to nearly two thousand dollars. She could cover that from her personal savings, but should she continue to shore up the stables? Why had the Royal Majestic Hotel stopped using Beachside Stables?

None of the recent invoices had 'PAID' stamps on them, and most of them were final demands. Puzzling her way through the accounts book, she pushed her glasses onto the top of her head and rubbed her eyes. The figures were tiny, and in places almost illegible, but it seemed that all the previous hotel bookings had stopped completely. The income simply didn't meet the outgoings.

The other animals would still need feed, vaccinations, and for the horses, there were also bills from the saddler, the cash and carry and the garden centre. Chloe finally pushed her chair back, and ran her hands through her hair in despair. This was a business in crisis.

Did Antoine realise his job was on the line? His salary seemed to be paid every month from the tiny amount of money that Dre had left, but that was dwindling fast. If she didn't do something fast she might end up accepting Jonas' offer.

The thought made her sit bolt upright. She couldn't sell this place. She was happier here than she had ever been and if she needed to fight to keep it then she would. Surely she must have some business skills she could use?

The thought of selling the horses, including gentle Goldie, of telling Antoine his job was going, was inconceivable. Not to mention Dre had trusted her with her home and animals, her neighbours had welcomed her as one of their own... No way would she let everyone down.

Her own savings, combined with Dre's, were just enough to keep the stables afloat for another month. During that time she would write a new business plan and find out if she could drum up more bookings, speak to Antoine and make new contacts. Possibly she could even get a bank loan if she could show an increase in clients.

With this in mind, she decided to combine exploring the island with saving her business and making those all-important new contacts. The fact that her place of interest today was the Royal Naval Dockyard, meant that she could also stop in at the new art gallery. It would mean spending what little cash she had changed up to bring with her, but Chloe felt it would be worthwhile, and the bus was inexpensive and safe.

Anyway, she told herself she would probably have popped over to the gallery, even if she hadn't just discovered the body of one of their artists. She would thank Jonas for being so kind that day.

Her last task before she left was to ring the SPCA about a dog. Again, money would be needed to look after a new pet, but in light of recent events, she thought a guard dog was essential. The woman who answered the phone introduced herself as Helen, and was brisk and friendly. Yes, they had several dogs who might suit Chloe. They would need to do a home visit and there was paperwork to be filled in. Could she pop over sometime tomorrow to discuss it?

Chloe said she could, and felt a rush of excitement as she finished her call. She would need to drop into the pet store she had seen next to the garden centre, and get food, a bed, a collar... She had always loved animals, and now she seemed to be acquiring more by the day.

Without her own vehicle, she took the very efficient public transport, and studied her new island home from the dusty windows of a large pink bus. The beaches, the multicoloured towns and villages stretched along every road, dotted along the coast, huddled under hills and perched on the very tops of rocky outcrops.

The bus driver trundled carefully along the narrow roads, and each turn revealed breathtaking views, or some point of historical interest. As it moved slowly through the parishes of Southampton and Sandys, Chloe drank in the mirror-like bays of the coastline, and on the other side, onion fields, majestic cedars and peaceful loquat woods.

Here and there, the dips in the road revealed farms with neatly planted red-earth fields, and on the shore side, rusty remains of half-submerged wrecks. Chloe slipped on her sunglasses and pulled out her maps, trying to trace the journey, to reacquaint herself with her home.

As she drew nearer to her destination she spotted luxury condos and apartments peeping out of foliage on their own islands. Small, white bobbing yachts and cruisers were moored along the bays. She allowed the colour and warmth to flood her senses, relaxing properly for the first time since the discovery of the body. It was tragic, but apart from finding the body, the murder didn't touch her personally. There was nothing she could do or could have done, to help the dead man.

Something she *did* remember from childhood was the sense of community that bonded the island's residents. Regular busgoers were greeted with a '*Good morning*' as they boarded the bus, and often people would get on, laden with children and shopping bags, calling a cheery '*Nice day everyone!*' to the whole bus. However, snatches of gossip that she caught were all about the murder.

It couldn't be more different from riding the Tube on her way to meetings in London. As a copywriter for a large advertising agency, she had been lucky that mostly she had worked from home, but a couple of times a week she was summoned to meetings, and fought her way through the inefficient, crowded London public transport system. Just now, it seemed far in the past, wispy grey memories eliminated by the bright sun.

Dockyard was the very last stop, on the western tip of Bermuda in Ireland Island (north), Sandys Parish. Chloe smiled to herself as she drank in the half-remembered limestone buildings. Perched on the clifftop was the magnificent former Commissioner's House, which dated from the 1820s and was the first ever cast-iron house in the world.

Little half-remembered facts and snippets of historical information floated up from Chloe's brain as she wandered across the stone roads and pavements. The Royal Navy had finally left Dockyard in 1951, but it wasn't until the seventies and eighties that the current transformation had begun. Many of the towering derelict workshop areas were now converted into thriving independent shops. There was an ice-cream shop, boutiques, eateries and a glassworks surrounding the marina.

Two huge cruise ships were in dock and the terminals at Heritage and King's Wharf swarmed with a colourful tidal wave of recently disembarked tourists. It seemed that trade was thriving, as every shop was crammed, and every eatery had queues stretching out the doors.

The renovation was ongoing, and Chloe soon found herself drawn to the former Victualling Yard, where it was possible to peek through storm-damaged doors, into the half derelict Victorian buildings.

Some of the roofs had gaping holes, and massive rusting iron machinery was suspended precariously from upper levels. As she walked slowly across the broken pavements, and peered into dark interiors, she couldn't help but notice the man.

Emerging from behind a group of tourists, he was wearing shorts and an England rugby sweatshirt and carried a small sports bag. Ignoring Chloe, he gave a quick look to either side, hopped over the *No Entry* barrier, and disappeared as quickly as he had appeared.

Chloe frowned after him. Perhaps he was an employee... But no, there was something furtive about his movements, and she was fairly sure she had seen him earlier, near the bus stop at the end of her drive. She remembered the shadow flitting behind the cracked window at Tranquility House... Surely it must be coincidence. Her nerves were shot to bits and she was jumping at ghosts, she told herself sternly.

But all the same, she shivered and walked to the corner. Leaning casually on the red barrier, she was just another tourist scanning the majestic buildings. She simply couldn't see where the man had vanished to. More rusting machinery and a pile of industrial rubbish blocked the way into the warehouse.

Chloe sipped her water, considering, then pulled out her phone and pretended to be photographing the panoramic view back across the yard as the man stepped out from behind the rubbish.

His movements still quick and furtive, he walked briskly down to the barrier, and put a hand down to vault over. Chloe, swinging her camera across to get the vista, managed to snap him as he joined a bustling hungry crowd gathering outside the Frog and Onion Pub.

His hair was close-shaven and blond, and he was young. Maybe in his late twenties. She realised that he had not returned with the bag he had been carrying on his outward journey.

This was definitely where Alexa would tell her not to be a nosy old bag, to keep out of someone else's business... But she found herself edging to the other side of the barrier. No way could she do an athletic vault over the top, so she ducked underneath, holding her breath, half expecting someone to shout that she wasn't allowed down there.

Unchallenged, Chloe stepped cautiously over the mossy flagstones, keeping to the shadow of the walls. The doorway she was certain the man had emerged from was barred with a *Keep Out* sign and a padlock. The half rotten door was leaning to one side, affording access to the building.

Chloe glanced back into the sunlight, before gathering her dress and slipping into the shadows with far less grace than the stranger had before her. She blinked, breathing in the smell of dust and cobwebs, mingled with oil and damp.

She could see footprints on the dirty floor. Recent footprints leading towards a staircase. The wind groaned through the building, making sheets of iron rattle and some winching machinery sway above her head. Her heart was pounding, but she could now see the sports bag, slipped under the first step.

Making it across the floor, she paused, half scared and wondering what she might find in the bag. Body parts? Drugs? What if this was the murderer hiding his knife? She dithered, and cursed herself for watching too many episodes of *CSI*... But she hesitated too long and a shout made her jump.

'Hey, lady, you shouldn't be in here! It's dangerous. Did you not see the signs?'

A tall man was beckoning to her from the doorway.

Reluctantly retracing her steps, she wondered if she should tell this man about the bag. But he was just another tourist, whose wife had seen her slip under the barrier.

'She saw you go in here, and she was worried,' he told her. 'The building isn't for tourists. It's derelict.'

Feeling suitably admonished, Chloe apologised. 'I just love old buildings, especially the insides and I wanted a few pictures.'

'Well you need to be careful. A danger sign is a danger sign,' the man said, seeing her under the barrier, where a plump, pretty lady in a green dress was waiting.

'You found her, Walter!'

'All safe and sound,' he said, giving Chloe a dubious look. 'She said she likes to photograph old buildings.'

'Goodness. Did you tell her it wasn't safe? Oh, there's Maria and Jack! Coooooeeeee!' Without a backwards glance the woman was off, waving wildly at her friends, dragging her husband with her.

Although intrigued by the mystery bag, Chloe decided she had better leave the mystery for later, and treated herself to a trip around the Commissioner's House, admiring the antiques, revelling in the rich history, and actually gasping at the view from the breezy balcony.

Leaving the walled area, she found herself heading for Clocktower Mall, mind back on the murder and those shapes carved in the man's skin. As she did so, she passed the man in the England rugby shirt, hurrying in the opposite direction. Crossing the road to keep him in sight, she slowed to see him approach a woman on a scooter. After a quick, heated conversation, he jumped on the back and they roared off.

So he *had* probably left the bag in the warehouse. Chloe hesitated, and then continued on her way. She would finish her visit to the mall and then walk back down towards the Victualling Yard, taking in the warehouse where the man had dumped his bag.

Jonas Aliente's new gallery was a large double unit, flanked by brightly painted T-shirt shops and glittering jewellery stores. *Stone Galleries* was etched in flashy black font across the signage, and the windows displayed various easels of work.

She bent down, enchanted by a selection of tiny canvases in jewel-bright colours. The artist had captured the richness of the sea and the sky perfectly. Chloe checked the name; Melissa Aliente. Jonas' wife perhaps? The canvases had discreet pink stickers underneath with *Half Price Sale!* printed on them.

The inside of the gallery was bright and airy with white-painted walls and huge artwork hanging alongside glass cabinets of sculptures and jewellery. Pretty bracelets and necklaces caught the light from artfully arranged spotlights, and the huge area was restful, inviting the customer to explore, to linger.

'Chloe Canton! How lovely to see you again.' Jonas appeared from a side door, his smile welcoming.

5

'Hi.' Chloe returned his greeting slightly awkwardly. 'I... I thought I'd treat myself to a day out. I was just admiring the artwork.' She really didn't feel she could confide in him about the mystery bag. He'd think she was crazy.

'Are you an art connoisseur?' Jonas asked. He wore an elegant cream suit today with a pink striped shirt and pale-pink tie. His dark hair was slicked back from his forehead.

'Not at all, I'm afraid. I collected a few pieces when I lived in London, but they're in storage. I just bought what I liked to look at. They don't really fit in my new home, but I can't bear to part with them,' Chloe told him, brushing a stray curl from her face. She had tied her long hair into a ponytail today, but suddenly felt the style was more suited to a younger woman. 'I... I heard the dead man was one of your artists?'

He frowned, forehead wrinkling, distress now evident in his grey eyes. 'Yes, the police have been asking lots of questions. I am beyond shocked and deeply saddened, of course. He was a brilliant artist... Look, I have several of his pieces displayed on this wall.'

'I'm so sorry. I did have a look at some of his work online...'

Chloe followed him, her long pink dress blessedly cool in the warmth of the gallery. The whirring overhead fans weren't doing a great job at air conditioning. Pushing away the all too vivid memory of the blood and the crumpled body, she peered at Matthew Georgias' work.

There were four canvases arranged in a row, and each linked by their subjects. Like many of the artists displayed in the gallery, Georgias had used the beaches and the sea in his work. Chloe had wondered if maybe the pictures didn't translate well online. Perhaps his was the kind of work that needed to be appreciated in the flesh. But she was disappointed. The pictures were not appealing. The slashes of red and black, the huge figures casting shadows across each canvas, lying underwater or etched in the sand were impressive but also quite frightening.

'Amazing, aren't they?' Jonas said proudly. 'I was so excited when Matthew's agent contacted me and asked if I would display his work. We sold one of his highest priced works at the launch party. I believe it went to a US collector. His legacy will live on, but imagine what more he could have achieved... So very sad. I hope the police are able to catch whoever did this very soon.'

'Yes, I heard about *The Painted Lady* being sold.' Chloe didn't feel she could say that she disliked the paintings immensely. They were disturbing and too reminiscent of violence and hatred. She stayed silent, examining some of the smaller paintings. They depicted the back view of a naked woman, her long hair tangling down her back, legs curled under her as she stared out to sea. Although the subject matter was different, the overall impression was one of depression, fear and anger. 'You were friends as well as colleagues, then?'

'I hadn't known him long but yes, I'd like to think he would have called me a friend.' He dropped his gaze to the smaller paintings. 'Maybe not what you were expecting?'

Disconcerted by his intuition, she changed the subject. 'I saw some lovely smaller pictures in your window, by Melissa Aliente?'

His expression brightened. 'My sister, yes. She has always been inspired by the sea, wherever we have lived. I have more of her work over here, if you'd like to see?'

'Yes, I'd love to. Have you been in Bermuda long?' Chloe asked, moving gratefully away from the dark paintings, and admiring the small, vivid canvases on another wall.

'Two years now, but it's really only in the last few months that I have found time to stay in Bermuda and focus on this gallery. I have, well my family has, other galleries in New York, Madrid, Los Angeles, Florida... Lots of work, but I love to travel. And you? Will you stay on the island now? I heard a little of your history from someone.'

She understood. Rumours were bound to be flying around, and to be fair, she had been just as curious about him. 'I don't know. At the moment I'm trying to just live in the present and take things as they come.' She bit her lip. 'About my house...'

He stopped her with a polite raised hand. 'Say no more. I had no idea that the other investors had been approaching residents already. All I was told was that your house had been inherited by a family member who might be willing to sell.' A flicker of annoyance crossed his aquiline features. 'I apologise on behalf of the other investors. Perhaps I could take you out for a drink to say sorry properly?'

'Oh! No you don't have to do that. I haven't really even moved in properly, let alone got started on a social life yet,' Chloe protested, feeling her cheeks redden, wishing she had put on make-up instead of sunscreen.

'This is Bermuda. You can't tell me that you don't already know at least ten people, and half of those will be neighbours.' He was smiling, clear grey eyes glinting now as he teased her.

'Well... you are right about that. Yes, thank you, that would be lovely,' Chloe told him, trying to regain her composure.

'Good. Do you have a telephone now, so I can call you?'

'I do.' Chloe scrabbled in her bag for her new mobile.

'Come into the office for a moment while I take the number down.'

She followed him through the door, nerves still jangling.

As she stepped through, a voice said, 'Another new girlfriend, Jonas, or is this an actual client?'

'Ah, Melissa, I didn't realise you were back. This is Chloe,' Jonas told the woman, his voice edged with annoyance.

'I came in the back door. Hallo, Chloe.' The voice was mocking and slightly amused. Melissa Aliente was sitting on a swivel chair, long tanned legs crossed, wearing a bright orange short silk sundress. Her shiny dark hair fell over her shoulders in perfect curls. 'Are you another art groupie? My brother collects them.'

'*Melissa!*' Jonas snapped at his sister, who glared at him.

Chloe, intensely uncomfortable, wondered if she should just make her excuses and leave. Melissa was far younger than her, and her ice-queen persona should have been amusing. But it was actually quite intimidating. Did she really think Chloe was after her brother? Had she heard him ask her out for a drink?

'I told you I met Chloe at her house the other day,' Jonas added, pouring iced water for all of them.

His sister waved her glass irritably away. 'I don't remember every single detail of your busy life.'

Chloe moistened her lips, before smiling at the girl. 'I was just saying that I like your paintings. The bird ones in the window.'

There was silence. Jonas was looking tense, sipping his water, clearly wondering what on earth his sibling would say next.

For a moment Melissa's eyes narrowed, lips pursed as though she expected some practical joke. But although her gaze was still assessing, enthusiasm warmed her voice. 'Did you really like my paintings?'

Chloe, now awkwardly reciting her new phone number for Jonas, turned back to the other woman. The girl couldn't be more than twenty-five, and beside her Chloe felt ancient. 'I do. I've just moved house and I'd like some smaller artwork for the walls. Your study of the birds and beach is just beautiful.' Her crumpled notes, her allotted spending money, wedged into her purse, would cover the paintings easily with the huge discount advertised.

Melissa leant forward eagerly, her hair swinging across her shoulders, clear grey eyes, so like her brother's, very bright. 'Most people want the bigger works, although actually recently everyone has wanted Matthew's stuff. Tragic, isn't it? He was a rising star, the golden boy of the gallery.' Something that might have been mockery touched her words.

'Chloe was the one who found the body,' Jonas told her, moving to open the door for Chloe, and indicating she should follow him.

The other woman's eyes widened, and the annoyance and brittleness fell away. 'How horrible for you. Sorry, Jonas did tell me a woman had found Matthew. I didn't realise... We are all deeply shocked. This kind of thing... It happens, but not to you, and you see it reported on social media, in the papers, but it doesn't touch you personally.'

It was almost an apology. 'I know what you mean,' Chloe said gently, wondering if she was imagining the wetness in Melissa's eyes, the taut jawline when she said the artist's name. Perhaps she and Matthew had been more than business colleagues? She *was* very beautiful. 'So, back to your work... I'd love to buy the three bird studies if that's okay? The sales tag said fifteen dollars for each painting...'

Melissa beamed at her, childlike now, all traces of reserve vanishing, and sprang to her feet. 'Of course! Would you like to take them now, or shall we get them wrapped and couriered to your home?'

'I can take them now,' Chloe told her, enjoying the reaction, the swiftness of the character transformation. She loved to make people happy, and her busy, motherly nature drew others to her. In Melissa's pleasure she could feel an instant bond, a shared enjoyment of the artwork. The paintings were beautiful, peaceful and would look perfect in her living room, but it was just as much of a pleasure to see the artist's reaction to her sale. Perhaps she didn't sell much.

Certainly fifty dollars fell far short of the thousands garnered by Matthew Georgias for his work. She was struck by a thought. Would his artwork be worth even more now he was dead? Could someone have killed him for that very reason?

6

Paintings neatly wrapped and placed in her cotton tote bag, Chloe soon added to her purchases – a few beaded bracelets, a flower-patterned sarong, and some beauty products from another local business. Each business she bought from, she was able to engage in chat with the salesperson and explain she had taken over Beachside Stables. Already, she had a definite booking from the man selling the jewellery, even if her supply of cash was steadily diminishing.

Dodging tourists, she wandered over to the Bone Fish Bar and Grill. She sat in the shade, watching the marina while she ate an open sandwich.

Someone had left a copy of *The Royal Gazette* on the table, and she winced at the front-page news of the murder. Matthew Georgios stared up at her from a publicity shot. She recognised his face from the shot online – his face was unsmiling, angular, with full jutting lips and angry eyes. The brown hair was messy and shoulder-length. There was something about the defensive, almost antagonistic expression that Chloe could see translated into his work. She felt he might have been a difficult person to know.

But then Melissa and Jonas were an odd couple too – the kind of jet set European upper class she remembered vaguely from boarding school, flitting from destination to destination as their parents enjoyed the social whirl of parties and polo. The siblings had that same veneer of sophistication, although Melissa's had been swiftly stripped away by the purchase of her artwork. Chloe wondered which was the real girl – the bored, scornful socialite, or the childish, eager-to-please artist. Was her self-confidence all an act?

She sighed and went back to Matthew. Clearly there was something in his life, past or present that had made the artist pour those kind of emotions or experiences onto canvas. Just as clearly they weren't pleasant memories.

'So who do you think killed him?'

Chloe jumped, and put out a hand to steady her drink, but the speaker was at the next table. A large lady with abundant grey hair barely contained in a yellow headscarf was questioning her companions.

Aware she was eavesdropping, Chloe sipped her iced pineapple juice, idly dividing her gaze between the boats in the marina, and the crowded table to her left.

'I should think it was a family member,' one of the men at the next table suggested, 'it nearly always is, isn't it? I saw a news snippet online that suggested he fell out with his siblings after an inheritance.'

'I bought some of his work this morning, you know. Honestly, I don't actually like it, but my husband says it will be worth a fortune now he's dead.' The woman in the yellow headscarf shook her head at the shocked murmurs. 'I know, I know, but I bought it because *The Painted Lady* went for twenty thousand dollars to that collector in Chicago. He must know about art, mustn't he?'

The other woman at the table was munching on her

burger, but she managed to speak out of the corner of her mouth and continue chewing at the same time. 'I'd say it was a good buy, Veronica, but I'd never buy art I didn't want to look at.'

Chloe had heard enough, although at the back of her mind she noted there had been nothing about those three shapes carved into Matthew's forehead. Maybe the police hadn't released that information? Surely it would be widely discussed if they had, she thought with distaste. It would sensationalise an already horrible murder case.

She paid for her sandwich and drink, left a tip for the friendly waiting staff, and wandered back along Maritime Way to the museum. After refreshing her memory on the history of the island, and respectfully peering at more antiques, she glanced at her watch.

There was just time to pop back into the community gift shop before the bus went. A tiny seed of an idea was growing at the back of her mind, sparked by her look at the Beachside Stables accounts.

It was true she knew nothing about running a riding stables, but she was only fifty. She could learn! It was the first time since her landmark birthday that she had caught herself thinking like this. Instead of writing herself off the page, and diving into imagined old age, why not begin a new career?

If the riding stables could provide an income, she could follow her heart and honour the trust Dre had placed in her. It might even be fun... It had been a long time since she felt like this – light and free instead of weighed down by broken promises and false expectations.

The community shop had more efficient fans than the gallery, and Chloe was able to browse in comfort, enjoying the cool breeze on her hot shoulders. There was a huge rack of jewellery, piles of books displayed in wooden crates, local rum cakes, soaps in colourful chunks, and some more artwork decorating the walls.

'Can I help you?' A tall woman with red hair cascading in wild curls approached her, smiling.

'I just wondered...' Chloe stopped. She'd only just had the idea. Maybe it was bit soon to be exploring sales outlets. 'I wondered how the shop worked? I mean, how do your craftspeople and artists get a space for their products?'

Far from being offended, as Chloe had feared, the woman seemed delighted to explain the workings of the shop. 'We only take things of a certain standard, but everyone who sells here puts in some time in the shop, and we all pull together to do the accounts, pay the rent. Everyone lives right here in Bermuda. It's a great place to get inspired. Do you have something you'd like to sell? Sorry, I never told you my name! I'm Emma.'

Chloe shook hands, hoping her palm wasn't sweaty. 'I'm Chloe. I've just moved to the island, and yes, I was thinking of setting up a small business. Well, actually more of growing a current one.' She laughed, finding the other woman's enthusiasm encouraging. 'I actually only thought of it the other day.'

'See!' Emma beamed. 'You were inspired by coming here. How wonderful! It was the same with me. I'm an artist. Not a fancy one with my own gallery, but I do cards and miniatures.'

Chloe bent down and examined the pretty watercolours, making approving noises. 'I own Beachside Stables,' Chloe explained, slightly shocked now she was actually putting her idea into words, 'and I would like to try and promote the business a little bit. One idea I had was perhaps inviting artists to visit for the day and draw the horses?'

'Sounds like a fabulous idea! Beachside Stables...' Emma tapped her teeth with a long, glossy red fingernail. 'Can't say that rings a bell... I'm not a horse person though.'

'It's off South Shore Road. I can send you an email with the details if you think anyone might be interested?'

'No problem. Look, and I can give you this sheet with all our products and contact details on, and my phone number is at the top. We try to have a general meeting once a month, usually at a pub, so you're welcome to come along when you feel like the time is right. We've got a Facebook page too, so do feel free to have a browse,' Emma told her.

'Thank you.' Chloe popped the information into the bag containing her artwork.

'I see you've been over to the Stone Gallery,' Emma remarked, glancing at the discreet logo on the packaging.

Was she annoyed Chloe hadn't bought something in her shop? Her bubbly friendliness seemed to have faded slightly. Chloe quickly picked a couple of bars of the gorgeous-smelling soap, and two of Emma's postcards. 'Yes, I just got a couple of pictures for my living room... I'd like to take these, please.'

Emma popped behind the till, her long turquoise dress catching the sunlight, red curls bouncing on her shoulders. She quickly totted up the bill, made the entry into the till, and began wrapping Chloe's purchases in brown paper and string. 'You know that one of their artists was murdered?' Her voice was still a little cool.

'Yes. Matthew Georgias.' Chloe accepted her change and fiddled with her purse. 'I did see some of his work when I was in the gallery, but I bought some pieces by Melissa Aliente. Do you know her?'

'His sister.' Emma frowned. 'She's a bit of a madam. Easy to have an art career if you're a trust-fund kid with time and money to dabble. She always used to row with the other artists. And with Matthew. I saw them together late one evening last week. She actually slapped his face, so it must have been quite a conversation.'

Melissa and Matthew? Chloe wasn't quite sure what to say in response to this piece of gossip. 'Did you tell the police about the row? After he was murdered, I mean?'

Emma nodded meaningfully. 'Of course. She's got a temper, and they're a funny family, that's all I'm saying. Jonas is all right, I suppose, but so smooth and polite you can never tell what he's really thinking.'

Other customers were beginning to drift towards the till point now, so Chloe thanked the other woman and headed back out into the sunshine. Standing at the bus stop, enjoying the sun-drenched walls, dotted with pretty mosses and flowers, she couldn't help but wonder why Emma had been so quick to share this particular piece of gossip with a stranger. Certainly her friendliness had cooled pretty quickly at the mention of the Stone Gallery. Or was it because of Melissa? Professional rivalry amongst the artistic community? Or was she just being respectful after such a horrific event?

Jonas' sister was utterly gorgeous, and Chloe could imagine that family wealth could either help or hinder a career. There would also be those, like Emma, who said that you had achieved what you had because of the money. Yet from what she had seen, Melissa was genuinely very talented. Not in the intense abstract way of Matthew Georgias, but her seascapes and bird paintings had the intricacy of a photograph.

Emma hadn't seemed the type of person to suddenly confide, but then the murder would have affected the close-knit local community, so perhaps the woman was just treating her like a local. There was clearly some friction between Emma and Melissa...

7

The tourist crowds were swelling as more people poured into Dockyard from a recently arrived ferry. Chloe supposed perhaps they had been on a day trip to St George's. Taking advantage, she slipped in amongst them and when they passed the warehouses, she nipped round the barrier and squeezed into the musty darkness.

Heart pounding, she stepped across the filthy floor and bent down to the bag. It was a medium-sized sports bag with the logo printed on the front pocket.

Very carefully, she undid the zip, hoping with everything she had that she wasn't about to discover sawn-up body parts or something equally horrid. Instead, she let out a sharp breath of relief. Camera equipment! All at once she felt embarrassed. The murder had clearly been playing on her mind to such an extent she was seeing villains everywhere she looked.

It seemed a strange place to stash what must be expensive equipment, but the bag would have been awkward to carry on a scooter – too large to sling over the shoulders. Chloe paused for a moment, before neatly zipping up the bag and turning her back on the mystery.

Her imagination was in overdrive, and it was none of her business if the man was planning a photoshoot in the derelict building. Perhaps he shared her interest. Or maybe the camera was stolen and awaiting collection... Feeling quite cross with herself for allowing her nosiness to get the better of her, Chloe managed to join the crowds admiring two restored cannons which stood next to the path.

She snapped her own picture of them before walking quickly towards the bus stop. Maybe, she thought, she needed to get home and focus on something else to stop her nerves jangling.

~

When Chloe finally walked up the hill, Ailsa was waiting on the porch with a chicken under her arm. The bus stop was a mile or so from her house, but the walk, with stunning views of the sea and the chance to peek at the pretty church, was hardly arduous.

'Did you have a nice day at Dockyard?' her neighbour inquired.

'Lovely, thanks... Um, Ailsa, why are you holding a chicken?'

'This is Betsy. She likes a little cuddle, and I wanted to make sure I was here when you got home.' Ailsa was puffed up with excitement, clearly bursting with gossip. The chicken sat peacefully in her arms, scaly feet dangling, bright beady eyes fixed on the new arrival.

'Do you want to come in? I could really do with an iced drink after that walk,' Chloe said, shoving her keys in the door. 'Do you mind leaving the chicken outside though?' Chloe's own chickens seemed to be quite happy wandering around the yard, not really venturing into her garden, but Ailsa's flock seemed rather more sociable.

Ailsa put the bird carefully on the rocker chair, where it sat balefully on a red cushion. Chloe and the chicken looked at one another for a long moment, before she sighed and followed her neighbour across the cool tiled floor into the house.

'You've been to Jonas' gallery?' Ailsa commented, as Chloe put her bag on the table.

'Yes. I bought some of his sister's artwork.' There was no reason why she should be blushing, and Chloe quickly hid her face in the freezer, digging out ice for their drinks. 'She seemed nice.'

'They're an odd pair,' Ailsa said, frowning. 'Funny you should have been over to the gallery today...'

'Why?' Chloe sat opposite her, unpacking the paintings, setting them carefully across the table. 'Aren't they beautiful?'

Her neighbour tapped a wrinkled finger on the nearest picture, and nodded. 'Pretty. Dre would have liked them too. I saw Peter today... You know, the taxi driver who brought you from the airport?'

'Yes, of course, I remember.'

'He told me that Melissa Aliente was seeing Matthew Georgias and that they had a big row the night before he was murdered. He said there's a rumour she owed him money.' She sat back, eyes glittering with excitement. 'Which means she's now a suspect, doesn't it?'

Chloe paused in her unpacking. 'I suppose it might. How does Peter know?'

'His son is a friend of Josonne's. He's with the Bermuda Fire and Rescue Service. Melissa's never been that friendly, not with the local boys. But she usually has some rich older man in tow when she does go out. That's what he said anyway.'

'I met Josonne the other day. He's also Antoine's cousin, isn't he?'

'He is. They look very alike. They've always got so many girls chasing them, but they're good boys, both of them. Melissa and

Jonas have been coming to the island on and off for years, but since the Clocktower gallery opened they've made this more of a base. Their mother passed away when they were quite young, and I believe their stepfather raised them. He's a lot older than his sister, of course, but they seem very close. I heard their stepfather was the one who gave them all the money to open galleries.'

'Right.' Chloe's first thought was one of pity. Clearly Melissa wasn't well liked, but she must be – what? Early twenties tops, and the haughty, spoilt-little-rich-girl persona had dropped so quickly when Chloe had admired her work she felt compelled to defend a girl she hardly knew. The frosty antagonist attitude had melted like ice in the Bermuda sunshine, leaving a glimpse of someone quite different. 'Well, she was very charming to me.'

'How did you find Finn, then? Did he ask you lots of questions?'

'He was very professional,' Chloe said. 'I'm sure the police will catch whoever committed the murder soon, and we can all relax a bit. He did reassure me this is very unusual, and not something I can expect living here.'

Ailsa was watching her, her head slightly angled, a quizzical expression on her wrinkled face. With her bright beady eyes, and small energetic figure, she really was very similar to her beloved chickens. 'You know he's a widower?'

'Yes. His wife was killed in a road accident, wasn't she? Antoine told me the other day.'

'Awful, that was. That poor man, and his boy was devastated too, of course. Daniel, he's called. He lives and works in England now. Hasn't been back for years, I don't think.'

'I can't imagine how terrible something like that would be,' Chloe said soberly. She changed the subject. 'It turns out we were at school together. How strange is that?'

'Oh? You already know each other from before, then?'

Clearly pleased, eyes sparkling with interest, Ailsa finished her drink in one gulp and focused all her attention on her neighbour, her thoughts as transparent as though she had spoken out loud.

'No... I mean I don't remember him, he just saw a photo on the wall and...' Chloe was interrupted by a chicken screech from further down the drive.

Ailsa swung around, clearly torn between a bit of rather-too-obvious matchmaking and the desire to sort her birds out. Another screech, followed by a cockerel crowing sent her swiftly out the front door. 'That stupid bird! Always hassling my chickens. Next door need to keep him under control.' She was glaring at the offending bird.

'Did Cheryl come and visit you today?' Chloe asked, quickly changing the subject.

'No, she was too busy in the end, and Jordan's still causing trouble... If that boy focused on his sport he could go the same way as Alfie did, with a scholarship and prospects, he'd be okay.' Ailsa sighed. 'But as it is he prefers to run wild. Cheryl is tearing her hair out, and his dad's so busy at work he hardly sees the boy.'

Ailsa's daughter and son-in-law were both solicitors, working in Hamilton for a big firm. She was clearly very proud of them, but her worry for her grandchildren was now dimming her natural effervescence.

'I can't be too snidey about rich people not giving a bit back, because that was what funded Alfie's trip to the UK. It's one called the Skylight Foundation. We never could have afforded his fees if he hadn't got the scholarship.'

'I'm sure Jordan will settle down. Maybe he'll see how well his brother's doing and be inspired to follow in his footsteps.' Chloe had followed her out onto the porch, still holding her drink. She was about to make a soothing comment about Jordan maybe just needing to grow up a little, and teenagers in general not knowing which career path to take, when there was another screech.

'I'm going to sort that wretched bird out! Sorry, Chloe, we'll catch up later?' Her neighbour gathered up her own chicken, which once again hung as placidly as a feathered puppet and she scooted off.

The marauding cockerel was dancing up and down, crowing at the edge of Chloe's drive, and, not wanting to offend Ailsa, she suppressed a giggle. She really was becoming very fond of her big-hearted neighbour.

'Actually, I'll see you tomorrow. I need to go and tell Adrienne her bird's out *again!*' Ailsa called, moving with surprising speed and agility, making her exit through a gap in the hedge. Her bright-green dress floated out behind her as she and the chicken vanished from sight.

Chores completed, Chloe wandered out for her evening stroll. It had become a routine to take a walk around her property last thing, to pet the horses, check the chickens and goats were locked up for the night. Tonight, as darkness began to fall, the wind had picked up, and she could see the distant waves were now topped with frothy white.

Darker clouds scudded across the sky, and she shivered, moving back towards the house. The garden gate shut behind her with a sharp click, and she jumped, heart accelerating in fear, palms sweaty.

'*Idiot,*' she told herself, moving quickly inside, locking the door firmly behind her. But Matthew Georgias' face was back, the bloody, grotesque body on her mind once more. Two squares and a triangle? Why?

To distract herself, as the rain started outside, she hunted down a hammer and hooks, and began to hang her new paintings.

Her home was bright and cosy, filled with electric light, and the cheerful flicker of candles. Pausing in her labours, she bent down and took a sniff of the candles. They were pleasant, but... she felt sure she could do better. Last year, Alexa had given her a gift voucher for a candle-making course.

Chloe had enjoyed the weekend but never really made time to pursue her new hobby. But now, perhaps she could make some candles for her new home? A tiny spurt of excitement replaced her anxiety and she hung the last picture quickly, standing back to admire the view.

Perfect. It was past ten now, so she made some toast, and switched on her laptop. The files were still there. All her course notes, and all the instructions she would need to start making her own candles again.

Chloe sighed with pleasure, saved her file for later, and turned her creative energies towards saving Beachside Stables. It was going to be a challenge. To start with, the website was one page in a very odd font, with no contact details save the address, and there was no social media. Well, she could certainly sort that out.

A crash from outside made her lose concentration. The rain was pelting down, hurling against windows and doors, battering the roof. As a precaution, and as instructed by Ailsa, she had closed the shutters. Peering out, she could only see shadowy bars, and a vague image of furiously waving trees.

A buzz from her phone told her Alexa was calling, and she grabbed the mobile phone with relief.

'Chloe darling! How are you? Just thought I'd ring for a quick chat.' Alexa's sharp tones cut through Chloe's rising panic.

'Oh it's going well. I think. No word from the police on the murder but everyone seems very confident that whoever did it will be caught soon.' Chloe made herself speak briskly, confidently, but her friend knew her well.

'Must have been an awful shock. I couldn't believe it when I got your email... Sure you're okay?'

'Yes, really I am. It's so lovely here and I'm going to make a real go of turning the riding stables into a profitable business.' Chloe paused. 'Actually, something strange did happen...' She told Alexa about the man and the camera equipment.

'You are such a nosy old bag!' Alexa said affectionately. 'Honestly, what did you *think* he was up to?'

'Hiding stolen goods?'

Alexa snorted with laughter. 'Or he could just be someone taking photographs. But if you are worried, Chloe, you should have mentioned it to the police.'

'I didn't want to. I've already caused enough trouble by finding a dead body!' Chloe said.

'Hardly, but I can't imagine this is anything sinister,' Alexa said comfortably. 'And if it is, let them get on with it. Sounds like you've got enough on your plate without chasing after would-be villains. Did you say you were getting a dog?'

'Yes! Well, I hope so. I'm going to the rescue centre tomorrow, and if I pass the home visit I should be able to pick one up by next week.'

'Sounds perfect. You've always been an animal person, even stuck in the city you kept fussing over that damned bird feeder, not to mention picking worms off the path in the park so they didn't get trodden on...'

Chloe giggled. 'The bird feeder that fell on that man's head on the balcony below mine, you mean?'

She could hear the amusement in Alexa's voice. 'Exactly the one. It happened while you, me, and Maria were having a girls' night in and drinking rather a lot of wine as I recall. Well you seem happy, darling, but do get in touch if you need anything at all, and I'm planning a summer holiday at yours so make sure the guest bedroom is ready! Do keep me updated, and remember you don't have to pretend it's all perfect if you have any days when it isn't going well. Just call me.'

'I know, and thank you, but I am honestly okay. Maria and Mandy are coming over for dinner next weekend, so I'll give them your love.'

Reassured by Alexa, Chloe finished the call far happier. Alexa had suffered from depression for a number of years, and Chloe had early on made her promise to call when she felt low. The two women, along with Maria, had also supported each other through numerous traumatic life events.

It would be lovely, too, when Alexa visited to have her in her new house. She could introduce her to her new friends, show her around Bermuda... Another gust of wind buffeted her house, followed by the steady drumbeat of a downpour.

She tried to go back to her business plan, but instead found herself checking the weather forecast, watching the orange-and-red swirls across the online radar. It was just a spring storm, and would have blown over by tomorrow afternoon. But she was still jittery. Unable to concentrate, she googled *Matthew Georgias/Melissa Aliente*.

Most of the articles were from gossip blogs, or art reviews. *The Royal Gazette* had another piece on the murder, stating that Georgias' family were devastated and planning a memorial service in Bermuda... No mention of a feud between siblings.

There was a whole load of information on the galleries owned by the Stone family, the artists that had been signed, the jet-set circles the family moved within. Numerous pictures of Jonas and Melissa at events, and yes, it seemed Jonas did indeed play polo. There was no family history on the website. Chloe was idly curious about the siblings' parents. Their mother was dead, but where was their father? There was also a photograph of Melissa with Matthew at a glitzy charity ball.

Chloe studied them with interest. Glamorous, glossy, and almost a matching pair with their high cheekbones and sharp features. They were leaning into each other, smiling for the camera. The photograph was dated March this year. Six weeks ago.

There was nothing else of interest, but Chloe did find a few lines on a community forum, art-based, and seemingly for anyone to post thoughts or opinions. The thread was about the tragic demise of Matthew Georgias. Everyone offered respectful condolences, until the last post.

> Matt and Melissa have been mixing art with drugs so what do you expect? She got him into something he couldn't handle and now he's paid the price.

Could that be true? Or was it just another piece of speculation? The shortening of Matthew's name suggested familiarity, but being online it was so easy to stir up gossip and lies without any truth. Chloe took a quick screenshot, just in case. In case of what, she didn't know, she was acting on instinct. Perhaps she would show Finn... Perhaps he already knew. The carving up of Matthew's face could have been a warning to Melissa?

At midnight the lights went out with a snap, plunging Chloe into darkness apart from her flickering candles. She took a shaky breath, one hand clutching the table, blinking hard as her eyes adjusted. It was just a power cut, not anything sinister. She had a spare torch in the kitchen cupboard, so she got to her feet and felt her way carefully towards the sink.

The torch was there, along with an emergency stash of plain candles, bottled water and canned food. Ailsa had told her on the very first day, to expect a few spring storms, and had even given her a basic list of store-cupboard essentials in the likelihood of it happening.

Not for the first time, Chloe felt a rush of gratitude towards her neighbour. She was certainly prepared, but that didn't make the darkness any less oppressive.

As she stood, peering uncertainly around the room, in the powerful beam of her torch, the noise of the storm seemed to intensify. The whole house seemed to be buffeted by the wind, and the torrential rain was so loud it drowned out any noise from the sea. Chloe hoped the animals were all right.

The sensible option would be to go to bed, instead of standing here, spooked, clutching her torch. It was just a storm, and she was a grown woman, in her own house, not a scared child. She turned to blow out the candles in the kitchen, pushing down the irrational rising panic.

A sudden hammering at the back door made her freeze in terror.

8

Her heart was beating so hard she almost forgot to breathe. The panic in her chest seemed to blossom and images of the dead body shot to the forefront of her mind.

The hammering came again, and she inched towards the door, keeping the torch pointed downwards. Her hand was shaking so much, the beam of yellow light made crazy patterns on the tiled floor.

Perhaps it was one of her neighbours come to check she was all right? No, she glanced at her watch, not at this time of night. Who, then? It wasn't debris from the storm, like a fallen branch, it was a fist against her door. Well there was no way she was going to make the classic mistake and open her door to an axe murderer.

For some reason the image of the man at Dockyard who had carefully stashed away his camera equipment popped into her head. Maybe she should have reported it to the police? Perhaps it was stolen and somebody had seen her looking and followed her back... Chloe took a firm hold of her irrational thoughts before they turned down an even crazier path. For instance, that whoever killed the artist was now after her.

The hammering came again.

She would ignore it. Whoever it was would go away. Five minutes later she was at the door, pressing her hand to the wood panelling. They were still there, she was sure of it. There was no further hammering, but during a lull in the wind and rain, she thought she heard sobbing. A woman?

'*Chloe? Please open the door if you can hear me!*'

She couldn't place the voice, but felt her confidence return a little. *Should she?* Could she open the door? The definite sound of sobbing decided her. It might be an axe murderer, but she couldn't ignore the pleas for help. She knows my name, Chloe thought as she wrestled with the bolt and lock, attempting to hold the torch steady as she did so.

The door came open with a jerk and a girl fell through, breathing heavily and shivering. Her hair was lank with rain, and drops streamed off her thin dress, pooling on Chloe's tiled floor.

'*Melissa?*'

She was clutching a large flat parcel to her chest. Unlike her, it was swathed in waterproof wrapping. Her breath came in gasps and her grey eyes were wild and terrified. 'Haven't you got any electricity?'

'No, it went out about half an hour ago,' Chloe told her. 'Look, why don't you come and sit over here. I can get you some towels and a drink...' She was already rummaging in a cupboard, for once grateful for her ever practical nature. Panic was quickly replaced with concern for the girl.

Melissa sat clutching her package, teeth chattering, watching her in the light of the torch. There was a bruise on one side of her forehead and her bare arms and legs were smeared in mud.

By the time she was swathed in towels and a blanket, wearing a pair of Chloe's thick socks, and sipping Gosling's Black Seal rum, colour was beginning to return to her cheeks.

'Sorry. For turning up here, I mean. You must have thought I was a loony, or drunk or something. But...' – she glanced into the living room, taking in her newly hung paintings – 'Jonas told me where you lived. I didn't know where else to go.'

'Does Jonas know you're here?' Chloe, sipping her own generous tot of alcohol, sat next to her.

The girl shrugged, her cocoon slipping slightly. She tugged at the blanket with long, thin fingers, shifting so she could smooth a hand over her package. 'No. Nobody knows I'm here. I didn't...' She bit her lip, clearly struggling to find the right words to explain. 'I didn't know I was coming until afterwards.'

'Until after what? Do you want to tell me what happened?' Chloe suggested gently. Melissa looked younger than ever, her hair drying in long dark wisps, her silver-grey eyes still big and scared. Now that her arms were clean, Chloe could see other bruises above her elbows, as though someone had held her tightly – fingerprints of red and blue.

'No.' Her chin came up, shoulders squaring defiantly, as she noted the direction of Chloe's glance. 'I can't tell you. But... I need you to do something for me. This package is really important. So important that I can't trust anyone else to have it. I want you to keep it safe, hide it for me.'

'But you only met me today! You don't know anything about me,' Chloe protested. And, she added to herself, I don't know you at all. The memory of the online forum worried her too, but her instinct was always to help and it often overrode her common sense.

Melissa leant forward, her face thrown into dramatic lines by the torchlight. 'That's exactly why. You aren't a part of any of this. You're a stranger, so I know I can trust you.'

'Part of what? That's crazy! What about your brother, or a friend...' Chloe's voice trailed off, disbelief edging her words.

She really hoped the girl wasn't into drugs, or was this package stolen goods?

The girl sat watching her, calm now, surer of herself and whatever plan she had hatched. 'Jonas likes you too.'

'That's irrelevant. Melissa, if you need help we could go to the police. Someone has obviously scared you, hurt you even...' Her eyes strayed again to the bruises.

She shook her head. 'I know you must be wondering if I killed Matthew. Everyone else seems to be thinking that. The police did interview me, and I could tell they were thinking that too.'

'That idea hadn't actually crossed my mind. Why would it?' Chloe asked her gently. 'I'm going to take a wild stab in the dark here and suggest you and Matthew might have been into something way over your head... It's okay, you don't have to tell me, but if you know who killed him you should tell the police.'

There was silence, broken only by the sound of the wind outside, before Melissa nodded. 'You're right, and let's say I might *suspect* I know who killed him.' Her voice trembled. 'But I can't go to the police because I don't have any evidence.'

'Is someone blackmailing you?' Chloe tried a different tack. She didn't want to ask outright about the drugs and destroy whatever fragile trust the girl had placed in her. 'Are you in danger?'

'I... All I need you to do is hide this painting for me.' She gasped and put a hand to her mouth at her mistake.

'It's all right, I'm not stupid. Even wrapped up tight like that, it looks like a piece of artwork.' Chloe smiled at her, coaxing the warmth back into her eyes. She'd prefer it to be art than drugs, but still... There were laws about handling stolen goods and if she agreed to hide the parcel, she would be breaking the law too.

She gave a tight little smile that didn't reach her eyes. 'So will you do it?'

'I...' *Should she?* Surely the best thing would be to take the package, give Melissa a bed for the night, so she was safe, and persuade her to go down to the police station in the morning. She could even call Finn on his mobile, if the girl felt safer doing that. 'I will help you, although I can't say why. I have a question though.'

'Okay. Thank you.'

'Who does this painting I'm going to be hiding belong to?' Chloe was careful not to let her tone sound accusing, but she figured it was a fair question.

Relief flickered in Melissa's eyes, followed by defiance. 'Me. It belongs to *me*.' A trace of irritation touched her voice. 'I didn't *steal* it!'

9

Was she telling the truth? Chloe studied the girl's tense face. 'I wasn't suggesting that you did, I just wanted to know. Look, Melissa, are you sure you don't want to at least chat with the police?'

'No!' She sat up straighter and grabbed Chloe's wrists. Her grip was strong, but her fingers were still cold, and shaking slightly.

'All right.' Chloe decided not to enquire any further. The storm sounded like it was moving away now and the rain had ceased. She stood up and flicked the light switch hopefully, but her house remained in darkness.

'They'll probably get it back on tomorrow. The electricity, I mean,' Melissa said from the sofa. 'I should be going. My scooter's outside.'

'Why don't you stay? At least until it gets light and the weather improves,' Chloe suggested. 'We can dry your dress, and shoes, and you can have the spare room. Honestly, I'd prefer to know that you're safe.'

The searching grey gaze tracked around the room, touching

on the framed photographs, before it settled on Chloe's face again. 'Have you got any children?'

'No.' Usually she felt the need to launch into endless uncomfortable explanations about this, but just now, she suddenly felt an overwhelming urge to go to sleep.

But Melissa just shrugged at her answer. 'I haven't either.'

Surprised, and a bit relieved at her response, she gently took the wrapped picture and put it in the cedar chest at the back of the room, laying a grey-and-white striped blanket on top. 'There, it's safe. Now give me a minute to find you something to wear and I can hang your things above the sink in the bathroom to dry out.'

Despite leaving Melissa tucked up in bed in the spare room, Chloe wasn't altogether surprised to find her unexpected guest had vanished by the time she woke. The sun was high in the sky and a fresh breeze chased away the ragged remnants of storm clouds.

The spare-room bed was neatly made, with the borrowed oversized T-shirt laid on the pillow. Padding to the kitchen, the tiles cool against her bare feet, Chloe poured a glass of water, sipping it slowly.

Her next stop was the cedar chest. She half expected Melissa to have retrieved her painting, but it was still there, wrapped and hidden under the blanket.

Curiosity made her hold it carefully up to the light, just to see if she could make out the picture. But the wrapping was thick waterproof plastic, stapled at the edges, so she gave up. The whole thing was bizarre. Should she speak to Finn?

But Melissa trusted her. It seemed rather sad that the girl had nowhere else to hide her treasure, except at the house of a stranger she had only met the day previously. The bruises bothered her. Somebody had hurt the girl, frightened her. The same person who murdered Matthew? Melissa had certainly implied she *did* know who the killer was. Or could she have killed him herself after a lovers' quarrel?

The possibilities made Chloe's head spin, but she thought it was really the drugs element that was bothering her most. Visions of an international drugs cartel descending on her home made her shiver with fear. A school friend in her teenage years had been duped into muling money for a large-scale operation. As someone who travelled on a regular basis, the girl had brought money, and drugs in and out of the UK at the beginning and end of school terms. She had also, through a boyfriend, sampled some of the 'products'. Eventually she was caught by UK Customs and endured a nightmare of threats and punishments from both the law and those involved in the drugs operation.

It was not a situation Chloe wanted to get into if she could avoid it. She could still hear her erstwhile friend's voice pleading with her to lie for her, so the supposed boyfriend wouldn't cut her face as he had threatened.

'Chloe? Are you up yet?' Ailsa's cheerful voice broke into her whirling thoughts. She was knocking on the kitchen window, a steaming kettle in her hand. The usual noise of clucking followed her round the house as Chloe opened the door.

'Thanks, Ailsa, I was just thinking about a cup of coffee,' she said, gratefully taking the kettle. 'How did you manage this?'

'I've got a little stove for emergencies. You should get one as well. Very useful in hurricane season. The power will be back on by lunchtime though, so don't fret,' her neighbour said confidently, settling down at the kitchen table. 'I brought you an extra box of eggs, too, just in case your girls are put off laying by the storm. Did you sleep all right?'

'Not too bad,' Chloe lied, grateful her back was turned as she reached for mugs from the cupboard. 'I must get out and check the stables for storm damage when I've had a drink.'

'They all look fine and Antoine's already in the yard feeding the horses,' Ailsa told her. 'Just a few branches down in my garden, and the usual buckets and the like blown all over the place. The spice tree at the end of the drive has taken a battering, but it's still standing.'

Chloe shut the door firmly on six brown chickens who were edging their way over the threshold. 'Oh good. I don't normally sleep in this late, but it was a bit of a disturbed night, wasn't it?'

Ailsa launched into a story about the hurricane from a previous year, when the island had been badly hit, losing many buildings and a large proportion of ancient cedar trees. Chloe half-listened, feeling her gaze move over to the chest, and back again. *Could* this all be down to drugs? She hoped not. Melissa, despite the gossip, had seemed so vulnerable. Maybe Matthew had forced her into whatever trouble she was in? After all, he was the one dead. With knife marks on his face. Oh God...

She could ring the gallery, she realised with relief, to check Melissa got home safely. It could be on the pretext of buying another painting, and if Jonas answered she could suggest a drink or something. If his sister was in trouble, did he know? Or, she thought suddenly, was *he* part of the trouble?

'I can see you're away with the fairies this morning. Don't worry, I told you, the power will be back on soon. This is just part of island life.' Her eyes narrowed perceptively. 'Or are you still worried about the murder?'

'Sort of, I suppose,' Chloe said apologetically. 'I just hope they find out what happened and catch whoever is responsible.'

Ailsa stood up, picking up her kettle. 'Whatever it was about, you've only been living back here five minutes so it can't touch you!'

That's what you think, Chloe thought, as she bid her neighbour goodbye and went to check on her property.

Antoine greeted her cheerfully as she made her usual round of the animals. Her own chickens had been joined by at least half a dozen more, and seemed to be having a noisy party on the muck-heap. A few cats were lurking around the feed room.

'No storm damage to the house?' Antoine asked, as he scrubbed out the feed bowls.

'Nothing that I can see,' Chloe said. She was keen to get back inside and phone the gallery, but checking the flyer, she had noticed they didn't open until ten. Probably they wouldn't even arrive to open up until half nine... and they wouldn't answer the phone before then. 'Do you need any help with the mucking out or anything?' She felt almost shy asking, especially as he seemed rather surprised by her question.

'Well... If you really want to it would be great if you could do Star's stable for me. Not being rude, but I wasn't sure how involved you'd want to be with the stables.' His tone was hesitant. 'Do you know how to muck out?'

She grinned. 'I remember, and I can see where the muck-heap is, so I'll be fine. Did Dre not muck out?'

He finished the food bowls and started on the water buckets. 'She did everything, but as she got older, her arthritis was very bad. She got very frustrated having to watch me do the things she used to' – he flashed a grin at Chloe – 'and she was a perfectionist, so everything had to be done right.'

Chloe smiled, imagining Dre sitting on the wooden bench near the gate rapping out orders like a drill sergeant. 'She always was. When I was younger, whatever I did she'd say to make the best of it, because you never know when things will come in useful.' She grabbed the barrow, added a pitchfork and broom and headed for the end stable.

They worked companionably for a while, against the

background noise of waves on the beach and birds chattering in the spice tree, before Chloe said casually, 'Antoine, do you know Melissa Aliente?'

He shrugged, setting down the clean bowls to dry in the sun. 'The artist? She's Jonas' sister, isn't she? I've seen her around.'

'Yes. I bought some of her paintings yesterday.' Chloe finished her share of the chores, propped the brush against the wall, and picked up a ginger-striped cat, who purred with pleasure.

'She was dating Matthew Georgias, but it was a bit on and off. I think the police questioned her,' Antoine said. 'Josonne thinks she's hot, but she only ever hangs out with the artists, or society people. You know, the "it crowd".'

Chloe cradled the cat, and leant back against the fence, enjoying the heat on her shoulders, the view of the sea. But she was still dithering. She'd forgotten Antoine's connections via his cousin Josonne. Perhaps she could talk to Josonne. But say what? Interfering could make things worse. The bruises on Melissa's forehead and arms were still worrying her. It *hadn't* been an accident. The pattern of the redness and bruising had clearly shown someone's finger marks.

As Melissa herself must have seen when she looked in Chloe's bathroom mirror this morning. Just the thought of the girl making her bed so neatly, creeping carefully out of the house, driving off alone into the storm-tossed morning, made Chloe uneasy and worried.

The first thing she needed to do was make sure Melissa was safe. Afterwards, she would decide whether to tell the police about the package, and the girl's midnight visit.

10

By mid-afternoon the sea was restored to its usual state of smooth, rich blueness, and the electricity was back on.

Chloe's tentative call to the gallery had been answered by Jonas.

'Melissa isn't in today. She's flying out to New York tomorrow for some meetings, so she's packing,' Jonas told her. Was his tone a little flat, a little rehearsed or was she completely paranoid?

'Is she... is she okay?'

'Of course. Why wouldn't she be?' He sounded normal enough. Curious even, but still with that formal icy tone that seemed to come so naturally.

Chloe thought fast. 'Just that I heard she had been interviewed by the police about the murder, and I hoped she wasn't too upset.' It sounded lame, but it was worth a shot. She found she couldn't tell Jonas what had happened. What if he was responsible for the fear and the bruises? Melissa hadn't said who she was hiding the package from, only that Chloe 'wasn't involved'. So did that mean Jonas was?

'She was upset naturally, we all are, but business must go on, and her trip to the New York gallery has been in the diary for a while.' His voice was warmer now, more genuine in tone. 'But thank you for asking after her.'

'Oh, well perhaps I can catch up with her when she gets back,' Chloe said. 'I just wanted to tell her a friend of mine is interested in buying some of her work.' It was a flash of inspiration, and she would persuade Alexa to buy a painting if she had too. '...She's based in London, but I sent her a few photographs, and she loves them.'

'That's great news.'

Another quirk of Chloe's was listening to voices. When she was eighteen she had been involved in a car accident. The subsequent head injury had rendered her deaf in both ears for several months. When her hearing returned she found she could pick out tone and nuances in voices that she hadn't noticed before. It was a random quirk she had been left with, and sometimes it was useful.

As she listened to Jonas now, she felt his tone warm from cool and polite to friendly. He even asked if she would like to come to a small party tomorrow night to celebrate three new artists. 'It will be just drinks and canapés, but it would be lovely to see you. Both as an art lover and as a... friend.'

'Of course, I'll put it in my diary,' Chloe told him, both pleased and relieved. 'Thank you for asking me.'

Pleasantries over, there was an awkward pause, before she invented a fictional knock at the front door, and put the phone down. She found herself analysing the call, much as she used to do with various boyfriends when she was younger. Had he really sounded strained in the beginning, or had she been projecting her worries onto the call? And Melissa. Was she really okay and off to New York, or... Or what? She cursed herself now for not demanding the girl's mobile number when she had her in the house.

As a distraction, she turned her laptop on and started to

write a business plan for her stables. Apart from everything else, if she followed up on her idea of allowing artists into the stables, it would bring her into the creative circle at Dockyard, and therefore closer to the Stone family.

Relaunching Beachside Stables was going to be expensive, depending on how ambitious she was going to be with her plans. She bit the end of her pen, trying to stop her mind drifting to the package sitting in the chest.

After adding another few columns to her spreadsheets on the laptop, she reluctantly concluded that only the most pressing bills could be paid this month. That was the farrier, the vet and the feed merchant.

Taking a deep breath, she made the money transfers, watching the numbers dwindle as she paid the debts. But at least it was done now, and her rough business plan was taking shape.

She got up and made herself a coffee, as usual taking a moment to sip reflectively, staring out of the window at the blue-and-gold day.

It was so different to her London home, which had looked out onto other tower blocks, onto roads and cars and the relentless march of hundreds of people.

A quick call to the SPCA confirmed that she could pop in later for a chat, and to look at the dogs Helen had selected for her. Pleased, Chloe downloaded and filled in the adoption forms from their website, ready for her trip. The rescue centre was on Valley Road, near the Paget Marsh Nature Reserve, and not far from the bus stop.

Chloe tidied the house, put the washing on, and then remembered a box that arrived with her belongings. With no claims on her time until the SPCA visit, and following that, the soothing routine of settling the animals for the evening, she could make a few candles for the house.

Soon she was busy melting soy flakes in an old pan. The kit and instructions sat open on the table, along with a couple of pretty teacups she had found.

Clothes pegs clipped the wicks in place while she poured the hot wax. The only fragrance she had available was peppermint, and once the wax had melted she added a teaspoonful to her mixture. It smelt heavenly but did she need something more Bermuda-inspired for her new home?

There were a few labels and some string in the bag, but she left the candles to set and headed out to the beach. It was a short scramble down to the high-tide mark, where she took deep breaths of the warm, rich air, trying to analyse the smell. Salt, obviously, but there was a fragrant depth to the island air, and a tinge of sweetness. Clearly she would need to experiment with scents.

A rush of excitement filled her heart with happiness. She hadn't been excited about hobbies or work for years. But now the challenge of saving the stables had caught her heart. And she would make candles scented with sunshine and sea, for a beautifully smelling home. Perhaps she might even join that yoga class too.

The sea tempted her, and she kicked off her shoes and paddled in the surf. Clear water bubbled and sucked at her toes, and her long pale hair lifted in the breeze. Heaven. And a perfect distraction.

The sand on the beaches varied in colour, but the distinct pink blush seen in abundance, but mainly on the South Shore, was due to geographic make-up as a volcanic archipelago, and the location in the Atlantic Ocean. She could remember Dre telling her that some kind of miniscule insect-like creatures living in the coral left behind tiny pink shells when they died.

These shells, Dre had lectured in her schoolmistress tone, scooping up a handful of sand, were then broken up by the tides and washed up on the beaches, giving them that beautiful colour.

Dre could have been standing on the beach in front of her, her long hair streaming out behind her, so strong was the memory. Chloe bit her lip in sudden wistfulness. Further out she could see boats, and along the coast the bob of swimmers' heads on the waves, paddleboarders making the most of a glorious day, and someone flying a kite on the next beach. She could swim, she really could... But another wave brought coloured strands of seaweed that tangled around her ankles and she felt a twinge of fear. Not today, she thought, the inclination dying. But maybe soon.

Walking back up the cliff path, panting slightly from the climb, she waved at Antoine, who was saddling Star and Jupiter for a young couple. Must be honeymooners, she thought, smiling at their linked hands and gooey glances.

Leaving the horses tied up, Antoine shouted over, 'Hey, Mrs C! Finn called into the house about half an hour ago.'

Chloe frowned, pausing at the gate, her heart rate speeding up. Had he discovered Melissa had been here last night, or was there news on Matthew's killer? 'Did he say what he wanted?'

Antoine walked over, a riding hat in one hand, lead rein in the other. 'No, just to call him when you had a minute. He did say it wasn't urgent, and he only popped in because he was passing.' Antoine's brown eyes lingered on the clients, and he lowered his voice. 'They've never ridden before, so I hope they can untangle themselves long enough to balance on the horses.'

Chloe grinned. The couple were now taking selfies with Star, trying to get the grumpy bay mare to put her ears forward for a photo. 'They're onto a loser with Star.'

'Yeah. We're going out for two hours, so I'll see you at six.' He raised his hand in farewell and went back to his charges.

Chloe went back inside, pleased to see her candles had set and a luscious minty smell permeated the house. Without giving herself time to think, she called Finn.

'Chloe. How are you?'

'Hi, Finn. Sorry I missed you, I went for a walk along the beach,' she said, trying to keep her tone light and breezy. It wasn't lying, and it wasn't withholding information on a murder case. Oh God, she hadn't thought of that one. 'Sorry, what were you saying?'

'No trouble. I was just passing. I've got the day off tomorrow and I wondered if you might fancy a trip to St George's?'

'Oh... Yes, that would be lovely. Thank you.' Chloe was totally thrown, having expected questions about Melissa. Her guilty conscience was making her sound like a certifiable loony, she thought. Also, should she mention the man and the bag from Dockyard? She had almost forgotten about that after Melissa's visit.

But Alexa's advice rang in her ears. She had only just moved to the island, and she thought she should definitely be careful about stirring up any trouble, if only for the sake of the business she was hoping to revitalise. Hang on, though, was Finn asking her out on a date?

'Are you sure? Don't worry if you're busy,' he said, having clearly picked up on her confusion.

'No, I'm not. Thank you very much for asking.'

They arranged to meet outside Chloe's house at ten, and she felt a pleasant buzz of anticipation. She hadn't managed to get up to St George's yet, and it would be lovely to have Finn's company as she played tourist for a day. His easy conversation and friendliness made him very attractive.

She could also maybe offload her worries about Melissa. Jonas didn't seem bothered. The trip had been planned, he said, and in the diary, so she certainly wasn't missing. If the girl was indeed AWOL surely her brother would be worried, Chloe told herself firmly. It seemed Melissa had gone straight from Chloe's house to get ready for her business trip. But that still left so many questions. Mainly, who had hurt her and scared her so much?

Eventually, having designed a basic couple of pages for the new Beachside Stables website, Chloe could stand it no longer. Checking that her doors were locked, and none of her neighbours were in their gardens, she fetched the package from the old chest.

A knife cut through the heavy plastic wrapping with ease, and she carefully slid away the string to reveal a cardboard box. Reasoning with her guilty conscience, she told herself that it could still be drugs Melissa had left. She needed to check for her own safety. And if it was drugs, she was going straight to Finn, no questions asked.

It wasn't drugs. It *was* a painting, as the girl had insisted. Very beautiful, oil on canvas, and depicting the same figure as *The Painted Lady*. It fact it *was The Painted Lady*, but in miniature and slightly different. It was lighter, softer too, with more pale ribbons of pink and scarlet merging with the blackness of the sea at night. At least that was what she thought she saw. It was definitely one of those pictures where what you saw was personal. To her, a woman's naked body, under the waves, with perhaps a ribbon or rope winding gently around the figure, tangling in the long dark hair?

As with the other paintings, and the larger *Painted Lady*, she couldn't say she liked it. It was still too dark and still stirred unwelcome fears and memories, but wasn't that the point of creativity? To evoke emotion and response?

She moved the painting aside. Neatly stacked in the back of the canvas were packages of bank notes. Hundreds, probably thousands of US dollars, wedged carefully into the package. Now what was she going to do?

11

Chloe flicked through the notes with a fingernail, and saw that her initial assumption of the amount was correct. This was the kind of money anyone would kill for. Perhaps, though, a miniature of *The Painted Lady* might be worth even more? She remembered the woman at Dockyard, who had bought a Matthew Georgias painting simply because it was a good investment now he was dead.

Quickly, she picked up her phone and snapped photos of the painting and the money. Melissa had been adamant that this belonged to her, so why was she hiding it? Nothing made any sense. If the drugs rumour *was* true perhaps she and Matthew owed money and this was to have been a payment.

The bus dropped Chloe a little way from the rescue centre, and she walked quickly in the late-afternoon sun, hair hot and heavy on her shoulders.

Helen was waiting at the white-painted gate, and showed her in. 'I knew your grandmother. I didn't twig until I looked up the address, but she once brought me a stray dog she found dumped on the edge of the road.'

'Sounds like Dre,' Chloe said, smiling at her. 'Any animal or human in distress and she was the first to look after them.'

'So come and have a look around. I've got a couple of dogs that might suit you' – she consulted the paperwork Chloe passed her – 'I remember Dre had chickens and goats. We stayed in touch and I went over a couple of times. Lovely place she had out there.'

'Yes. I'm very lucky to have inherited it,' Chloe agreed.

'Shouldn't be any difficulties with the home visit, but we do need to check... Now come this way and meet your new dog!'

Chloe followed her round a square, white-painted building, already hearing excited yaps and barks from behind the wire netting, feeling a rush of excitement, coupled with a feeling of sorrow. She knew perfectly well that it would be a tough decision and that she would want to take all the rescue dogs home with her!

By the time she got home, rushing down the yard for evening stables, Antoine was already halfway through the mucking out.

'I'm so sorry, I've been down to the SPCA to choose a dog!' she explained, quickly collecting the dirty feed bowls.

'It's fine. Did you get one, then?'

'They have to approve the paperwork, and do a home visit but yes, I reserved one.' Chloe found herself beaming at him as she rinsed the bowls under the tap. 'She's called Hilda, and she's a Staffie cross, five years old and just adorable. Helen – that's the owner – said she had been kicked out because the family she belonged to had a new baby.'

'A Staffie cross? Will she be okay with the horses?' A slight shade of doubt crept into Antoine's voice.

'Oh yes. That's one of the reasons Helen chose her for me. She came from a smallholding with ducks and chickens and cows. I can't wait to get her home now.'

'Do you think she'll be a good guard dog?'

'Is that a subtle way of asking if I'm still nervous?' she teased him. 'No, it's fine, I'm joking. Yes, she's not big and imposing but I think she's certainly got a loud enough bark,' Chloe said, remembering the excited dog putting her paws up against the wire fence, looking imploringly at Chloe. It had been love at first sight when Hilda was allowed to meet her properly, and she had hated leaving her behind.

With the animals attended to and the chickens shut up for the night, Chloe made herself cheese on toast and a mug of coffee, before she curled up in bed with her pile of books.

This time she did browse through one of Serena Gibbons' titles, but only managed to get through a few chapters, before she drifted off, book in hand.

Chloe slept badly, despite her exhaustion, and she woke early. The first rays of sunlight were pushing through the blinds, and the beach was calling her.

At five in the morning, at low tide, the beach was perfection. Hers were the first footprints in the creamy pink sand, and she was quite alone for as far as she could see. Inhaling long breaths of the sweet, salty air, she tried to calm her racing thoughts. Was Melissa in trouble, or had *she* killed Georgias?

The earlier thought returning to her troubled mind made her stop dead. Despite her assurances to the girl that she didn't think she was the murderer, the discovery of the money made her edgy. It was such a lot of cash. This was not something she should get involved in, and yet she was already out of her depth. Her mother hen instinct to rush around rescuing everyone and everything, dimmed by her marriage, was now back in full force. She smiled ruefully to herself, thinking of the lovely Staffie cross who would soon be taking up residence in her home.

But she was a newcomer to the island, despite her connections, and if she was serious about the stables, it really wouldn't do to get tangled up with something illegal when she had barely settled in.

The sensible thing to do would be to hand the package over to Finn when he picked her up today. But again she saw in her mind's eye, Melissa's tearful face, her assertion that the package was hers and her ill-concealed terror when Chloe mentioned talking to the police. Chloe had felt sure at the time the emotion was genuine, and if the poor girl couldn't turn to her family or friends.

She turned slowly, wandering back along the beach, pausing to examine the tiny blueish blobs that were man o' war jellyfish washed up by the tide. Before the heat of the day arrived, the breeze was blissfully cool, tugging gently at her long skirt as she walked.

Antoine was busy in the yard when she returned. 'You're out early, Mrs C. You all right?' Goldie was tied up outside her stable as he forked soiled bedding into a wheelbarrow.

'Yes, thanks. I just couldn't sleep.' She paused, unsure how to frame her next question. 'I... I keep thinking of that poor artist. They haven't caught the murderer yet, have they?' She grabbed the second wheelbarrow and started on Jupiter's stable. The comforting smell of horse and hay calmed her jitters a little, and she turned straw with vigour.

'Not that I've heard. It's shaken everyone up. We get trouble like anywhere else, but this is... bad,' he said, leaning against the stable door.

'I heard a rumour Melissa and Matthew were into drugs and the murder could be something to do with a deal gone wrong,' she said, in what she hoped was a casual manner.

She had underestimated his intelligence, and he raised a sceptical eyebrow. 'Where did you hear that?'

'It was on a chat forum,' she confessed. 'I was just looking... I can't get it out of my mind most days.'

He studied her face for a moment, before nodding. 'We don't do drugs round here, but Matthew was definitely a party boy. He liked his pills, but he wasn't dealing as far as I know. Melissa, well, I don't know about her. I've never really talked to her, but she's always been a bit of an ice queen. Doesn't drink, doesn't hang out at the all-night parties... Yeah, the ice queen.'

Chloe considered this. 'And her brother, Jonas?'

'He's always friendly enough. Bit like Melissa in that he's very guarded, and icy when he wants to be. They're a funny pair, but I do know they lost both their parents. Their dad in the last year, I think.' He shrugged. 'Who can judge how grief affects a person?'

'I didn't know they lost their father too,' Chloe said, thinking grief may well have impaired Melissa's recent decisions.

Antoine fidgeted with the broom handle, and then met her gaze and burst out with, 'Mrs C, if you don't mind me asking, have you made any firm decisions about the horses?'

She blinked, confused at the rapid change in subject. 'What do you mean?'

He put the broom down, slid a hand along Goldie's neck and gave her an affectionate pat. 'I'm just thinking about the future, you know like long term, if I'm going to have a job or need to find something else...' He trailed off, obviously embarrassed.

She set down her hay fork with a clang and studied his

worried face. 'I wanted to get things a bit more organised before we had a chat, but yes I have had a look at the books and I know we're in trouble.'

He glanced down at his feet, scuffing a toe on the concrete.

'But I have plans and we're going to relaunch Beachside Stables with a website, flyers and a whole lot of networking. The horses are beautiful and well-trained, we have the perfect location, and we have you and me!' She grinned at him.

His own grin of relief was just beginning to break through. 'I thought you were going to say you'd decided to shut everything down and sell up. I've been wanting to ask for ages, but the timing never seemed right, and then there was the murder.'

'I never back down on a challenge,' Chloe promised him. 'And I'll go through everything with you tomorrow, if that's okay? I mean, you've been the manager for a couple of years now, so you must have a brilliant insight into what we need and how to take this forward.'

'I do!' His eyes were sparkling now, and his enthusiasm matched her own. 'I was saying to Dre about a website and social media, and about Louisa's contacts on the tourist board, but she wasn't having any of it.'

Chloe laughed. 'I can't imagine Dre bothering with all that nonsense. But don't worry, we're going to make it work, I'm sure of it.'

'I must text Louisa. She's been waiting to hear if I've been made redundant these last few weeks,' Antoine told her, reaching for his phone. 'What are you doing today?'

'When I've finished Star and Candy's stables, I'll do the water buckets, and then I'm going up to St George's.' She didn't say who with and he didn't ask. 'I promise I'll sort out all the paperwork and things this week. I suppose I've just been a bit thrown by all this. You know, with everything that's been happening.'

'Not surprising' – he turned back to his chores, still beaming and tapping out texts – 'Enjoy your day.'

She paused on her way through the gate. 'Just one thing I was curious about, Antoine, the investors who want to buy the property... Did Dre say why she wouldn't sell?'

His head jerked up. 'Not really. She didn't have anything against them, just said that this place was hers and she wasn't selling. Got pretty annoyed when they kept on pestering, but you can see how this would be a great area for redevelopment. Cliffside, access to the beach and all that. Plus they already did those new apartments further down the road. Your place would link it all up nicely.'

Chloe could see why he had been so worried. 'Okay, thanks.'

He gave her the thumbs up, and she felt pleased to have set his mind at rest. Chloe went back inside for a shower, shooing the inevitable chickens from her doorstep. She thought again of the investors that wanted to buy her land. And Jonas had been going to ask her to sell the day she found Matthew Georgias' body. Was it too much of a jump to consider that somebody might be trying to drive her out? Money, these things always came down to money. Was the gallery making a profit?

Chloe gathered up her hair, her brain still ticking over. Surely not though. They couldn't have guessed she would find the body, but it had been dumped on the trail below her house. For a second her mind flickered over the movement in Tranquility House as she'd ridden past...

But it was one of two trails that Antoine used regularly for rides. Perhaps somebody had hoped her clients would stumble across Georgias. Whatever had happened, Georgias could have been murdered for money. But whose money?

Chloe chided herself once again for having an overactive imagination, but her mind kept going over and over the same pieces of information. Where did Melissa, a painting and thousands of dollars fit into this picture? Jonas surely couldn't be part of this. As a gallery owner and art dealer, Matthew would be worth more to him alive, especially since his work appeared to be gaining in popularity.

A quick check on her emails revealed one from Helen at the SPCA saying her paperwork all checked out, and could she send someone over to tick off the home visit tomorrow?

Chloe tapped out a reply in the affirmative, and hastily pegged the washing out to dry, before going inside again to pull off her baggy sweatpants and T-shirt, and agonise over what to wear for her day trip.

Finn arrived promptly at ten, and Chloe, after brief panicky indecision over the pink dress or the blue one, was waiting at the top of her driveway. Off duty, he was dressed in a blue shirt and cargo shorts, sunglasses pushed up on top of his head.

'All ready for me to be tour guide for the day?'

She laughed, nerves vanishing. 'I think I might be able to cope with you for the morning, but I'll let you know if it gets too much!'

The car moved smoothly through the morning traffic. Scooters hurtled past, overtaking on narrow bends, making Finn mutter about tourists. The roads in Bermuda were all narrow, and twisting by necessity, covering as they did the rocky areas inland and the shoreline that linked the parishes. They were certainly not designed for a large volume of traffic.

'So how have you been? Are you managing to find everything you need?' Finn asked, as they reached St George's and parked in a convenient empty space at the side of the road.

Chloe got out, relishing the warmth on her bare shoulders. She was glad she was wearing the thin pink cotton dress, instead of the long-sleeved blue one, as the sun was now high in the sky, and she could feel beads of sweat starting on her neck and back. 'Yes, thanks. I'm going to relaunch Beachside Stables and as I get properly settled run it as a profitable business.' She explained about the website and her idea of welcoming artists for drawing classes, and he was enthusiastic.

'That's a great idea. And Dockyard is a proper hub for small businesses, so I'm sure there will be lots of other ways to boost your profits.' He glanced sideways at her. 'Not to mention Jonas Aliente's gallery. That has been a big success.'

Something in the way he said it made her look at him. 'You sound like that's not such a good thing?'

He sighed. 'It is and it isn't a good thing. There are a lot of people who feel Jonas should be helping to launch careers of Bermudian artists, but he focuses solely on foreigners. I know a few very talented up-and-coming artists who were turned away when the gallery first opened.'

'Aaah, I see. I met the lady who runs the community shop at Dockyard... Emma? She hinted at much of the same. I suppose it might have got people's backs up when Georgias became so successful?' It would explain why Emma had seemed so cool towards the siblings. Or partly, anyway.

He grinned. 'Is that a leading question?'

She could feel her cheeks burning, and bit her lip before answering. 'Well you started it. Obviously I've been thinking about who killed him. I think the entire island has.' Chloe glanced at him again, squashing the random thought that he looked very handsome striding along in the sunshine.

They started to walk along narrow streets, edged with colourful houses; peppermint-green, candy-pink, and a vivid blue that rivalled the sky for depth and richness of colour.

'I can't comment in an official capacity, especially as it's an ongoing investigation. Are you all right by yourself at the house? You're not worried, are you?'

'For myself?' Chloe was touched by his concern. 'Oh no, I'm fine. Ailsa practically lives at my house anyway, and Antoine's around all day.'

'She lives next door, doesn't she?' He grinned. 'I've had to sort her grandsons out a few times in the past. Little hellraisers when they were younger, but they've calmed down a bit now. It's amazing what a bit of sport can do.'

'She mentioned one of them is in the UK on a cricket scholarship. Alfie, wasn't it? Her daughter has twin boys, and she did say they were a bit of a handful,' Chloe commented, pausing at a shop doorway. 'This is so pretty. Do you mind if we stop for a bit?'

He shrugged good-naturedly. 'Of course not. We can do whatever you like. Yes, Alfie went when he was fourteen. He was another tearaway, but once he got into cricket properly, he was totally committed. Super-talented kid. Jordan could do the same but he's less focused.'

His voice had a slight edge, and Chloe glanced at him, surprised, but he just smiled and indicated she should go ahead of him through the doorway. 'Ladies first.'

The shop was filled with wire racks. On each tier neat piles of soap were stacked geometrically, so they looked like spiked sculptures, with corners pointing outward. Coloured blocks that smelt heavenly, and tempted Chloe's purse.

The owner was young, energetic and delighted with her praise. 'These are all made by hand, and I sell all over the island. I got a grant to start exporting to a couple of boutiques in the US, so I guess I'll have to expand soon.'

'That's great news, Claire.' Finn smiled at her.

'Yeah, I was over the moon when I heard. I got the money from the Skylight Foundation.'

Chloe looked up from her browsing. 'Isn't that the same one that funds the sports scholarships?'

Finn nodded. 'There are lots of charities and community-interest projects on Bermuda, and many of them are set up specifically for one area or another. The Skylight Foundation is a little different, in that it will help any young person to achieve growth. It could be in business, or sport, or academically.'

'Sounds like an excellent idea.' Chloe bought a small gift box of citrus soaps to send to Alexa. The thought of her friend opening the box on a grey, gloomy London day, and her pleasure at the vibrantly-coloured present, made her smile.

Claire took the money and popped the box into a string bag. 'Yeah, I'm doing good at the moment, thanks to Arron Stone.'

Chloe gave Finn a querying look, and he supplied the answer. 'He's the head of the foundation. Although he isn't from Bermuda he has spent a lot of time over here. And he has family on the island.'

'Oh?'

They were walking out the door now, into the burst of sunshine.

'Yes. Arron Stone is Jonas' and Melissa Aliente's stepfather.'

She wasn't sure why she was shocked by this. Everyone seemed to know everyone in Bermuda, and it made sense that there would be family connections. Melissa's stepfather. *Stone Galleries*. Of course. 'What's he like?'

'Arron?' Another shrug as they strolled uphill now, away from the dock, through more tiny streets, dotted with cafes and shops. 'I don't really know him. I've seen him at benefits and other events. He lives mainly in New York, I believe. The family are very wealthy, and I do like it when those who have money, are compelled to use it for good. Seems like a top bloke all in all.'

'I agree with the wealth thing.' Chloe pushed a sweaty strand of hair out of her eyes. 'If I had lots of money I'd donate to a whole bunch of charities and maybe start my own animal rescue centre.'

Taking her lead, Finn grinned. 'I'd help out some charities too, and then maybe buy my own boatyard. That would be the dream! Oh, to change the subject, I saw Helen from the SPCA yesterday and we talked about you. She mentioned you were getting a dog.'

'This island!' Chloe exclaimed, but she was laughing. 'Everyone knows everything, don't they? Yes, I am. She's called Hilda and she's a Staffie cross. I liked Helen a lot.'

'She's great and I'm glad you're getting yourself a guard dog.'

She looked at him quizzically. 'You're the second person who's said that. Do you think I need one?'

'No,' he hastened to reassure her, 'I just meant it might make you feel more secure having one.'

'Aah, okay.' Chloe felt it was time to change the subject. She had already made up her mind to tell him about both the sports-bag man and Melissa, but felt the need to prolong their normal conversation for a while before she got down to business. She was enjoying herself, she realised, in surprise. It was nice not to feel awkward or silly around Finn, as she had often done around men friends at home, and certainly around Mark...

'Which way do you want to go now?' Finn asked, as they reached a crossroads.

'Can we go up and look at the Unfinished Church?' Chloe turned towards Government Hill Road.

'Are you all right walking? I know you mentioned that you wanted to see St Catherine's Fort and that's a good four-mile hike.'

'I'm fine. As long as we can stop somewhere for lunch before we start the long climb.' She smiled. 'Dre used to take me for trips out to the beach up there, and I'd love to see if I remember it properly.'

The church was halfway up the hill, on Blockade Alley, and Chloe marched at a brisk pace despite the heat. Majestic in semi-completion, even though the roofs had never been added to the various corridors and halls, the church had been built on the site of the former Governor's House. The impressive gateposts were survivors of that era, and Chloe ran a gentle hand down the sun-warmed stone.

Finn assumed the role of tour guide. 'It was intended to have been a magnificent example of Victorian Gothic architecture. But after building began in 1874 there were continuous problems. I believe several workers died, a storm wiped out a lot of the half-finished structure, and then they just ran out of money.'

Chloe studied the stone walls, the half-finished roof and outlines that should have one day been windows. The gate was shut with a big sign stating that the structure was unsafe. 'It's very atmospheric, even half built. Such a shame it was never finished though, the lines are beautiful.'

It was funny, after worrying about their day together, she thought again how she felt perfectly happy she was with Finn. He was kind and considerate, funny, and, of course, drop-dead gorgeous too.

'My wife used to love it. She was a fan of old buildings, and we have a lot of history on the island.'

It was the first time he had mentioned his wife, and Chloe put a gentle hand on his arm. 'I'm so sorry. Antoine told me she died. It must be awful.'

He guided them both back down to the road, and they began the long climb. 'Yes, it was. It is. She was killed down in Sandys Parish in a road accident. The other driver was coming far too fast and hit her head-on. She must have swerved to avoid him and lost control. She never had a chance.'

12

She was silent. It seemed easier to confide side by side rather than face-to-face and perhaps it would help him to talk about it. She felt a tiny bit ashamed for thinking he was gorgeous earlier, when he was clearly suffering. When had Antoine said it happened? Four years ago, that was it. Horrible.

'It does get easier. I have a lot of happy memories. Our son, Daniel, lives and works in London now. He's engaged to a British girl, and they want a wedding in Bermuda in a couple of years.' He glanced down at her. 'I suppose you should know, if you haven't already been told, that the driver who pushed my wife off the road was Jordan, Ailsa's grandson.'

'My God, that's awful. Was he... in prison?' Chloe thought of Ailsa's worries about her grandson, but she had never mentioned this.

'He was only thirteen so he did time in a juvenile detention centre. It's over and it was an accident. Do you want to stop for a bit and admire the view?'

The abrupt change of subject told her he had shared enough, and she quickly took her cue from him, despite her mind still spinning with the horror of this new information.

'Love to. It's just so stunning, and I could do with five minutes in the shade.'

They paused under a line of pine trees, and looked back down at St George's. The sprawling town basked in the spring heat, inhabitants turned to little dots as they scurried about their business.

'Tobacco Bay Beach,' Chloe said, when they walked on. 'We must stop there if we have time. We used to get fish for lunch and ice creams after we went snorkelling.'

'It'll be quite busy now. Probably far more touristy than you remember it,' Finn warned.

The bay was busy. With Easter approaching, locals and tourists were making the most of the first real burst of hot weather. The bluey-green water, the dark rocks encircling pools, and the cheerful gaudy umbrellas brought back Chloe's childhood.

'I sometimes wonder what I would have been like if my mother hadn't taken me away from Bermuda,' she said. 'At the time it was a huge culture shock, but nobody ever mentioned leaving me with Dre permanently. I knew it wasn't forever, but I suppose I secretly hoped each time they came back that they might forget about me, and let me stay on the island.'

He smiled down at her. 'And now you're back. Older and wiser, and settling back in.'

'It is funny, but I do feel so much stronger here, much happier. Back home, my job was boring, and everything felt flat and grey. I would never have had the confidence to run my own business for instance. I...' Wondering if she was talking too much, she met his eyes, but saw nothing but keen interest. 'My ex-husband, Mark, left me on my birthday. My fiftieth. I know it shouldn't be such a big thing, your fiftieth, but for me it was.'

'Your husband, ex-husband, I presume, must be an idiot,' Finn said hotly.

She sat down on a rock, stretching her aching legs. 'Yes. I mean I think he is, obviously, but I didn't to start with or I wouldn't have ever married him. Other people like him, it just didn't work for us, I suppose. He's a journalist, and he certainly gets a lot of work. But I was in a bad place and Dre leaving me the house... It was like it was meant to be.'

'So you could start again?' The gleam in his eyes suggested he was also happy she had been left the house. 'Shall I get us a drink from the cafe?'

'Yes, please. Just a juice with lots of ice would be lovely.'

Chloe often worried that she was boring people during long conversations. She wasn't stupid, and she knew this feeling stemmed from a lack of self-confidence. Mark had been chipping away at her for years. Little remarks, little sighs, raised eyebrows at things she did. To some women, she supposed it wouldn't have mattered, but to her, it had been confirmation that she was indeed boring, not worth talking to, or taking out.

It was fun to be out in the sunshine, exploring half-remembered places, and not feel she was being a burden in any way. And then she also had the party at the gallery to look forward to. She had a feeling that might be rather more of a challenge. Her mind wandered back to the painting, to Melissa. It was time to bring up her worries. She so hoped that her confessions wouldn't ruin the day.

After a cold drink, the words popped out before she even planned to speak. 'Finn, there's something I need to tell you. In fact, a couple of things...'

They started walking up the hill again. Starting with the easiest one, she told him about the man and the sports bag at Dockyard.

He listened carefully, and as they walked under a row of shadowy pines, she showed him the photos on her phone. 'I think I know who you saw, and if it was him, he has already been in touch. He *was* at Tranquility House the morning you found the body.'

She stopped walking and stared at him.

'Shay Taylor. He's an American photographer. He and his girlfriend, Michelle, came into the station for a chat. They photograph derelict buildings around the world.' Finn smiled. 'They have a very active Instagram account, and from what I can see make a nice living from it.'

'I see,' Chloe said slowly, as they started walking again. 'That would be why he was sneaking around Dockyard?'

'Yes. A lot of their photography is done at night, and a good percentage is actually illegal. They break into the deserted buildings and set up for various shots, then get out before security find them.' Finn was looking disapproving now. 'It's pretty dangerous, some of it. I had a quick look at some of their pictures and they take a lot of risks.'

Chloe let out a long breath. 'I can kind of see it, and I'd like to have a look at their photos. I... I love old buildings myself, especially the kind where you don't pay to join a queue of tourists and get ushered round.'

He laughed. 'Is that a guilty secret?'

'It kind of is, I'm afraid, but I certainly don't have any plans for breaking and entering. So that's one mystery cleared up.'

'You have others?'

'Oh yes, I'm afraid so. Seriously, this is one I'm more worried about...' Chloe said, and blurted out the whole story. Melissa, the money, the painting, the packaging, her concerns about the possible drugs link. Finally, when he didn't speak, she nudged him. 'What do you think?'

He frowned. 'I don't know yet. Wow, I wasn't expecting that at all.'

They walked a little further in silence and just as Chloe was thinking she couldn't go any further, they reached the last bend.

Ahead and slightly to the left, lay the beach and St Catherine's Fort. The sand was like pink-and-white icing sugar, and the sea a ribbon of rippling turquoise with a wooden jetty stretching out into the water. The beauty of the scene, and her anxiety over her confession made her throat tighten.

'Chloe?'

She tore her gaze away from the scene in front of them, and back to Finn.

'Firstly, I'm glad you told me.' His brown eyes, the pupils threaded with amber, were fixed intently on hers. 'Secondly, as I said before, I can't make any comments on the ongoing investigation, but I am worried Melissa and Matthew could have been putting others in danger with their actions. And lastly...' He swallowed and just looked at her.

'And lastly?' she prompted, staring at him as though she could prise the secrets from his mind. Putting others in danger? He hadn't denied the drugs rumour.

'Lastly, I don't want to scare you, but you could also be in danger.'

'*Me*? Why?' Chloe said. 'Let's just go down to the beach for a bit.'

He led the way downhill, over the road and onto the sand. In the shade of the tree-fringed beach, Chloe pushed her sunglasses back onto her head and kicked off her sandals. They were comfortable, easy to walk in and very unfashionable, but her feet were now aching from the climb. She sat down, wriggled her toes in the sand and tried to ignore the icy shivers that raced up her spine at Finn's words.

'You have the painting and the money in your house,' he said. 'The first thing to do is to get it safely down to the police station.'

Chloe thought of Melissa's tearful pleas. 'But why would she give it to *me*? I feel so bad that I'm betraying her trust and handing it over. And come to that, it's been worrying me that she is supposedly in New York, but she never said a word about a trip when she was at my house.'

'Melissa seems to be a complex character, and Chloe, you seem to be a very kind, giving person. It may be that Melissa picked up on that...'

'She was faking?' Chloe thought back to that night. '*No!* She had bruises and she would have to be an incredible actress to give such a convincing performance.'

'Sorry, I didn't mean to sound patronising,' he said gently. There was an uncomfortable pause. 'You haven't seen her or heard from her since?'

'No, but I called the gallery the morning after it happened. Jonas doesn't seem bothered and surely if he thought his sister was in trouble, or if she really went missing he'd be the first to call you in?' Chloe pulled her bottle of water out of her bag and unscrewed the cap, frowning.

Finn leaned back on his elbows. 'We did interview Jonas as well. He and Melissa both have alibis. It's common knowledge, and Jonas will probably mention it himself when you go to the party tonight.'

Chloe spluttered water down her dress. 'How do you know I'm going to the party? Are you a mind reader or just MI5?'

'This is Bermuda, we don't need MI5.' He grinned at her suggestions. 'I was invited and I've seen the guest list. I get lots of invitations, so I always ask to see a guest list before I commit.'

She smiled, tickled by the idea. 'That's such a good way to deal with things. Don't people get offended?'

'I don't know. Maybe, but I see no point in going somewhere if there's nobody interesting to talk too. I might as well be working on my boat.'

'You have a boat?'

'A Bermuda rig. It's a fore-and-aft rig that uses a triangular mainsail. Working on it, or sailing it are both pretty therapeutic. I'll show you one day.'

'That's why you wanted to buy a boatyard!' She nodded, pleased at this promise of future excursions. They were silent for a long while, listening to the waves lazily crashing onto the beach, the whisper and rustle of the tree branches above their heads.

Eventually Finn spoke. 'Seriously though, as soon as we get back, you can give me the painting and money for safekeeping. I'll make a couple more quick phone calls as we walk back if you don't mind, and get a few people in the loop.'

'Of course I don't mind, I'm really just worried about Melissa.' Chloe took his extended hand and hauled herself to her feet, brushing sand from her dress, looking around for her sandals. 'I've had a heavenly day, so thank you so much, and I'm sorry I didn't tell you about the painting before. I was just... I don't know...'

His face softened. 'It's fine, I understand. But we need to make sure it's safe now, and find Melissa. As I said, it could be that she and Matthew *were* mixed up in something that led to his death.' Finn glanced at her, as though debating whether to say more. 'What was the forum you were reading?'

'I can send you the link. It was an art forum.'

'We also need to consider that the perpetrator of the crime is perhaps targeting those from the artist community.'

Chloe's hand flew to her mouth. 'I never thought of that! Wait, why would you think that though? Melissa only mentioned her and Matthew. Oh, I have a screenshot from the forum. Look...' She scrolled through her pictures and handed her phone to him.

'Yes, I see. We are spending time investigating possible drugs links, but you'll just have to trust me when I say that we might want to take a closer look at the artists themselves.'

He clearly felt he had said enough, and she wondered if he had perhaps told her even more than he intended in his efforts to reassure and comfort her.

Chloe just nodded in response, her mind whirling with crazy ideas. The craziest of them all was that perhaps another artist with a grudge might be responsible for Matthew Georgias' death. But she didn't voice any of this, respecting Finn's professional silence. He had certainly gone above and beyond for her, and she wouldn't pressure him for more information.

She dropped slightly back, pretending to take some more photographs of the spectacular bay behind them as he made his calls.

Most of the car journey back was spent in easy silence. Halfway to the stables, Chloe got a text from the SPCA saying that Helen would send someone to visit tomorrow at ten if that was convenient.

Chloe had a brief panic that she might not have time to prepare the house, and told herself not to be silly. She had already checked the fencing in the garden, and there was plenty of space for a dog bed in the corner of the kitchen. Not wanting to tempt fate, she decided against purchasing any of the necessities until she passed the home visit.

Chloe sat listening to Finn's phone calls, curt and brief. They ascertained that nobody knew there was a copy of *The Painted Lady* in existence, and so far his contacts had drawn a blank on large withdrawals from Matthew Georgias or Melissa Aliente's bank accounts. No robberies had been reported on the island involving vast sums of money either, which meant they were no closer to solving the mystery.

It was a relief to get home to her tangerine-coloured house, to show Finn into her cool kitchen, and open the cedar chest.

'Do you want some iced water or anything? I'll just get the painting. It's all packaged up...' She was leaning down, opening the lid and moving the striped blanket carefully to one side, but her face was turned towards Finn. Chloe looked down, hands outstretched.

The package was gone.

13

'Are you absolutely sure this is where you left it?' Finn queried. 'Sorry, I'm not being an ass, just checking.'

'Yes! It was wrapped in this blanket.' Chloe ran shaky hands through her hair. 'Thank goodness I took the photographs, or I might think I dreamt the whole thing.'

Finn was walking around the house now, checking doors and windows. 'Well it doesn't look like there's an obvious point of forced entry. Who has your spare key, if you have one?'

'Ailsa, but she would never have taken the picture! She only comes over to gossip and she's lovely anyway. What reason could she possibly have to...?'

'Calm down. I'm not pointing fingers, just asking. Did Melissa see where you put the package?'

'Yes. She watched while I laid it in the chest. Perhaps she came back for it? But if it was someone else, and they knew Melissa gave the package to me, but didn't know where to look for it, it wouldn't take long to search my house.' Chloe went quickly into her bedroom, checking her jewellery, her bank cards, and her laptop. 'Nothing else appears to be missing.' Her heart rate was slowing now, her breathing more even.

'Let's go and have a chat with Antoine. Maybe he saw something. And you need to check Ailsa still has your spare key,' Finn said.

Chloe opened the front door, and he followed her down to the stables. Antoine was just waving off a group of six into their hotel minibus.

'Did you have a good day out?' he asked cheerfully, his smile fading as he took in their serious faces.

Chloe explained that she thought she might have had a break-in, reassuring him that nothing was missing. Somehow she didn't want to mention the painting or Melissa.

'That's terrible! Not while I've been here, but that group that just left wanted a two-hour ride, so I've only just got back. Are you sure nothing was taken?' Antoine was clearly shocked.

'Nothing that I can see. It's just a bit strange,' Chloe said lamely, adding, 'Leave some of the tack and I'll clean it later if you like?'

'Don't worry, Mrs C, I like tack-cleaning,' Antoine said, and studied them both for a moment, apparently thinking hard. He unhooked metal bits from the bridles, dunking them into a bucket of water. Finally, he said, 'This isn't connected to the murder, but I did hear something from Louisa last night that I was going to mention... She works for the tourism board sometimes as well as her job in Dockyard, and she told me somebody had been spreading rumours that the stables are going bust.'

'My stables?'

'Yeah. Lou said it was just gossip and it was impossible to tell who started it, but, of course, if it gets back to the hotels, and the tourism board, we are less likely to get business sent our way.'

'That sounds like somebody is trying to get you closed down,' Finn commented, a serious expression on his face.

'There is a lot of competition for riding contracts,' Chloe said thoughtfully. 'I do know there are more stables up St George's way because I had a look online before I even came over. Since I looked at the accounts I noticed that Dre lost a big hotel contract recently. The Royal Majestic or something?'

'Yes, she did and that was a blow. They never said why but the business was divided up between two other stables on the island. I can't be sure, but we never had a problem with them before, so I would say this gossip might have had a lot to do with the fact we were dropped,' Antoine said.

'Surely if you had a good working relationship with the hotel they wouldn't have listened to a bit of gossip?' Finn suggested quietly.

'The old team wouldn't have, but there was a new manager brought in from outside Bermuda, and I suppose if he couldn't be sure we were reliable and had a future,' Antoine commented thoughtfully, shrugging as he spoke.

Finn nodded, understanding, as Chloe questioned, 'Can you ask Louisa if she can do a bit of discreet digging? Just to see if it leads us back to the source?'

'Yeah, she'd love that, a bit of detective work.' Antoine grinned. 'But seriously, it's a worry, so the sooner we get it sorted the better, especially if we're going to go all out to save the business.'

'Which we definitely are,' Chloe stated firmly.

'I agree with Antoine,' Finn said. 'If there is something going on, we'll find out, Chloe, and put a stop to it. Meanwhile, weren't you going to pop over to Ailsa's house?'

She nodded, and walked down the path between the two houses, slipping through the hedge, knocking on her neighbour's open door. Five brown chickens strutted out, but Ailsa was nowhere to be seen.

Pushing the door tentatively, Chloe went into the kitchen. 'Ailsa?'

A rangy, striped tabby cat wound around her feet, and she could tell by the soft clucking that the chickens had followed her inside. Puzzled, she called again, walking into the narrow hallway, gently pushing open the bedroom door.

Ailsa was lying on her bed, a blanket over her feet. Chloe would have retreated quickly and left her to her afternoon nap, if she hadn't noticed the sizeable bump and bruised face. She bent down and shook her neighbour's shoulder carefully. '*Ailsa?* Are you all right? Open your eyes!'

But Ailsa stayed unconscious, breathing deeply and rhythmically, as Chloe flew back outside, falling over chickens, shouting for Finn in panic.

When the ambulance arrived, Ailsa was awake, and clearly in pain. Her bruised face had swollen and her right eye was almost completely closed. 'What's going on? What happened?'

'We're going to get you sorted out first, and then you can tell us what happened,' Chloe soothed, squeezing her wrinkled brown hand gently.

'I don't... I don't remember what happened.' Ailsa tried to sit up, winced and was gently pushed back down by the paramedic. 'There was a knock on the door. I thought it was going to be Jordan arriving early. He was due to pop over... Cheryl was hoping I could talk some sense into him about this new job at the sports shop in Hamilton.'

'Could Jordan have hurt you?' Finn asked carefully.

Ailsa snorted in amusement, and then winced again. 'Of course not. It wasn't Jordan anyway. It was a stranger. Taller than my boy. I could see that much through the glass.' She pointed at her frosted-glass window next to the front door.

'Male or female?'

'I couldn't tell.' Ailsa winced again as the blood-pressure cuff inflated. 'I suppose a man by the size. I don't remember anything after that. I feel sick.'

'Your door was open when I came round,' Chloe noted.

By the time Ailsa was on her way to hospital, and Finn had gone down to the police station, Chloe realised it was already past four. The gallery drinks party was at eight. Should she still go? She was exhausted, and very worried about both Ailsa and Melissa.

Finn had told her that naturally he wouldn't be attending the party after this most recent incident, but he had urged her to go, to take her mind off things. He promised to call her when he located Melissa, or if anything urgent came up that she needed to know.

Undecided, Chloe had a quick shower and went out into the yard. Antoine was out with a single last-minute booking, and the other horses accepted her gifts of chopped carrots and apples. She stared out at the sea, watching the gentle swell of the waves, listening to the Longtails screaming over the ocean.

A text from Cheryl reassured her that Ailsa at least was safe and recovering:

Mum's fine and wants to go home. Will keep u updated. Thank u for helping out x

She hadn't asked Ailsa about the spare key, but she felt it was fairly obvious whoever had hit her neighbour, had taken the key, searched her own house, and taken the package. It sent chills along her arms, imagining somebody searching through her possessions.

If the SPCA were happy she thought she might go shopping for the dog bed and food tomorrow afternoon, and arrange to pick Hilda up on Wednesday. Would Peter allow her in the taxi with the dog? Oh God, she hadn't even thought of how she would actually get her home.

But it would be lovely to have the bouncy black-and-white dog around, and very comforting to have her solid presence in the evenings. Chloe did hope she really was okay with chickens, because Ailsa would be devastated if anything happened to her noisy feathered friends.

Star and Sunny were plodding back along the trail. She could see the bob of riders' heads further down the hill, towards the sea, and she turned quickly, decisively. It might be a mistake, but she would go to the party tonight, and see what she could find out. Any hesitation about sticking her nose in where it wasn't wanted was crushed by this latest incident. She was involved. Somehow. And somehow she would find out what was going on.

With an hour to kill before her taxi arrived, Chloe went back to her business plans. The file on her computer was now jammed with ideas, and the flyers were designed, ready for the Dockyard shop and Jonas' gallery. She would need to find a cheap printer and get those done in bulk, Chloe thought.

Glancing at her watch, she realised the hours had flown by, and this would have to wait. With a worried frown reflected in the mirror, she applied another coat of lipstick, and spritzed herself with her new perfume. It was a lovely light scent called South Water, from the Bermuda Perfumery. Dre had always treated herself to their beautiful perfumes, and bought Chloe little glass bottles of fragrance for her birthdays and Christmas presents as soon as she was old enough.

～

Murder on the Island

Peter was delighted to be taking Chloe to the party in his taxi, and clearly just as delighted to be catching up on the gossip.

'Everyone's been so friendly,' Chloe assured him, in response to his anxious enquiries about how she was settling in after finding a dead body, and finding Ailsa after her attack. 'Really. Antoine is just brilliant with the yard, and Ailsa has been sorting out everything else I need...' She trailed off. She had called Cheryl at the hospital just before she left, and been told her neighbour was 'comfortable'. At least Ailsa had a small army of family to look after her, Chloe thought.

'I hear it's just a minor head injury,' Peter said, driving slowly and carefully round another blind corner. 'She's tough as old boots, Ailsa. Must have been a big man to take her out. If anyone finds out who it is before the police do...'

'I just can't believe all this is going on,' Chloe said honestly, settling the silky folds of a long yellow skirt across the seat. Agonising over outfits for the second time that day, she had gone for a bright-yellow skirt and an embroidered white peasant blouse with puffed sleeves to hide her upper arms. 'It seems like it's been non-stop since I moved here.' She bit her lip, not voicing her latest worries.

'Well, it isn't like Bermuda to have a lot of violent crime I will say, and certainly not murder, but don't you worry. All things pass, and whatever is going on, whatever spat someone has had behind the scenes, I'm sure it will all be sorted out soon,' Peter said comfortingly, as he inched along the road behind a queue of traffic, tapping his fingers in time to the radio.

She told him about Hilda and was delighted when he agreed to take her down to the rescue centre, and bring both of them back.

'I shouldn't really have dogs in here, but it's only a short distance and you say you picked a small one?'

Chloe dithered. 'Yeeesss. I mean, she isn't tiny but she could probably lay down on my knee for the journey,' she finally agreed, still slightly uncertain.

'No problem, just let me know which day you want to pick her up,' Peter said agreeably.

'Hopefully Wednesday, but I just need to get the go-ahead after the home visit. Fingers crossed,' Chloe told him.

It took Chloe several goes to get through the doors of the gallery. There were so many elegant people mingling, chatting and sipping champagne that she nearly lost her nerve. Walking casually past for the fourth time, she saw that she could probably just sneak off to one of the other bars in Dockyard and nobody would notice.

Outside, the shadows were lengthening, and Dockyard was quieter, but enticing now with lights and laughter, as the night-time scene woke up. She could hear music, chatter from a group of teens leaning on their scooters, and she could see a bunch of people in evening dress boarding a sleek motor cruiser. Closer to the mall, a man stood smoking, and talking urgently into his mobile phone. He caught her glance and looked up, half smiling at her.

Chloe blushed and hastily turned back to the marina. She wondered if she should call the hospital to check on Ailsa again, or perhaps she should just get the bus home?

14

Cursing herself for her social anxiety, Chloe took a deep breath, held her head high, forcing herself to march, skirt swishing elegantly around her legs, straight back into the mall and into the party.

At first she couldn't see Jonas, but after accepting a glass of champagne from the waiter, she spotted him next to Matthew Georgias' paintings. He seemed to be arguing with a tall, well-dressed man, whose grey hair was slicked back from a large shiny forehead.

Intrigued, Chloe pushed her way through the crowds, smiling apologies, until she was right behind him. His face was set in annoyance, mouth downturned whilst the other man seemed to be half laughing.

'Hallo, Jonas,' Chloe said.

'Chloe!' He spun round, composing himself. 'I didn't see you arrive. How lovely to have you here.'

To give him credit, the charm returned in an instant, and she smiled back. 'Thank you so much for inviting me. Looks like a great party.'

The grey-haired man, wide shoulders barely contained in a

well-cut navy suit jacket, raised his glass to her, addressing Jonas. 'Who is this lovely lady? Another art collector?'

'More than just an art collector.' Chloe smiled. 'Jonas said that he had some new artists to introduce tonight and I was curious.'

'This is Chloe Canton. She bought some of Melissa's pieces the other day,' Jonas said silkily, his eyes still flashing with annoyance at the other man. 'Chloe, this is Arron. Arron Stone.'

The name was familiar, and Chloe searched for the link. He saved her the trouble. 'Delighted to meet you, Ms Canton, or Chloe if I may?'

She nodded. 'Of course.'

'I am Jonas and Melissa's stepfather. I expect they have mentioned me already.' The expectant smile, the warmth in the pale-blue eyes jolted Chloe. 'I am so proud of how well my stepchildren have been doing.'

Chloe's brain clicked the puzzle piece into place, even as Jonas stood looking slightly sulky, sipping his champagne. 'You have a foundation too, don't you? The Skylight Foundation.'

'Jonas *has* been talking!' the big man teased his stepson. His wide smile and genial manner was a total contrast to Jonas' stiff and icy response. He seemed to notice this, because a worry line creased his forehead and the blue eyes lost some of their sparkle.

There was an awkward pause, as Chloe wondered if she would make things better or worse by admitting it was actually Finn who had told her about Arron and his foundation. 'I expect Melissa will be disappointed to miss tonight. With you introducing new artists to the gallery. I mean... that must be a sign that things are going really well with the business?' Chloe stopped talking, aware of how awkward her words sounded.

Arron smiled gratefully at her, clearly still embarrassed by Jonas' lack of warmth. 'Melissa will be back from New York soon, if she behaves herself.' He laughed. 'My stepdaughter is a social butterfly, but sometimes she has to do some work!'

Jonas flashed another scowl at his stepfather. 'Melissa is also a very talented artist in her own right.'

'Of course she is!' Arron agreed hastily, apparently noticing he had made another gaffe. 'But I just mean nothing that's going to set the art world alight, like Matthew did. But she is talented...'

Chloe, clutching her glass, was trying to keep a pleasant, neutral expression on her face. She was riveted by the poisonous undercurrents in the conversation.

Arron seemed a likeable bear of a man, despite his size and reputation, he was made all the more appealing by his awkwardness around Jonas. It couldn't be more obvious that Jonas disliked his stepfather. Maybe Arron had tried to buy his affection with this gallery?

It must be a very strange situation, if the siblings' father had died fairly recently, to be left with two grown-up children. Had they ever formed a relationship? Chloe knew exactly how awkward the dynamic could be, having dealt with numerous step-parents in her life.

Jonas seemed to gather himself. 'I must take Chloe to meet a few people, Arron. She's new on the island and I'd like to introduce her to some friends. Perhaps we could continue our discussion later?' The edge was back in his voice, and he gently took Chloe's elbow, steering her away from his stepfather.

Arron smiled awkwardly and shambled over to another group of people, glass clasped in one large hand. There was a sadness in his eyes and his cheeks were slightly flushed, Chloe thought.

'I didn't really ever get on with my stepfather either,' she blurted out suddenly as Jonas led her away. 'Sorry, I couldn't help but get the feeling the atmosphere was a bit tense.'

To her relief he smiled, and the hard lines of his face relaxed into naturalness. 'Families! You love them or hate them, I suppose. Arron is a brilliant businessman, but he will try to interfere in the running of the galleries. Melissa and I are perfectly capable and the Bermuda gallery really is our baby.'

'It's okay, you don't have to tell me,' Chloe assured him, draining her glass.

He instantly passed her another from a polished wooden tray. 'No, honestly I'd be glad to. Melissa and I are a highly competent team, but I'm afraid he still thinks of us as ten-year-olds. And my sister's own painting is rather fresh and beautiful in its own way.'

'I suppose everyone has a different opinion of paintings, don't they? It's like books – it would be boring if we all liked the same thing. When is Melissa back?' Chloe asked in what she hoped was an artless fashion.

'Oh...' He broke eye contact and leant over to snag a plate of canapés. 'Do have something to eat... Perhaps in a few days. She was annoyed to miss tonight but we also have a week-long event in New York that demands her attention. She's excellent at all the finer details of planning, that kind of thing, dealing with the press and so on. Why?'

Chloe carefully selected what looked like a crab pastry from the plate of luscious offerings, and met his eyes innocently. 'No reason really... just that my friend in London looked at your website, and definitely wants to purchase some of her work. She has several small hotels, and might want to discuss a bespoke piece.' This was true, Alexa had been saying for ages she wanted some genuine pieces for her Devon and Brighton boutique hotels, but Chloe had totally forgotten to mention it last time they had spoken.

'That's wonderful,' Jonas said. 'She is welcome to call me at any time. And of course, as I say, Melissa will return to Bermuda soon.' But he was back to looking distant and cool.

'Of course.' Chloe tried to nibble her delicious pastry without making too much mess. She licked crumbs from her lips, hastily taking a sip of champagne to cover the action. She was beginning to wonder if Jonas was a bit of a spoilt brat. He was certainly far moodier and less cool and collected than she had initially thought.

Jonas checked his watch. 'I must keep an eye on the time because I need to make a little speech and introduce our newbies. Look, their work is displayed on this side.'

Chloe inspected the six vast canvases hung on the white wall. Very different works of art, but each splendid in their own way. She glanced down at the names and photographs underneath; Kaila Montana, Greg Landon, and Sheetal Araminta.

'What do you think?' Jonas asked.

There was a large crowd around the three artists, all of whom looked totally at ease, chatting to admirers. The man, Greg, was tall and stick thin, with a black beard, a mop of untidy black hair and very white teeth. He saw Jonas checking up and waved at him.

The two women, one with long, glossy black curls, the other with short white hair streaked with pink, were laughing with a group.

'We were only going to take two new artists this spring,' Jonas told Chloe in an undertone, 'but with Matthew gone...' He cleared his throat. 'Kaila was on the reserve list before we took Matthew, and her work is similar. I like to ensure my clients have the opportunity to view and buy an interesting selection.'

Chloe looked back at the paintings. Kaila's work *was* slightly reminiscent of the dead artist's in technique, but her subject matter was totally different, being cityscapes with streaks of neon lights. The buildings were morphing into shapes as they faded into the background; squares, triangles and long, thin rectangles of silver.

Sheetal's work was an incredible blur of colour and structure, and Greg's a striking contrast in black ink, so finely drawn he had woven what looked like a whole epic story onto his canvas. It brought to mind legends and ancient songs, and it was certainly unique.

Jonas was moving her on now, acknowledging several more acquaintances as they slipped through the crowd. 'Now you should come and meet Fiona. She organises the publicity for several businesses in the area, and she told me earlier she was looking for a horse for a photoshoot at short notice. Something about a top photographer being in the area just for a few days, I think.'

They walked across the room, dodging the waiters, the elegant, confident people in lace, sequins and thousand-dollar suits. Chloe was fascinated by the clientele. She had almost expected them to be more... more arty. But there were no paint splodges on this lot. When she had attended exhibitions or viewings at home in London, the crowd was far more diverse, with everyone from art students, to pensioners, to actors. But she had to admit the food was better here.

A group of younger, well-dressed people were swapping business cards, and talking intently. A couple of the men seemed to be arguing, or at least in intense conversation.

'Are they okay?' Chloe asked Jonas doubtfully.

He glanced over, a swift assessing gaze. 'Oh them. Yes, they flew in from New York yesterday. I think they're friends of Kaila's... They certainly like to flash their cash. The taller man on the left, with the red scarf... He told me this morning he'd bought a yacht before breakfast.'

'Wow...' Chloe widened her eyes in amazement at the idea of

having so much money to spend. They moved on across the room.

'Fiona! This is Chloe. She runs the riding stables I was telling you about,' Jonas called across the crowds.

A tiny, voluptuous blonde woman in a tight, green-silk dress, turned away from a laughing group and beamed. 'How wonderful to meet you, and thank you to darling Jonas for the tip-off. Now tell me *all* about your horses.'

Slightly overwhelmed by such enthusiasm, Chloe barely felt Jonas' gentle hand on her shoulder, or his murmur that he would catch up with her later. Puzzled by yet another change in mood, Chloe smiled at Fiona.

'Well it really depends what you are looking for in your photoshoot. I mean, all my horses are well-trained and very placid. Are you having professional models?' Chloe asked, racking her brains for sensible questions.

'Oh yes. We're shooting a honeymoon brochure for Palm Bay Hotel, so I'm really looking for a pretty horse who will stand nicely for a model in a wedding dress. I'm sure you can imagine the type of thing.' Fiona smiled at her. Her eyes were a strange colour, hazel threaded with brown, like marbles. 'It is absolutely at short notice because I've managed to nab a brilliant photographer who is only here for a couple of days.'

Chloe pulled her phone out of her bag, flicking through the photos of her horses. 'Goldie is very pretty, and she has a lovely nature,' she suggested.

'Oh goodness, a palomino! Isn't she stunning?' Fiona was in raptures. 'This is perfect, and I don't know if Jonas mentioned it, but we will pay a fee for all our models, horse and human.'

'I believe Goldie is the only true palomino on the island,' Chloe told her, remembering something Antoine had said. 'There are lots of cream, buckskin or dun colours, but to be a true palomino a horse needs be have that gorgeous golden coat and a perfectly white mane and tail.' She felt rather pleased to have been able to sound like a knowledgeable horse owner and businesswoman.

'Perfect. Bang on exactly what I'm looking for,' Fiona told her.

'That's great. I mean if you're happy...' Chloe beamed back, shocked and delighted by the speed of the transaction. How could she have thought Jonas cold? He might have just provided her with an introduction that saved her business. 'I'm not sure if Jonas mentioned but now I've taken over the stables, I'm looking to form a partnership with a local hotel... We have six horses in total, all well-trained, and our location is unrivalled. Not only for a photoshoot, but also because we can access excellent riding trails on our doorstep.' That sounded good, very businesslike, she thought, mentally crossing her fingers.

Fiona bent over Chloe's phone again as she flicked through more photographs of the yard, the views and the stable block. 'You're right, the location is stunning, and in Bermuda there's plenty of competition. Okay, you put together a package with rates and a potential partnership proposal. I'm very happy to go ahead with the photoshoot. We'll do it at your stables instead of at the hotel, because I've got a few ideas popping into my head as I look at these photos... We'll discuss the rest afterwards?'

'Yes, I'm happy.' Chloe beamed at her again. Her cheeks ached from smiling and she felt like doing a little victory dance. It really did seem too good to be true, but one of Dre's favourite sayings had been never to look a gift horse in the mouth, and it seemed pretty apt in this situation. She could almost imagine her grandmother cheering her on from wherever she now resided.

'Hallo, Chloe!' It was red-headed Emma from the community shop. 'So sorry to interrupt, but I only popped in for a few minutes because I have a meeting. It's always so nice to support another local business, isn't it?'

Chloe said she supposed it was, despite thinking that if Emma didn't really like the gallery, or Jonas and Melissa what was she doing here? She introduced Fiona.

'So, Chloe, I was thinking about your suggestion of art classes at the stables, and a friend of mine is very interested. He takes watercolour classes and has a solid following. Shall I put you in touch?' Emma said. 'I take it you have some prices in mind?'

Chloe said she did, and promised to get the flyers over to the shop as soon as they were printed. 'Thank you so much for thinking of me!'

Emma smiled back, muttered something polite and moved on. Her red hair was a vivid cloud of colour against her orange dress. She walked straight over to the noisy younger crowd, Chloe noted, and was soon in intense conversation with the taller man Jonas had pointed out. Was she giving him money? Or perhaps just her business card.

'Sounds like your lovely Goldie is going to be in demand,' Fiona said, reclaiming her attention. 'Glad I got in first!'

Jonas, clapping his hands, managed to claim everyone's attention, and charmingly introduced the three new artists, adding that he hoped they would be very happy exhibiting here in Bermuda at the Stone Gallery.

Emma, Chloe noticed, was right at the front, watching intently, a look of fierce concentration on her face. She seemed to be exuding pent-up energy, fidgeting with her hair, curling it around and around her fingers.

Greg and Sheetal made polite little speeches about how excited they were to be here, but when Kaila stepped up to the microphone, she looked sombre.

'Ladies and Gentlemen, I am so honoured to be here tonight.

Having my work exhibited by the Stone family of galleries is something I have dreamt about for years. But I feel I need to mention that we in the art community were very saddened to hear of Matthew's death, and I know Jonas and Arron will continue to show his work here, and in their other galleries. His legacy will remain, even as we move forward. Art is about fluidity and is neither pinned to past nor present.'

On this enigmatic note, Jonas took the microphone back. He handed it to Arron, who launched into a couple of sentences about how the Stone Galleries had an excellent track record in talent-spotting and he hoped that Greg, Sheetal and Kaila would all go on to achieve worldwide success. Arron ended his little speech by beaming round with uncomplicated delight and accidentally dropping the microphone as he handed it back to his stepson.

'Shame Jonas didn't take on any local artists. It would have been such a chance for some raw talent to get noticed.' Emma was back at Chloe's elbow, business cards in one hand, phone in the other.

'I don't know how these things work, but I do agree it would be nice to showcase an artist from the island. Perhaps...' Chloe cleared her throat. 'Perhaps it isn't down to Jonas and Melissa to decide?'

Emma frowned. 'No, you could be right. Those two are just puppets on a string. Arron Stone makes all the big decisions and he's showing no signs of retiring. How are you settling back in? Apart from getting the business going again, I mean.'

'Oh good, thanks. I'm formulating a plan. Slowly.' Chloe laughed. 'There is such a lot to sort out, but I'm loving it and I'm so grateful that everyone has been so welcoming.' It sounded a bit gushy but it was true, and the icing on the cake was that if she could pull this photoshoot off, the stables might be saved. She noticed Emma still seemed edgy, and her face had a sheen of sweat, making her make-up patchy. Well, it was hot despite the air conditioning.

'I can imagine. Well you know where I am, if I can help in any way.' Emma gave her arm a friendly squeeze and walked purposefully towards the new artists.

'Chloe! Can we get back to business?' Fiona tapped her arm and handed her another glass. 'I'd like to double-check dates and times, if that's okay with you?'

'Of course.'

Official photographers were snapping the happy group around the artists, and lots of people were taking pictures on their phones. Chloe could already see little red 'sold' stickers on Greg's two pieces, and one on Kaila's biggest painting.

Sheetal was now in deep conversation with the tall man from the noisy group in the corner. Maybe he was a young millionaire, and if he really had just bought a yacht, he could definitely afford to buy some of her paintings, Chloe thought.

Within minutes, she found that the photoshoot was booked, along with the photographer, hair and make-up stylist and models. Tiny, brisk Fiona was a whirlwind of efficiency and energy.

'Thank you so much and we'll look forward to seeing you at the shoot. Such a lovely location. We can maybe think of selling a package for our honeymooners... It looks like there would be room on that terrace area for a table and chairs, some champagne and cake maybe... Anyway, must grab Jonas again before I go, but I can't tell you how excited I am about all this. Ring me with any queries!' After patting Chloe's arm affectionately, Fiona whirled off.

Chloe glanced at her watch, surprised to find that it was past ten. Peter would be here to pick her up soon. Jonas was surrounded, and Arron was enthusing over two walls of new paintings, waving his arms around and roaring with laughter.

As she turned to put her empty glass on a silver tray, there was a scream from the far side of the gallery, followed by other shouts.

'*She's having a fit!*'

'*Has she taken drugs or something?*'

'*Give her some room and call an ambulance!*'

Chloe forced her way through the crowd of jostling bodies, and saw Sheetal, the new artist with the mass of black curls, was half sitting, half lying, gasping for breath. She was clutching at her throat with one hand and with the other, her fingers were scrabbling for her bag.

Jonas was kneeling next to her, Emma and Fiona helping to keep people back, and Arron was already pulling open the emergency exit.

'What's happening to her?' One of the party guests was kneeling beside the stricken artist.

'She can't breathe!' Jonas yelled in panic.

15

_____

Chloe was near enough to see that Sheetal's face seemed to be swollen, her skin blotchy, almost like a rash, and in an instant she understood what was happening. She pushed forward and reached the other woman, kneeling opposite Jonas.

'Sheetal, do you have an allergy? Are you having an allergic reaction?' Chloe asked urgently.

The black curls had fallen over her face now and the wheezing of her breathing was horrible to hear, but Sheetal gripped her wrist, nodding frantically, pointing at her bag.

Chloe grabbed the evening bag, upended it and dived for the contents. A small cylinder with a blue cap. An EpiPen. She yanked off the cap, wrapped Sheetal's limp fingers around it and jabbed it straight into her thigh. Ignoring more shouts of horror, and shrugging off Jonas' hand, Chloe pulled the needle out and began to massage the area where it had entered Sheetal's body.

Beneath the woman's long, flared, velvet sleeves Chloe found a MedicAlert bracelet, and she showed Jonas. 'She's had a massive allergic reaction. She should be okay until the paramedics get here now,' Chloe said, watching Sheetal's face.

She was lying down on her side, her eyes closed, but her breathing was definitely easier.

'Are you sure? How did you know?' Fiona was crouching next to Chloe now, her eyes bright, expression fearful.

'My best friend, Alexa, is allergic to peanuts. She carries an EpiPen and wears a MedicAlert bracelet. I've been with her when she's suffered an allergic reaction,' Chloe explained. She was still shaking. Although she had acted on instinct, she still couldn't quite believe what had happened. 'Sheetal must have come into contact with whatever she is allergic to. It can happen very quickly, and it only takes a very small amount. With my friend, even peanut *dust* is enough.'

The paramedics arrived, and, excitement over, partygoers began to drift away. Chloe moved back and leant against the wall. The excess adrenaline was still coursing through her veins, making her shake and feel slightly sick.

'Thank God you were here.' Jonas, with Arron at his elbow, was looking dishevelled and exhausted. 'I thought she was having some kind of fit.'

Chloe repeated her explanation and added that Alexa was always very careful to avoid peanuts, or anything that might have been contaminated by them. 'Most people with severe allergies know exactly how to manage them. I guess whatever Sheetal is allergic to, must be here in the gallery tonight.'

The artist was being wheeled out on a stretcher, her eyes still closed, and an oxygen mask across her face. They watched her soberly.

'She could have died, couldn't she?' Jonas said.

'Yes,' Chloe told him, watching his face, but seeing only concern.

Arron was also frowning, blustering that it was such an awful shock, that he would speak to the caterers, and adding, 'I think we need to inform the police.'

'Why?' Jonas was clearly shocked.

'Because we have had one artist killed this month already, and now another nearly dies right here in the gallery. I don't believe in coincidence,' Arron said, worry clear on his face. He strode off, pulling out his phone, knocking over a vase of flowers and stumbling slightly as he went.

Jonas watched him with icy eyes and compressed lips.

Chloe winced. 'That's probably a bit extreme, isn't it? I mean... It was an allergic reaction.'

Jonas nodded. 'I agree. There is no way I think it could be linked to Matthew, but Arron... Arron will do what he wants, and if he wants to be dramatic and waste police time, that's what he will do. Excuse me for a moment, Chloe, I need to make a call of my own. Sheetal's family should know.'

'Of course.' Chloe found herself with Emma again, and several overexcited gallery clients. It was a relief to excuse herself after a decent interval, and make her way home.

Exhausted now, she wriggled through the remaining crowd, and touched Jonas' shoulder gently. 'Thank you so much for a wonderful evening, but I'm afraid my taxi will be here now, so I need to go.'

He made apologies to the crowd around him, and turned to face her. 'Pleasure, Chloe. Thank you for saving Sheetal's life. If you hadn't been here... I never had the chance to ask – how did you get on with Fiona?'

Chloe smiled. It seemed like a long time ago since she had been talking business, not a mere hour. 'She's very enthusiastic. The photoshoot is all booked up for two days' time.'

Arron was suddenly back, phone still in hand, pushing into the group around Jonas and Chloe, murmuring apologies. 'I would like to add my thanks to you, Chloe. You saved a life and we are all very grateful.'

Uncomfortable, very aware of his intense grey gaze, Chloe

felt her cheeks burn. 'If it hadn't been me it would have been someone else. You will let me know how she is, won't you?'

Arron smiled. 'Of course. And, may I ask, what photoshoot were you talking about?'

'It's for Palm Bay Hotel,' Chloe said. 'They want to feature one of my horses. She's a lovely palomino, so perfect for modelling. If it goes well, Palm Bay want to talk about a potential partnership contract.'

'That's great news!' Arron beamed at her. His silver-grey hair was sticking up at the front and his jacket had a stain on the sleeve, but he exuded good humour. 'So you won't be selling up any time soon if business is going to be good?'

How totally crass, Chloe thought, registering yet another social blunder. Out the corner of her eyes, she saw Jonas wince. 'No. Even if business wasn't good, I wouldn't be selling up.'

Arron raised both hands, laughing. 'Sorry, sorry, if you don't ask you don't get. No offence taken I hope, Chloe? As my stepson knows, I do tend to rather put my foot in things a lot of the time.'

How was he such an astute businessman? This clumsy, bumbling bear of a man, who now stood with his tie askew, a perfect contrast to his still immaculate stepson. 'None at all' – she smiled sweetly – 'and now I really must go. Jonas, do let Melissa know I was asking after her. Maybe you could get her to call me about that potential client?'

He nodded, and beside him, Arron said quickly, almost humbly, 'I need her in New York quite a bit during the next few months, Jonas, so I doubt she'll have much time for her own paintings.'

The fury that flared and was abruptly quenched in Jonas' expression made Chloe widen her eyes. Crikey, what was going on with these two? Suddenly, though, she was too tired to care. It had been a hell of day, and she just wanted a bath and bed.

'Goodnight, Chloe. Come along, Jonas, let's see if you can

make a few sales tonight, even after all the drama,' Arron said cheerfully.

Chloe turned in time to see Jonas shrug off the other man's hand from his shoulders, and the hurt in Arron's face as he registered the snub had been noted.

The lights at the rear of the gallery were being dimmed, and Chloe took a last look at the wall of new works. Only one wasn't sporting a 'sold' sticker, so clearly a good night's work for the Stone Gallery. Even as she turned to go, Kaila's paintings caught her eye again and she stopped, puzzled. Something had been niggling at her brain ever since she first saw them, but now it clicked into place.

The buildings morphing into shapes on the largest piece, ended on a silver-and-gold horizon, blocked by a triangle flanked by two squares. It was unmistakably the same alignment carved into Matthew's forehead.

'Oh my God,' Chloe whispered to herself, taking deep breaths to calm her rapid heartbeat. Finn had hinted the murder was linked to the artists themselves, and here was a painting replicating part of a murder scene.

She quickly continued with her exit, resolving to ring Finn first thing in the morning. It could be a coincidence. The shapes of buildings could really only be interpreted in a few ways, but the alignment was exactly the same.

Pushing Kaila's painting from her mind – it was far too late to do anything about it now, even if she was right – Chloe watched the flickering lights of the coastal paths on her way home.

She texted Antoine with the good news about Goldie, and the even better news that it was a profit-making venture. She smiled fondly as he texted back:

Wow, that's sick. Gotta be in early to give her a bath!

There was a message from Finn on her voicemail, telling her Ailsa would be home tomorrow and the scans were clear. He added that he had spoken to Jonas and Arron earlier in the evening, and managed to fit in a video call to Melissa in New York. According to Finn, her brother and stepfather had been telling the truth about her visit to the States. She seemed absolutely normal.

There was just one thing... when he had brought up the package, she denied being in possession of it, and insisted she had never visited Chloe's house that night.

16

—————

'**M**rs C!'

She jerked awake, torn from her dreams, flinging her legs out of bed. The late night, and her subsequent nightmares meant she seemed to have only just fallen asleep. Yet sunlight was streaming in through the slits in the shutters. Her bedside clock said it was just past six.

Antoine was standing at her bedroom window. Chloe fumbled with the shutters and window catches, still half asleep. But the urgency in his voice was starting to send shivers down her arms.

'It's Goldie. She's been stolen!' Antoine was distraught, sweat soaking through his T-shirt, beading his face and bare shoulders. He wiped a hand across his shorts.

'Are you sure? Couldn't she just have got out?' Chloe grasped wildly for a sensible solution. Goldie wasn't a Derby-winning racehorse, she was a hack for hire. Her value wasn't any more than any of the other horses in the stables.

Antoine nodded. 'I thought the same thing. But she hasn't just let herself out and wandered off. The stable door was closed and bolted behind her. Someone took her and didn't care that we knew it.'

'Is her tack gone?'

He shook his head. 'No, I checked, but if they can ride, she's easy bareback in halter... she'd go with anyone.'

'I can't believe this. I only arranged the photoshoot last night!' Her mind was whirling, remembering the gossip that Louisa had passed on. 'Oh my God, I've just thought... You don't think she's been stolen to prevent us doing the photoshoot do you?'

Antoine stared at her, wide-eyed and confused.

Chloe said decisively, 'Let me get some clothes on and I'll call Finn. I suppose you've been out looking?'

'For ages.' He glanced down at his watch. 'Over an hour. I got here early again because Louisa is supervising a delivery and she had to leave at four... There were fresh hoofprints heading down the Railway Trail, but then I lost them across the road at the five-mile point.'

'I'll be out as soon as I can. Do you want to come in and make yourself a coffee or something?'

He nodded gratefully, and Chloe padded out of her bedroom in bare feet to open the front door. Who knew about Goldie being chosen for the photoshoot? Fiona at the hotel, of course. Jonas knew. He had been right there when the offer had been made... Arron had made a clumsy crack about selling the land, too.

She called Finn and he promised to send someone over. 'Oh and Chloe, I heard you saved Sheetal Araminta's life last night. Well done.'

'I didn't do anything really... She would have done it herself if she could.' Chloe stopped gabbling. 'Arron said he was going to report the incident to you, to the police anyway, because he seems to think somebody is targeting his artists.' She remembered the shapes in Kaila's painting and was about to tell him, when she heard the crackle of a radio in the background.

'Sorry, I've got a possible incident in Hamilton I need to deal with, but sit tight, Chloe. Is Antoine with you?' Finn, as usual, sounded calm and in control.

'Yes. He's been out looking for Goldie. But we're fine. You get out to that traffic accident.'

Had Finn heard her comment about Arron, or was he just unable to say anything? Dressed, with a cup of coffee in her hand, Chloe went out to the yard with Antoine striding anxiously beside her.

'See? There's no way she got out and then shut the bolt neatly afterwards,' he said angrily, kicking a tuft of grass.

She did see. The sea breeze was fresh and cool this early in the morning, and the tide far below was rolling up the beach with dancing breakers. There was no sign of a palomino horse, but as Antoine pointed out, her stable was neatly shut and bolted. 'The police will be here soon.'

'Ailsa's still in hospital until this afternoon, and her house is empty, isn't it?'

'Yes. Why?'

'Do you sleep lightly? I mean, would you have heard a van?' Antoine asked quickly.

'A horse van? Yes, and somebody would have seen it. There are houses all along the driveway, and those things make a lot of noise,' Chloe considered. By the time she had arrived home, shattered from the events of the day, it must have been past eleven. 'I didn't sleep well, but I think that was more because of last night than because anything outside disturbed me.' She told him more about Sheetal, trying to distract from his obvious worry about one of his beloved horses.

'Wow. That's bad. Will she really be all right now? Did they find out what she was allergic to?'

'No. Finn never said when he called, just that she was okay,' Chloe reassured him.

'You told Finn that Arron Stone doesn't think it was an accident.' His dark eyes were watchful, thoughtful. 'Because of Matthew getting murdered?'

Chloe had forgotten, in her sleep-befuddled state, that Antoine had been with her while she made the call, sipping his coffee. 'I think he's being overcautious but then, I suppose that's better than ignoring a potential problem,' she said carefully.

He shrugged, clearly less interested in the potential of another murder, than the theft of Goldie. 'So we go back to the theory she was led, or more likely, ridden away, down the Railway Trail.' Antoine ran a hand through his hair, frustration clear in his face. 'We need to find her, Mrs C!'

The sound of a vehicle on the driveway made them both jump and Chloe spilt hot coffee on her hand.

'You made an early start!' It was Josonne, Antoine's cousin, bright-eyed and alert.

He was riding shotgun with a police officer, who introduced himself as Charlie. 'We're short-handed just now, and Josonne shares a house with me, so he tagged along when he heard it was you.'

Antoine launched into a description of what they surmised had happened, before looking guiltily at Chloe. 'Sorry, Mrs C, I should have let you tell him, really.'

She shook her head. 'No, it's fine. I was trying to think who knew about the photoshoot, and who would know it was so important to us.'

Charlie nodded, taking quick notes as she spoke.

'At the party, we were in a little group when Fiona and I started talking about horses, and I showed her pictures of ours. That was when she made her offer. Some women I don't know probably heard, but Emma, who runs the community shop, and Jonas who runs the gallery, both heard. Arron Stone...' She faltered to a halt. It seemed terrible to name these people as suspects, but what else could she think?

'So you set this up at the party last night? Did you speak to anyone else since?' Josonne queried. 'I'm guessing Fiona at the hotel would have brought in a photographer and an assistant. She would have called them last night maybe? Short notice so she would have wanted to get everything sorted out. Some models too, if it's for their website? Suddenly the field opens up quite a bit.'

'Yes, she did arrange it all last night. Literally made phone calls at the party, and it was done.' Chloe nodded. She hadn't considered any of those possibilities. Murder was playing so heavily on her mind that all her suspicions seemed to spring automatically from the little community at Dockyard.

The sun was already warming the yard, and the remaining horses began to neigh and kick at their doors.

'I haven't fed them all yet,' Antoine explained.

Something was niggling at Chloe's brain. 'Why didn't they make a fuss when Goldie was taken last night? Isn't Star her best pal? Surely they would have called for each other. Surely, wherever Goldie is now, she'd be calling for Star?'

'Good point. Unless someone fed them to shut them up, until Goldie was well clear?'

'More than one person involved, then?' Charlie suggested. 'Okay, I'll get back and file a report. We've already got a call out, with a description of the horse, but if you send me a few photos I can start sending them out around the island.'

'It isn't like she could have left the island, is it?' Chloe said.

Both men frowned. 'Not by air, and it would have been tricky loading a horse onto a boat without being seen. Any cargo is inspected before it leaves and when it arrives at the destination.

Seems like that would be an awful lot of trouble to go to for a horse.'

⁓

Finn appeared at the house two hours later, on his way back to the station. 'Sorry, Chloe. I had to get everything sorted out. Turns out it wasn't a shooting incident, thank goodness, just a row after an RTC, and...'

'Don't be silly, Finn. A missing horse is nothing compared to people's lives. One of your officers, Charlie, turned up with Josonne. They were very competent. Was everyone okay at the traffic accident?'

He nodded, accepting a glass of iced water. 'The two drivers have been taken to hospital, but they should be fine.'

Every road traffic accident must remind him of his wife, Chloe thought sadly. She changed the subject. 'Was Melissa really all right when you spoke to her?'

'Seemed to be.'

Chloe was silent, mulling things over in her head. Why had Melissa denied knowledge of the package? A sudden dark thought flashed into her mind – had Finn really spoken to her? She didn't know him and although her gut said he was definitely to be trusted, there were such things as corrupt police officers.

'Chloe?'

'Did you tell her the package was missing?'

'No. I didn't want to give too much away. It was more of a welfare check than anything. Despite the rumours currently circulating, as I told you, Melissa isn't a suspect in the Georgias murder. Her alibi checks out. Now tell me about the horse.'

He had changed the subject pretty quickly, which certainly did nothing to dull her sudden suspicions. Chloe gave him a quick rundown of events, adding that Josonne and Antoine were both out searching. 'Antoine is devastated. He loves the horses, but it's more than that. If we miss this chance for the photoshoot it might screw up our chance to pull the business back from the brink.'

'Are things really that bad?' Finn raised an eyebrow.

'Yes, they are. I checked the accounts, and unless Beachside Stables lands a really good contract with assured income, we'll have to close by the end of the year. It just isn't sustainable at the moment. This is our make-or-break moment.'

'I knew Dre had let things run down, but I had no idea...' Finn whistled softly. 'Do you still think someone is trying to get you to sell up?'

17

She shrugged. 'What else can I think with Goldie suddenly vanishing the moment I get a sniff at changing the fortunes of the stables? Developers have been knocking at the door, and from the bookings I can see that the business has been nosediving for a while. Even if Dre was winding down a little, the serious downturn has all been in the last six months.'

'All right, I'll see what I can do. When's the photoshoot?'

'Tomorrow afternoon.'

Finn's radio crackled and he glanced down, listening. 'Sorry, I need to head off now, but keep in touch about this, won't you? Charlie is very good, so fingers crossed he pulls up some clues. Make sure you let me know if you get any ransom calls or anything.'

'*Ransom calls?* You think Goldie's been kidnapped?' Chloe was shocked.

He was halfway out the door. 'Possibly. I wouldn't rule anything out at this stage.'

After Finn had gone, Chloe went out over the headland, picking her way along steep paths, edging past the newly painted walls of the luxury development. The buildings were empty at the moment, but she was sure they would soon be filled by people drawn to this area of the island.

Her mobile phone was in her pocket, and every few metres she stopped and pulled it out, checking she had a signal. Goldie being kidnapped didn't make any kind of sense, but she wasn't taking any chances. There was the home phone, but she wasn't hanging around all day on the off-chance somebody would call and demand a ransom. The answerphone was on anyway. She realised suddenly that she had missed her chance to tell Finn about the shapes in the painting, but fear for her livelihood and her beautiful horse had driven the discovery from her mind. She hesitated to call Finn again. She had bothered him enough recently.

Standing in the shade of a cluster of trees, she paused to get her breath. Her plaited hair lay heavy on her shoulder blades, and her shirt was wet with sweat. The view was spectacular. The beach a mere strip of white sand, the sea smooth and turquoise. She could see her own house, further down the cliffs, nestling in the cleft, green paddocks stretching up the next hill. Ailsa and her other neighbours were further inland, hidden by the pines that edged the headland.

From this vantage point she could easily see why the developers were keen to get their hands on her property. The road she had just passed, could lead downwards, and her land would provide at least two apartment blocks, or several large luxury homes. Being lower down, the paths to the beach and trails were more accessible, the line of trees would provide further privacy and the views were breathtaking.

Walking back two hours later, weary and dispirited, Chloe found Antoine and Josonne in deep conversation in the yard. They both shook their heads at her hopeful glance. Goldie's empty stable stuck out like a pulled tooth. The men were gulping water from large bottles, and Antoine was munching on an energy bar.

'Charlie had to go and attend another incident, but I've got the afternoon off so I thought I'd stick around. I was saying that we put an alert out to the other stables on the island. Just in case they've seen anything unusual or had any thefts themselves,' Josonne told her.

'They haven't,' Antoine said, 'but Ellis Jack at Green Ridge said they had a lad grooming for them for a few months on a working visa. He was supposed to be getting experience, but they sacked him for misconduct. He left the grooms' accommodation two days ago, and as far as they all knew he was going home to Kentucky.'

'Okay?' Chloe didn't see the connection.

'When he left, he stole some tack. A saddle and bridle.'

'But not a horse?'

'Nope. Weird isn't it?'

'Green Ridge is in St George's, isn't it?' Chloe queried. She remembered looking up all the other stables on Bermuda, just to compare them with her own. 'And Ellis Jack is some kind of celebrity horse whisperer?'

Josonne pulled a face. 'Yeah, he did some tours in the USA. He was pretty popular.'

'Was?'

'He got a lot of flack when someone reported him for cruelty last year. The charges didn't stick but that kind of press was very bad for business. That's why he's spending more time at home on the island. He hasn't toured since it all blew up,' Antoine informed her.

'Oh...' Again Chloe wasn't sure what to say, but she didn't think Ellis's missing stable lad could be connected to Goldie's disappearance. If he wanted a horse surely the boy would have pinched one of his ex-employer's? Her money was on the developers, which, if Arron and Jonas were investors, meant they both had the chance to pass on the information about the shoot.

But Jonas had introduced her to Fiona, obviously knowing full well that Chloe would make some money from a photoshoot, and Arron, although he joked about her selling up, seemed to spread his largesse around. The Skylight Foundation, and other beneficiaries, seemed to suggest he used his wealth for good, as Finn had said. Would a little development on Bermuda matter that much to someone who was rich beyond Chloe's wildest imaginings? 'I might go and visit Ellis when all this is over. His stables looked really smart on the website.'

The two men exchanged glances and Josonne shook his head. 'You might not want to do that. You see the person who reported Ellis to the animal welfare people was Dre.'

'Oh my God! Really?'

'Yeah. They never really spoke after that,' Antoine said. 'Dre was adamant that she dropped in for a chat, and saw him using illegal training aids, but he denied it when the welfare people pitched up.'

'I suppose he couldn't have taken Goldie, could he? For revenge or something?' Chloe queried.

Josonne leant back against the fence, considering. 'Don't see why he should have. I mean, the row was between him and Dre, not you, and if there were going to be any repercussions it would have been last year when the incident occurred. He's a nice bloke as it goes.'

'If he had taken Goldie, he'd hardly volunteer information about his ex-employee, would he? He'd keep a low profile, surely.'

'Charlie said he promised Ellis someone would pop in later and take details of the tack theft and the missing lad anyway,'

Josonne added, finishing his drink. 'Come on, Ant, let's get back to it!'

Chloe dropped back into the house for a drink. She sipped the iced water, so lost in thought that she jumped in fright at the banging on her front door.

'Hallo, you must be Chloe?'

'Yes?' Chloe stared blankly at the smiling, bearded man outside.

Confusion crossed his face. 'I'm Andie. I'm from the SPCA to do your home visit check?'

Chloe put her hand to her head. 'I'm so sorry, I totally forgot you were coming.' She invited him in, and explained about Goldie.

'That's terrible.' He gulped down the orange juice she offered. 'Look, this is obviously a bad time for you. Shall I go and we can rearrange?'

'No!' Chloe said, surprised by the strength of her feelings. 'No, I would like to show you around. There are people out searching and the police will call if they find Goldie.'

Andie stood up, still looking doubtful. 'If you're sure...'

He left an hour later, and informed her that the house and land had passed the check and her home was certainly suitable for Hilda to take up residence. After she had signed more forms, and promised to deal with the small hole in the hedge which Ailsa liked to use as her own personal entrance and exit to Chloe's garden, Chloe sank down on the sofa with exhaustion.

There was delight, of course, that she could go and pick up Hilda. She had hated leaving her at the rescue centre, despite the fact it was obvious she had been well cared for. But the worry for Goldie, and for her business suddenly made her feel like crying. How could things have gone so wrong in the space of a few hours?

Pulling herself together, she made sandwiches for herself and Antoine, piled cartons of iced drinks on a tray and took them down to the stable yard.

Antoine tucked straight into the sandwiches. 'Thanks, Mrs C. Any news?'

She shook her head, and went to fuss over Star and Candy. Both mares seemed slightly subdued. Even Star accepted her cuddle, without nipping her owner as she was prone to do. 'If I had managed to get Hilda earlier she would have heard the horse thief and barked.'

Antoine stuffed another sandwich in his mouth and shoved the paper straw into his juice. 'Was that the bloke from the SPCA earlier?'

'Yes, I passed the home check which means I can pick her up,' Chloe said, gulping down her own drink. 'I'll leave the tray in the shade, that way anyone who comes to help look for Goldie can help themselves.'

'I'm going out again now,' Antoine announced, leaping up after apparently swallowing the last of his sandwich without chewing, and with visible effort.

'I've got something to do, but I'll be out again later. Call me if you find anything, won't you?'

He nodded and headed for the gate.

Luckily, word had spread and Chloe was grateful to find messages on her answerphone that several local people were now out searching the surrounding area for Goldie.

She popped over to welcome Ailsa back home with a bunch of flowers and one of her home-made candles, before rejoining the search parties.

Ailsa was sitting on her porch in the rocking chair, chickens clustered around her feet, pecking her shoes. She jumped up as

Chloe appeared via the usual way through the interconnecting hedge. 'I was going to come over when I saw you were back home. Any news of the horse?'

It was typical of her neighbour to have her finger firmly on the pulse of local news, even when she was recovering from an injury. Chloe sighed with relief at having her closest ally on the island back in the fight, so to speak. 'Not yet, but I'm sure we'll find her. How are you feeling?'

Ailsa brushed off her enquires, and went inside to make coffee. She ignored Chloe's protests that she should be resting. 'I only got a clout round the head. It didn't affect my brain, and my legs and arms still work, so don't fuss. I've only just got rid of my Cheryl. She would have had me in bed for the week if she could.'

'I expect she's worried about you.'

'No need.'

Despite her words, Chloe winced at the sight of the purple-and-yellow bruise that decorated Ailsa's forehead and her left eye. Neat Steri-Strips stretched like a ladder across the cut on her cheek. 'Any news of your attacker?'

'No. It's always busy down here at that time of day, so there were a lot of people. Nobody spotted anything out of the ordinary. Mind you, if he walloped me and then strolled off, who could tell?'

'You think it was a man?'

Ailsa shrugged, and put two steaming mugs, plus a plate of rum cake, on the table. 'Let's have this in the kitchen, it's a bit hot outside. I don't know. I suppose so. I remember seeing the outline in the glass, opening the door to him, and then... nothing.'

Chloe, feeling that she needed to lighten the mood, told her neighbour about Hilda, adding, 'Don't worry, she's totally okay with chickens, horses and goats.'

'Oh I don't mind dogs. I used to have a couple of rottweilers.' Ailsa smiled. 'Jack and Jill. Lovely creatures, they were.'

They chatted a bit about dog breeds, before Chloe decided she must ask the question that had been bothering her since she discovered the break-in. She felt a bit bad about broaching the subject when Ailsa was only just out of hospital, but she needed to know. 'You remember the spare key I gave you?'

'Of course.' The dark eyes were shrewd, worried. 'Someone been in your place who shouldn't have been?'

'Yes. I just wondered if the key is still here?'

Ailsa indicated a key rack next to her front door. 'Yours is the one with the pink ribbon. I got my daughter to check everything was safe and secure because the police wanted to know if anything had been stolen. Seems like maybe I just got unlucky. Someone off their head on drink or drugs who thought I might have something to steal, maybe… Perhaps they went to your house first to try their luck.'

Chloe didn't think this was at all likely, and she couldn't help feeling Ailsa was being very blasé about the whole incident. Strange behaviour would have been noted by the other residents, as would any shouting or sounds of a struggle. She sipped her drink, thinking hard. There was no other way her own house could have been broken into. Finn had checked the locks and windows carefully.

'You all right?'

'Just thinking that somebody else has a key to my house,' Chloe told her soberly.

18

There was no sign of Goldie by nightfall, and Chloe stood in the warm garden, facing the sea. She desperately hoped the horse was okay. They were such friendly, undemanding beasts, and the thought that their trusting nature might be abused was horrible.

Antoine and the other searchers had gone home, and the yard was peaceful. Chloe looked down at the beach, the sea... She felt restless and ill at ease. The locksmith was booked for tomorrow evening, which was the only appointment he had. She had bolts, which she would use tonight. It would be fine. Tomorrow she would also pick up Hilda and her little guard dog would be there warn her of any intruders.

Fiona had been brilliant about the news that her equine model was missing, saying how awful it was, but she was sure that Goldie would turn up. One thing she couldn't do, however, was postpone the shoot, so if Goldie wasn't found they would need another horse. Another palomino or something equally striking, so none of Chloe's other horses would do.

She googled Ellis Jack's place at Green Ridge Stable. The website was full of photos and there was lots of information about his status as a horse whisperer, his sell-out tours. Just out of interest, she found herself clicking on the photos of his horses for hire. No palominos. It was silly anyway. Antoine and Josonne were right, the bad blood had been with Dre, not herself.

Checking her emails she picked up one from Alexa:

```
Hi Chloe,
Just checking in. Hope all okay in sunny
Bermuda. Before you see anything on social
media, Mark has moved in with a new
girlfriend. You are well shot of that bastard,
so I hope you will just be pleased he's out of
your hair. Her name is Tamsin and she's a
photographer he met on an assignment
apparently. Don't worry, Maria is away in
Ireland doing another celeb wedding, so she
hasn't gone round to kill him!
Alexa x
```

Chloe read the email several times, and the words seemed to ring in her head. She had known her ex would move on, known that they both would, but her heart was pounding as she tapped through his social media. Sure enough, on his Instagram page, there were several photos of him entwined with a pretty blonde girl. She looked very young. Early twenties at a guess.

The curse of social media, Chloe thought, unsure if she was craving information on the new girlfriend because she was jealous, or because she was being masochistic. The girl was young, pretty and slim, all things Chloe felt she was not, and it wasn't doing her confidence any good at all. Deciding it was the latter, she forced herself to reply to Alex:

```
Hi Lex,
```

All good here, and thanks for the info. He can do what he wants, and I'm fine, honestly.
Still hurts but I'm back in a happy place so I really should thank him.
Still got papers to sign re divorce but I'll get it finished soon. Spare room all ready for you. I'll message Maria and tell her not to put out a hit on Mark. Yet!
Love,
Chloe x
Ps. Found an amazing artist who could do some pieces for your hotels. See att pix.

She shut down the computer, went back into her living room and picked up the framed photo of Dre. Her grandmother's dark eyes stared back, her wide, tomboyish grin and tousled black hair so typical of her in her younger days. Chloe felt tears again. Dre would have understood how she was feeling. She had been through it herself.

She sighed. She should have come back, should have written letters. But who wrote letters these days? Life had always been so busy she had allowed the most important things to slip away, unchallenged. And now she had lost one of Dre's horses. Horses that had been entrusted to her.

On impulse, encouraged by the warm evening air, and the low tide, Chloe went in and changed into her swimsuit. She looked in the mirror for a long moment, and then pulled on a loose dress and flip-flops. Dre had loved to swim and dive.

As a child she had swum all the time, and even as a teenager she had swum at school. It was only in her twenties that all forms of exercise had tailed off, and for some reason the longer she left getting back in the water, the more anxious she became.

It didn't matter how many times she told herself it was

totally irrational to be afraid of the water, she still panicked about submerging, about water stinging her eyes, about not being able to breathe. But now, today, the tanned, slightly more muscular woman in the mirror looked ready to brave the ocean.

Taking deep calming breaths, Chloe stood with her feet in the water. The little wavelets frothed and danced across her toes. She waded across to inspect the rock pools, enchanted by the marine life that inhabited them.

Then she walked in deeper, pushing the cool, silky waters apart, watching her hands, pale under the waves. Without any further thought she stepped off a sandbank and out of her depth.

The water was far colder out here, but the waves were still gentle. She was swimming, gasping at the sudden exercise, carefully keeping an eye on her landmarks, the lights of her house shining like a beacon.

It was foolhardy, even dangerous, but it was exciting, and her body revelled in the darkness of the sea. The moon provided a silver path towards the horizon, and the stars glittered full and bright, making cloud shadows flutter across the beach.

Chloe rolled onto her back and floated. '*I can still do it!*' She wouldn't have dreamt of swimming in the sea at night six months ago. If she had suggested it, Mark would have scoffed at her stupid ideas, would have told her she was scared of the water anyway, so why bother?

'*I'm not scared, just not familiar with myself anymore. Now that I have to cope on my own, with a murder, with a break-in and a horse thief, I've realised how strong I really am.*'

The sound of her own voice brought Chloe back from her night-time adventure and she started for the beach, her strokes rusty but purposeful. In no time she was rubbing down quickly with a towel, shivering at the change in temperature, and dragging the dress over her head.

Back in the house, after another quick check on the yard, she had a shower and pulled on her pyjamas. Finally, she made a tour of the house, checking every window and shooting every bolt. Her phone and the heavy torch rested by her bed, just in case. In the living room, Dre's photographs smiled down at her, silvered by the moonlight.

Whether it was the late evening exercise, or Dre watching over her, there were no nightmares to disturb her sleep, and no intruders, real or imagined. She woke early, ready to continue the search.

There was no news from the police station, and Chloe didn't like to ring and check up. She was causing enough trouble as it was, and although she had met with nothing but welcome and kindness since her arrival on the island, she really didn't want any further trouble.

Surprisingly, Jonas rang her mobile as she finished a piece of toast. 'Chloe! I'm so sorry about the horse. I bumped into Fiona last night and she told me what happened. Any news?'

'No.' Chloe tried to stop herself from sounding unfriendly. After all, she had no proof it was anything to do with Jonas. 'I'm sure we'll find her.'

'I hope so. Let me know if I can do anything. After all, you saved the life of one of my artists, the least I could do is join in the search.'

'How is Sheetal?' Chloe realised with a jolt of guilt that she hadn't given the woman a thought in the last twenty-four hours.

'She's fine. Discharged from hospital and gone to stay back with her parents for a while.'

'Good, I'm glad she's okay. Don't worry about me, Jonas, I

have lots of people searching, and whoever is trying to drive me out, won't succeed.'

He was silent for a moment, then, 'You think someone is doing that?'

'What else can I think? It seems very strange to have a missing horse just as I book in a photoshoot with it. And I've heard gossip saying that my stables isn't doing well, that we are unreliable. Which is a load of rubbish!'

'Chloe, I know I was the one who asked if your house is for sale, and I know the Skylight Foundation has some investments in this particular development, but please be assured I would *never*, *we* would *never* try to force you to sell. Those kind of tactics are for idiots and cowards. It isn't the type of thing our family would be involved in.'

'Thank you, Jonas.' She wasn't sure how to answer that. Should she say that the developers were fast becoming her number one suspect? Maybe not.

'Melissa is coming back to Bermuda tomorrow,' Jonas added.

'She is? That's great I mean, I can speak to her about the commission.'

'Yes. You do that. And, Chloe, I meant what I said. If you need help, you can call me anytime.'

'Thank you.'

After she ended the call she let out a long breath she hadn't realised she was holding. 'That was awkward,' she told a chicken, which had shimmied in through her front door. She dumped her plate in the sink and gently prodded the chicken back out. It scurried over to join its fellows under the spice tree, clucking crossly at the eviction.

After a quick tidy up, Chloe shoved her clothes in the washing machine, and swept the kitchen floor. Her phone buzzed with a text as she put the broom down and she pulled it out of her pocket.

Chloe. Don't get too cosy with Melissa Aliente. She isn't who you think she is and might bring you bad luck. I'm watching out for you.

Chloe sank down onto a kitchen chair, her hands shaking as she reread the text several times. It was sent from an unknown number. She felt nausea creeping across her stomach. What was going on? Was *Melissa* spreading rumours and trying to wreck her business, and if so, why come to her with vast amounts of cash and a valuable painting?

'Just us to start with today,' Antoine told her. 'We've got a booking of three at lunchtime, and I'll take Star, Jupiter and Sunny. Look, I plotted out a new route of the map for us to search.'

Chloe, having decided not to mention the text, was ready to go, in navy cargo shorts she would never have worn last year, and a white shirt. She pushed her strands of blonde hair from her hot face, and laced up her trainers. 'Let's go now. I've got to get Hilda's food and bed before I pick her up this afternoon.'

They took the trail down to the beach, but turned westerly, clambering across hidden coves. Occasionally Antoine would stretch out a hand to give Chloe a pull up the steeper inclines.

Eventually they stopped to rest, and unscrewed water bottles. Chloe wiped her forehead, sweat pouring down her neck, making her shirt stick to her back.

'You okay to finish off this section?' Antoine asked.

'Fine. Didn't you come this way yesterday?'

'No. Someone did cover it, but I'm going to double-check every single place until I've found her,' he said.

Chloe nodded in agreement, thinking once again how lucky she had been that chance had brought her together with such lovely, warm people. Ailsa, Antoine, Peter and Finn had all been so welcoming. No way would she let everyone down by failing Dre's legacy. But to stand any hope of carrying on she had to find her equine star, her gentle Goldie.

They separated briefly. Antoine went to look at the caves near the high-water mark, and Chloe clambered over sandbanks and crispy seaweed, peering up at the clifftops.

She was just getting exhausted again when she heard it. A horse. She froze, listening hard. The wind was getting up, and whipped the noise away from her.

'*Goldie!*'

She yelled for Antoine next, and he came running lightly down the beach, expression worried. 'Are you all right?'

'She's here! I can hear Goldie. *Listen.*' Chloe's heart was thumping hard, her hands clenched tightly.

The whinny was faint, but definitely there. The beach was empty, and the shoreline was sheer rock in most places. Bewildered, Chloe and Antoine began to scramble along the rock face, edging their way between the coves. The rocks were sharp and plentiful.

'Where the hell is she?' Antoine exclaimed in frustration.

The answer came as they rounded another bluff. Here, the cliff doubled back, almost folded in on itself to create a small sandy area, hung with a curtain of plants and vines. Seabirds flew in and out of nesting holes on the rocks, fluttering high above the palomino horse trapped in a pen of twisted wire.

'*Goldie!*' Chloe called again, her voice almost hoarse from yelling and emotion.

19

They climbed further along, dropping down and racing across the sand to the horse. Goldie was muzzled and hobbled, and penned by several feet of barbed wire fencing. There was an empty bucket outside the fence, suggesting perhaps somebody had been providing food and water.

'My poor baby girl. It's okay, we've come to get you,' Antoine was crooning. He leapt lightly over the wire, reaching back to hastily haul Chloe over.

Landing with a thump in the soft sand, she gently held out a hand to Goldie, stroking the mare's neck as Antoine got busy removing her bonds.

The horse had obviously been fighting to get away, because she had deep scratches on her forelegs, and there were drag marks in the sand, where she had been around and around her prison. Her flanks were drawn and her beautiful golden coat was dull.

They had almost finished when a shout drew their attention. Two men were coming down a narrow path from the top of the cliff.

'Quick, get that wire out of the way,' Chloe told Antoine. 'Is she lame?'

'No, I don't think so.'

'Okay, jump on and get her away from here. You can go along the beaches now the tide's out, can't you?'

'No. Absolutely no way am I leaving you here by yourself, Mrs C.'

'They won't hurt me.'

'How do you know?' He squinted at the men. 'Oh it's them. I see, but how do we know they aren't involved?'

'We don't, but trust me. You and Goldie are probably in more danger than I am if something *is* going on. We need her back and checked out. Now go!'

With a backward glance, he vaulted onto Goldie's back, and guided her through the wire, out onto the sand. She pranced a little, shaking her white mane, clearly delighted to be free.

'*Go!*'

The pair shot off across the beach, heading homewards. The dull thud of swift hooves on sand echoed in her ears, and she breathed a sigh of relief. Antoine had his phone on him, would call the police as soon as he got Goldie to safety. And she had been telling the truth, she didn't think these men would hurt her.

Chloe shook sand out of her shoes and waited at the bottom of the cliff. For a moment she had wondered if she was wrong, if it was a trick of the light. But no, as they approached she saw she was correct. Walking towards her were Arron Stone and Jonas Aliente.

It had been gut instinct, and the urge to protect Antoine and Goldie, that led her to claim she wasn't in any danger, but seeing their set faces, in reality she wasn't so sure. Was this really about her selling up?

'Chloe? My God, what's going on? Was that your missing

horse?' Jonas asked. He looked flustered, worried even. His shirt and one side of his shorts were covered in sand.

'We were looking at a couple of properties, and checking on progress at the new development when we thought we heard a horse,' Arron explained. 'We searched the top of the cliff, but we couldn't work out where the creature was. Jonas thought it might have fallen down a gulley and gotten trapped.'

She stared back at them for a long moment. Both men *were* formally dressed in shorts and suit jackets, their polished brown shoes sliding in the sand. Arron had sand on his trousers and the top button on his shirt was undone. It was a good story. It could even be true, Chloe thought.

'Are you all right? Was that your manager? Why did he gallop off like that? The horse could be hurt,' Jonas suggested anxiously.

'I don't know who put her in that pen, but thankfully she's okay. I told my manager to take her straight home and call the vet. Best get her checked out. Of course, I've let the police know as well. They're on their way over to see if they can find any clues as to who could have done this.' Chloe mentally crossed her fingers and hoped Antoine had a good mobile phone signal further along the beach.

'Dreadful. I still don't understand why somebody would do this! Especially just before the photoshoot. I spoke to Fiona earlier and she was devastated that they would have to use another horse. Apparently yours is the only palomino on the island.' Jonas did look genuinely concerned as he surveyed the remains of Goldie's prison. 'You certainly have been through it recently. Do you think someone is trying to put you out of business?'

'It's a possibility...' Chloe said slowly, as though the thought had just occurred to her. 'I didn't realise there was a path back up the cliff.'

'It's very steep. You'd be better off going back round the coves,' Arron told her. 'You must have had such a shock, finding the horse here. I do hope she is all right. And how is your poor neighbour doing?' His expression was charming, with just the right amount of concern. There didn't seem to be any falseness in his tone, just genuine interest.

'Ailsa? Oh she's doing well. Thank you for coming to Goldie's rescue, but I'll just walk along to the next cove and guide the police down.'

Both men seemed slightly at a loss in the face of this somewhat curt dismissal, and Arron looked disappointed. 'If you're sure we can't help in any way?'

'No, thank you, it's all sorted now we have Goldie back, but it's kind of you to offer,' she said.

Arron smiled, seemingly appeased. 'No problem.'

'I'll call you later, Chloe. Perhaps I could take you out to dinner? You know, to take your mind of this run of bad luck.' Jonas had reverted to his usual charming persona, smiling at her in the sunlight.

'Thank you, Jonas, that would be good. I'll look forward to it.' Chloe, exhausted, and struggling to observe any niceties, took her leave, heart still pounding far too hard. It was a surreal little scene and she really wasn't sure what to make of it. 'And thank you for racing to the rescue.'

Her exit was slightly spoiled as she tripped on a vine root, but all in all, she just felt glad to have escaped. What the hell was going on?

20

The vet was summoned and both Chloe and Antoine watched anxiously as Goldie was given a thorough examination. She stood quietly, but her ears still twitched nervously at the slightest sound.

'Is she okay?' Chloe asked, unable to bear it any longer. She was almost holding her breath, just as she had when she was a little girl waiting for bad news. Some childhood superstitions just never died.

The vet, Simon, grinned. 'She'll be fine. A little dehydrated, but the scratches are superficial.'

'Thank goodness!' Chloe sagged with relief, suddenly realising she'd been clutching Antoine's arm in an iron grip. 'Sorry.'

'No worries.' He was as delighted as she was. 'Does this mean she can do the photoshoot?'

Simon packed his gear away in the back of his truck. 'Don't see why not.'

'Thank goodness! I mean, her welfare comes first, of course, but this is such a great chance for the business,' Chloe said, relief making her weak at the knees. 'I must call Fiona. She was so sweet about the whole thing, but she did give me a deadline before they went with another horse.'

'No other palominos on the island,' Antoine said proudly, feeding Goldie a carrot.

'No, that's why she was hanging on for us, but with the photographer and everyone booked, she was just going to have to use a mare from Green Ridge and shoot at the hotel. I hope Ellis Jack doesn't mind,' Chloe said with a niggle of worry.

'Ellis is a good man, and I'm sure Fiona would have told him his horse was a reserve candidate.' Simon smiled at her. 'Look, I'll leave you with these rehydration salts. Just put them in her water, and of course, do give me a shout if you have any other concerns. But she's a tough mare, so she should come out of this absolutely fine. Do the police know who took her yet?'

'No. But they did say Ellis had a lad who went AWOL with some tack on the night she went missing. It seems like that might be connected, although why and how, I have no idea,' Chloe told him, fussing over the horse. She didn't want to go into the strange coincidence that seemed to have led Arron and Jonas to Goldie's prison. The police knew, but she would let them unravel the mystery. Just now, they had a photoshoot to prepare for.

'I'm actually seeing Ellis next. He's got four booked in for vaccinations, so I'll pass on the good news,' Simon offered.

'Sure,' Antoine said, untying Goldie and leading her towards the hosepipe. 'I'll get her bathed and beautified, then.' He clapped an affectionate hand on the golden neck, and the mare shook her mane.

Ailsa came over at lunchtime, trailing chickens, and eager for a gossip. 'She's back then!'

'Yes, we found her down on the beach.' Chloe explained the circumstances of the discovery, once again feeling that flood of relief that Goldie was safe. Not only that but her grand plans to save the business seemed to be back on track. Almost giddy with emotion and exhaustion, she beamed at Ailsa. 'It was so good of everyone to go out looking, and Antoine cares for those horses like they were his own children.'

Her neighbour nodded thoughtfully. 'At least you have her home now. Photoshoot still going ahead, I take it?'

Chloe made coffee and carried two steaming mugs to the table. Despite the glorious sunshine outside, and the heat stretching gentle fingers into the cool interior, this had become a ritual. 'It really was a last-minute thing, but Fiona wanted Goldie so much, she was hanging on to hear what the vet said. Now she has a clean bill of health, Antoine's getting her ready.'

'Oh good. Are you still getting your dog today?'

'Yes, but I rang and made an appointment for later this evening. It's been chaos, and I want to make sure I can spend a bit of time getting her used to her new surroundings,' Chloe said. Helen had been very understanding.

'Have you heard about Sheetal Araminta?' Ailsa changed the subject.

'The artist who had anaphylactic shock? No, is she okay?' Chloe was immediately concerned, her happy daydreams pushed aside.

A chicken slipped in through the doorway, settling unnoticed, under Ailsa's chair. 'She's fine, don't panic! You're more of a mother hen than I am, Chloe...' She smiled indulgently at her neighbour. 'I heard the police are treating her allergic reaction as attempted murder.' She beamed, clearly thrilled to be passing on this nugget.

'But why?' Chloe noticed the chicken, but was too busy thinking about this new information.

'You need to ask Finn, but word is that Kaila Montana has been arrested, or at least questioned. Apparently there's evidence that links her to the murder and to this allergic reaction. *And* she has a conviction for dealing drugs, so she's a criminal already,' Ailsa said triumphantly. Clearly, by the emphasis she had given this last piece of information to her, dealing drugs was almost worse than murder.

'Wow.' Chloe was stuck for words, trying to remember the night at the gallery. Kaila's picture with the shapes, the bloody carvings in Matthew's forehead... 'Oh, Matthew was chosen over Kaila, wasn't he? I think Jonas said something about her being on the reserve list. But now she's being exhibited by the Stone galleries, so why attack Sheetal?'

Ailsa shrugged. 'No idea, but if Kaila was bumping off artists to get rid of the competition, it makes sense, doesn't it?'

She supposed it did, and made a mental note to share her discovery in the painting with Finn, although if Kaila had already been arrested maybe the police had discovered the symbolism for themselves.

Despite her eagerness to share the gossip, Ailsa seemed slightly less than her usual self today. Chloe supposed she might be feeling the after-effects of the attack more than she was letting on, but she knew any offers of help would be met with a stubborn refusal. 'I suppose it does. I had no idea the art world was so cut-throat.'

'Neither did I. I expect the police are glad to have a result though. Finn can rest easy knowing he's got his man, or woman in this case.'

'Yes. I just hope whoever took Goldie is brought to justice too. I've got a funny feeling that everything to do with me and the stables is all about trying to drive me out,' Chloe said.

'Well I hope you're wrong but those developers would be my

obvious choice. Get Finn to take a look at them again if you're worried.'

'How are Cheryl and the boys?'

'Fine. Alfie's doing really well and Jordan's not been in any trouble for a while.' She sighed, and in the bright sunlight that streamed through the window, suddenly looked old and tired.

'I'd better get down to the garden centre and sort out that dog bed,' Chloe said eventually. She wanted to add that she hoped her friend would get some rest to help herself heal after the attack, but decided although the thought sprang from genuine concern, this sounded patronising.

Not meeting Chloe's eyes, Ailsa shifted in her seat. 'Yes, I'd better go now. Jordan's coming over after his cricket practice to clear my drains for me. In fact, if you want to save a bit of time and you know what you want, I can send him down the road to pick up your dog stuff if you like?'

'Oh yes, that would be wonderful.' Chloe, massively relieved at the offer, had already made a list and seen a lovely tweed bed stacked with the pet supplies on her last trip down to the shops. 'I'll ring up and place the order. Are you sure he won't mind? I'll probably be busy but he can leave it by the back door and I'll sort it out when the photoshoot is over.'

'It'll do him good to run a few errands,' Ailsa said, her lips pursed, gaze far away and worried.

'Is he back into cricket now then?' Chloe enquired, puzzled by the dimming of Ailsa's spirits. She stood up to clear away the mugs, and glanced at her watch. She hadn't met Jordan, but from everything Ailsa had shared during their chats, she felt like she knew him really well, not to mention Alfie and Cheryl.

'Seems so. Alfie's doing really well, and they've started FaceTiming each other again. I think Cheryl was right and it was just jealousy that caused the rift. Anyway, he's back on track now and it looks like I might have both grandchildren as sporting heroes!'

'I'm so pleased!' Chloe beamed at her, as she marched out of the door. The chicken stretched its wings, and followed, clucking softly. 'Now we just need to get that lunatic who assaulted you.'

Ailsa, on her way towards the hole in the hedge, turned back, her glow fading once again. 'Oh well, you know even if the police don't catch him, I'm fine and nothing was taken. See you later!'

Chloe realised she was standing in her doorway with her mouth open. It wasn't her imagination, Ailsa was hiding something.

She wondered what her straight-talking neighbour deemed necessary to keep secret. Ailsa *had* been cagey about the assault all along. She had been more worked up about Goldie's disappearance than her own bruises.

Chloe didn't want to pry, but she also didn't like to think of her neighbour being so troubled. She went back to the sink and washed up the few plates and bits of cutlery from last night.

As she worked, she came to the reluctant conclusion that Ailsa had indeed recognised her attacker, but was choosing to keep quiet about it. Jordan?

Wiping the last plate and popping it in the wooden rack to dry, Chloe thought she was very glad she was getting her locks changed tonight. It would mean peace of mind at the very least. No random text messages either, and it wasn't like she had changed her number or anything.

She rang the garden centre and paid for her order, explaining it would be picked up later and by whom. She did experience a moment's unease over using Jordan as an errand boy, and she noted that Ailsa, who had the spare key and could easily have suggested letting the boy in to deliver the goods, had not even broached the subject. Could her grandson have attacked her? If he had she certainly wasn't going to let on.

She switched on her laptop and pulled up the news pages. There did seem to be a flurry of excitement over Kaila Montana. Opinion was divided over whether she had been taken in for formal questioning, or if she had actually been arrested.

The Royal Gazette led with an exclusive, revealing Kaila had previously been in a relationship with Matthew. She had also apparently been seen on the island the night he was murdered. There was a bit about the rivalry between artists and the prestige and assured income that came from being part of the Stone Gallery family.

A US paper had picked up the story, and offered more of the same, including the fact that Matthew's work had been chosen over Kaila's for both the Bermuda gallery and the Madrid gallery. There was also a few lines about her previous drug conviction, leading to a theory that a gang of artists had been trying to break into an international drug ring.

The fact that Kaila was now proudly displaying work in Madrid and Bermuda, a week after her ex-boyfriend's death, was deemed by the press to indicate quite enough motive for murder. A B&B owner, who had a place on Harbour Road, was quoted as saying Kaila had flown into Bermuda the previous month, stayed one night at his B&B and flown out again the day after.

Another source, American photographer Shay Taylor, appeared to have reported another sighting of someone driving very fast late the night Matthew was killed, in the vicinity of Chloe's house. No doubt he had been out taking photographs of some ruined buildings, she thought.

Remembering her chat with Finn, which now felt like weeks ago, Chloe tapped the name Shay Taylor on Instagram, and wasn't at all surprised to see photos of Dockyard at night.

Looking more closely, she could see they were beautifully staged and really very professional. In some, a young woman she took to be Shay's girlfriend appeared in the shadows, looking dreamy or dramatic, depending on the shot.

Scrolling down, noting the many thousands of followers, Chloe thought she could understand the lure of photographing these old ruins. It seemed that Shay and his girlfriend travelled constantly. There were pictures of abandoned hospitals in Europe, great derelict houses in the USA and a whole lost village somewhere in Russia.

Some of the more recent pictures, apart from the Dockyard ones, looked familiar, and it was a while before Chloe realised that it must be Tranquility House, her neighbourhood *Sleeping Beauty* ruin. The views from the unboarded window showed the stone gateway, and the moon over the sea.

Looking at the time, Chloe hastily left the laptop, picked up the basket and went into the garden to peg her washing out. Could Kaila be responsible for Melissa's bruise, her insistence that Chloe hide the painting and money for her and keep her secret? And a great job she had done of that, she thought with a stab of remorse. She'd told the police about both and lost the whole package.

Melissa would be back soon, but she had made no effort to get in touch. Chloe, pegging up a blue shirt with quick, efficient fingers, supposed she would just have to be patient.

As the clock ticked towards the time arranged for the photoshoot, Chloe was overwhelmed with support from her neighbours, who had now all heard Goldie was back. Peter the taxi driver sweetly popped in mid-afternoon.

'It's just a bad run. You'll be fine now you've settled in, and I've told everyone you're making a real go of things,' Peter said, smiling at her as he leant against his taxi. 'And look, I've got a couple of bits from the wife. She always thought a lot of Dre and she was pleased when she heard you were making a go of the stables.'

He reached into the boot of the taxi and brought out a bottle of rum in a paper bag and a jewellery box.

Chloe thanked him profusely for the rum – she was definitely acquiring a taste for it! Intrigued by the square wooden box, she flicked it open and gasped. A pretty necklace on a silver chain nestled amongst shredded paper. The star-shaped pendant was clear glass, and filled with pink Bermuda sand.

'I hope you're right and thank you so much for the gifts.' Chloe was especially delighted with the necklace, and almost embarrassed. 'Please thank your wife too.'

'No problem. Her best friend has a jewellery store in Hamilton. Dre had one just like that. Wore it all the time. You know, your grandmother would be proud of you, Chloe.'

'I hope so,' Chloe said softly, 'I really do.'

'So. When do you want to pick up your dog?'

'I've managed to get a lift from... from a friend to pick her up tonight but thank you so much for offering. Sorry to keep messing you around and I'm sure Helen thinks I'm mad, but everything keeps going wrong, and I can't pick her up and then leave her in the house alone while I go off to the photoshoot,' Chloe explained. 'So Helen said I could go tonight after the centre is closed.'

'Special treatment?' Peter winked at her. 'Helen knew Dre, didn't she?'

'Yes, I'm very lucky,' Chloe agreed.

'It'll be nice for you to have a dog around the place. I don't think Dre ever had one, but she had a few cats along with her other animals. Mainly for her it was the horses that were number one though!'

Having finally waved Peter off down the driveway, Chloe,

clutching her gifts, walked slowly back inside. She put the bottle on the table and carefully drew out the necklace. It glittered in the rays of sunlight that danced through her shutters. Very gently, she traced the lines of the star, before turning to the opposite wall and her photographs.

Sure enough, in one picture Dre was wearing an open-neck shirt. Hair and shirt were billowing in the wind and the star-shaped necklace could clearly be seen against her tanned skin.

Chloe smiled at her grandmother, her eyes wet. 'Are you really watching what I do? I think you'd like it that Goldie's going to be a model horse... And I want you to know that I'm going to save the business. Whatever it takes.'

The sound of her own voice brought her back into the room, and she wiped her eyes before fastening her new necklace around her neck. It lay cool and heavy against her breastbone, the chain just the right length to show it off.

Her phone beeped, and Chloe's heart jumped briefly, before she smiled in relief at a text from Finn, confirming their dinner tonight. It would be good to unwind after the chaos of the last few days, and she could catch up on his cases.

With an hour left till the photoshoot, Chloe popped down to the yard to roll her sleeves up and make sure everything was spick and span.

Antoine had worked wonders with Goldie and her coat gleamed like pure gold, her white mane and tail floating like candyfloss in the breeze. He was now hard at work grooming the other horses.

'Do you want me to help with the grooming, or tidying the yard?' Chloe asked.

'The horses are pretty much ready, so you can do the yard,' Antoine told her. He was stripped to the waist, combing out Star's long black tail.

Chloe seized the broom and barrow and started sweeping

the concrete. The dust and sand made her sneeze, but she kept at it, hearing Antoine murmuring endearments to the horses as he groomed.

She found a stepladder and tied up the bougainvillea, which was draped in swags across the white stable roof. A yellow hibiscus was climbing across the tack room, and in the afternoon sunshine it looked wonderful. Chloe fetched a couple of metal chairs and a little round table from her garden, and put them next to the fence overlooking the sea.

'Fiona said something about a champagne and romance package,' she explained when Antoine came out of Candy's box and gave the furniture a look of surprise.

Chloe snipped a few hibiscus flowers and filled a pretty vase from the yard tap, arranging them as a centrepiece on the table.

'If they drink a bottle of champagne before they ride, they'll probably fall off,' Antoine pointed out, grinning.

'Not for us to worry about. That's Fiona's department. Perhaps they just have a glass when they get back from a romantic gallop along the beach?' Chloe suggested.

'Galloping is not romantic,' Antoine informed her, ducking as she chucked a sponge at him. 'Bad luck, Mrs C. Bet you never played cricket at school!'

'Back to work, and actually I did play cricket,' Chloe told him, laughing. 'Sport was my favourite thing at school, but I was better at hockey and football.' She glanced at her watch. 'Oh help, we've only got twenty minutes!'

Together, they tidied the muck-heap, arranged the buckets in neat piles and finally, sweating and filthy, checked each horse. Shiny bay, chestnut and gold heads looked eagerly from each stable. Chloe picked up a few stray petals from the immaculate yard.

'Perfect! Do you want an iced drink, Antoine?'

'Please.' He was pulling his shirt back over his head.

'Help yourself while I get changed,' Chloe told him as they headed for the house. Her stomach was churning with nerves. The moment had arrived. This was make or break for the business. At least she was satisfied that the horses and yard looked as good as they possibly could.

The goats and chickens had been moved into the field for the day, and the weather was absolutely perfect. Just a light breeze ruffling the smooth golden warmth of the afternoon.

Back in the house, Chloe quickly checked her voicemail. Nothing. That was good. After everything that had happened, she was still expecting something to go wrong. Fiona not to turn up at all perhaps, or one of the models down with food poisoning. Cursing herself for being negative, she showered briskly and changed into a smart flower-print dress, feeling she should make an effort as Goldie's owner. Her damp hair went into a long plait and she added a quick dash of make-up.

Antoine had just finished his drink when they heard vehicles on the driveway. The photographer's assistant and the models were bumping slowly over the ruts.

'Showtime.' Antoine grinned at her as they went outside.

Her stomach was full of butterflies, and she could feel her jaw clenched and the beginnings of a headache. This had to work...

Gradually, as introductions were made, Chloe began to feel better. The sick feelings receded and there was real pride in showing off the results of their hard work.

The photographer was delighted with Goldie, and Fiona was in raptures about the whole thing. Under the circumstances, Chloe and Beachside Stables were garnering a lot of sympathy and a lot of press.

'It's put you on the map, and people want you to succeed,' Fiona told Chloe. 'Oh your yard looks beautiful! This is just perfect for honeymooners. A little rest from everything before they plunge into the grim reality of married life.'

Chloe glanced at her, startled by the comment. Although she was laughing, Chloe thought she could detect a definite air of bitterness and exchanged a quick look with Antoine. Goodness, what a business to be in if you had been unlucky in love yourself!

The photographer, Stewart, was setting up his equipment, and taking test shots, while the models started hair and make-up in the shade of the tack room.

Chloe tried to stay out of the way, but soon found herself fussing over the horses, combing out Goldie's forelock just so, and giving the metal buckles on her bridle a last polish. One of the models was chatting to Antoine, asking him if he was in the business and recommending agents. He was laughing and shaking his head at the idea.

The whole group was soon gossiping about Goldie's kidnap. According to Vera, the model who would be portrayed as the bride, rumours were now rife about who was trying to put them out of business.

'And people asked me who would have wanted to stop the photoshoot, and if I had any enemies,' Stewart said. 'Or even if there was some kind of vendetta directed at Palm Bay Hotel and the new management.'

Fiona, who had been admiring the view, and setting up the inevitable bottle of champagne and crystal glasses, looked up sharply at this. 'How ridiculous,' she snapped, 'I think we need to focus on the job in hand.'

Gossip died to a murmur and Chloe, now leaning on the fence, watched Fiona tapping efficiently on her tablet. She caught Chloe looking and winked at her. 'Got to keep up with social media. It's terrible what happened, but Goldie has become a bit of a heroine. A PR gift horse!' She laughed, but this time the warmth was back and the bitterness gone.

Chloe smiled back, but her mind was questioning Fiona's words. It had undeniably been good PR for the stables, and Palm Bay Hotel had made no secret they were using Goldie for their brochure. Surely that wouldn't be a reason to steal a horse though?

21

Chloe tried very hard to put her worries aside, watching with pride as her horse was photographed on the beach. The pink and gold from the sun turned the waves into a magical fairy tale setting. Goldie was behaving beautifully, despite her misadventures.

The models, dressed up in wedding clothes, went through a variety of poses, and ended up with Vera, her long lace dress floating in the breeze, riding Goldie bareback along the pink sand, while her 'husband' looked on admiringly from the rocks.

'Perfect! Just what I wanted,' Fiona said, beaming at the photographer as she looked through the shots. 'In fact, it's going to be hard to know which ones to choose. Chloe, thank you for loaning us the horse. I'll make sure you get a credit on our website, and on the print brochure.'

'I took some shots of your yard as well, so if you want to use them in your own publicity, you're more than welcome.' Stewart smiled at Chloe. 'I'll send them over when I've done the final edits.'

'Oh thank you, that would be wonderful,' Chloe told him,

slightly dizzy with relief and happiness. They had done it! The first step to saving the yard and all its occupants was completed.

'We'll get going, then. I'll email you the links tomorrow,' Fiona said briskly as they arrived back at the yard. 'And I think the whole set-up is just perfect for what we discussed. The romance package? The hotel is only five miles from here, and your little yard on the top of the cliff is very intimate. It'll be a welcome addition to our brochure.'

'Thank you so much, Fiona. I'm just glad we got Goldie back in time!' Chloe said. Having been so keyed up and stressed, the whole event couldn't have run more smoothly, and as the adrenaline faded she began to feel drained and exhausted.

Antoine had been ready to take Goldie back to her stable as soon as the shoot was over. He fussed over her, taking extra care to rub her down until her golden coat was once again soft and gleaming. She hadn't settled completely, despite her exemplary behaviour at the photoshoot.

Chloe gave all the horses carrots and waved goodbye to Fiona and her team as the vehicles trundled off down the dusty driveway.

All she really wanted was a soak in the bath and a glass of wine before she got ready for dinner with Finn. Oh God, and the locksmith was coming. She'd nearly forgotten!

Antoine offered to do the horses, but she was determined to continue doing more, making it a real team effort, so she stayed outside, turning the mares out into their paddock, bringing the chickens and their coop back into the safety of the yard for the night.

'Hey, they left the champagne!' Antoine noticed, as they finally, wearily, locked the tack room and prepared to leave.

'You take it,' Chloe told him. 'It was opened so it would be such a waste to just leave it. Treat Louisa to a few glasses.' Out the corner of her eye she could see a young man walking round the corner of her house, bag in hand. That must be the locksmith.

'If you're sure...' Antoine grinned, his eyes sparkling with mischief, as he picked up his rucksack. 'She always says I'm never romantic enough.'

'Well there you go. Surprise her. See you tomorrow,' Chloe said, lifting a hand in farewell, and whisking through the gate towards the house. So much for her long soak, she was going to have to get a move on to be ready in time.

Next to the back door was a smart, red tweed dog bed, a bag of dry food and a cardboard box. This, when she peeked inside, contained red bowls marked *DOG*, and the brown leather collar and lead she'd picked out. She smiled, and made a note to slip Ailsa a few dollars to give to the boy. It was a lot to carry and he had brought everything she'd ordered.

The locksmith, whose name was Benji, was waiting patiently for her, ready to change all the locks on both her windows and doors. She let him in, and made him a cup of tea and having arranged Hilda's corner of the kitchen to her liking, started ironing her dress for tonight.

'I read in the paper about your horse being stolen,' he said conversationally, as he started work.

'Yes. She's back now though, thank goodness.' Chloe wasn't in the mood for chit-chat, but she thought he seemed a sweet boy and it would be awful to appear rude when he had done her a favour and come out so late.

'Well that's one way to get the police to visit!' He laughed.

'What do you mean?' Chloe asked sharply.

Benji shrugged, and flushed. 'Sorry, I shouldn't have said that. It's just that my sister said with everything going on at Beachside Stables people will wonder if you've got a thing going with Inspector Harlow.'

Chloe was furious. 'Tell your sister that she shouldn't listen to idiots. Perhaps she'd like to be the one dealing with all this?' Her rage died at his squirming embarrassment. 'Sorry, Benji, it isn't your fault, but I'm trying so hard to make a go of things, and it isn't easy. Sorry, you really must excuse me, I need to hang this dress up.'

But as she stepped into her bedroom, thoughts switching from missing horses, malicious gossip and murder to panic over whether the dress she planned to wear was still creased, she stopped dead.

Laid neatly on the clean sheets was a familiar package. *The Painted Lady* was back. Her phone buzzed with a text and she raised a hand to study the screen, her attention still riveted on the painting:

Be careful, Chloe. This isn't over. Watch your back because you never know who's behind you.

22

Great. Was somebody watching the house, waiting for her to go through to the bedroom and discover the painting, so they could send the text at the optimum time?

She threw the phone on the bed, her earlier anger breaking through again. She turned her attention back to the painting, fumbling through the plastic with shaking hands. The painting was undamaged at least. But the money was gone. Clearly whoever had taken it stole what they wanted and returned what they deemed to be useless. This surely must narrow down the thief? Trouble was, she had been in and out of the house all day, with plenty of visitors, not to mention the whole team Fiona had brought along. And Jordan... Jordan could have delivered the dog packages and used Ailsa's key to let himself in while they were all out on the beach. It would have been a perfect opportunity. He might not know enough about art to realise the picture was more valuable than the cash. But harder to dispose of?

She went back out to the kitchen, running a frustrated hand through her hair. 'Benji, did you see anyone when you arrived?'

'Here? No. There was a bloke packing up equipment next to

that blue van' – he paused in his work, thinking – 'but nobody near your house. Are you all right, Mrs Canton?'

'I'm fine, thank you.' She went into the bathroom and closed the door, but made no attempt to put her make-up on or do her hair. Her pulse was racing, and her reflection showed her normally rosy cheeks were pale and her mouth pursed with worry.

The painting, if it was another version of *The Painted Lady* was now safe with her. Matthew was dead... And yet the painting had been returned. Kaila had been arrested. Someone was either threatening her or trying to warn her, about Melissa. What *was* the link between these tremors in the artistic community?

She was dragged back from her thoughts by the ticking on the large cream clock on the wall. Half an hour to get ready, pay Benji, lock up and go. At least she could tell Finn she had the painting back. And Melissa would need to know too.

She forced herself into action, but in the bedroom her gaze kept drifting towards the painting. Melissa's painting. Was the money really hers too? The girl had been very insistent that she hadn't stolen the painting, but what of the hard cash? There had been no mention of Melissa in any of the recent speculative pieces online, just jealousy, art, love and drugs. A potent and almost sexy mix if you saw things in that light. Irresistible to the tabloids.

Her hand went to her mouth as the thought occurred to her. What if it was a love triangle; plain and not so simple; *Matthew, Kaila and Melissa*? The names seemed to be branded on the dressing table in front of her. She definitely needed to see Finn but she would be careful what she told him. Chloe was stronger than she had ever thought, and just at that moment she felt the need to prove it.

Finn's car arrived just as she was fastening her star necklace.

It genuinely made her feel closer to her grandmother. She did so hope that she could make a go of things, and make Dre proud, as Peter had so sweetly said. Dre had been strong too. Independent and proud.

She and Finn were eating at The Ocean Club tonight. It was a lovely venue and they had a table outside on the terrace, overlooking the sea. They barely broke in their conversation as they were seated and ordered drinks.

'Whoever took it must have slipped it back sometime after I changed for the photoshoot. But I don't get why they didn't hang on to the painting. There was a lot of money but the miniature *Painted Lady* must be worth more?'

Finn sipped his white wine thoughtfully. 'It might mean somebody is watching the house.'

'That's a horrible thought. Have you heard if Melissa's back yet?' Chloe glanced around. They were speaking in lowered tones, and only four of the other tables were occupied, but she was taking no chances. She had decided not to mention the texts.

There were no direct threats in them, and it really did feel ever since she arrived on the island, trouble had followed her around. If she could deal with things herself, nobody else would think of her as a drama queen, or an attention-seeker.

'She's come back a day early. I was down at the gallery today as part of our ongoing investigation. Melissa was there. She was shocked by the recent revelations.'

'Kaila Montana.'

'Yes,' he said. 'But back to the painting, Melissa would hardly take and then return her own property, would she? Is that what you're getting at?'

'I suppose not. I'm glad I had the locks changed though.' Another problem. Chloe was fiercely loyal to Ailsa now, and the last thing she was going to do was suggest her grandson might have stolen property. Not unless she was absolutely sure it was Jordan.

He sighed. 'To reassure you, I also checked in with Jonas and Arron. They have purchased the four properties on the cliff above the pen where you found Goldie. It was a logical step to move their apartment development in that direction. They did have a meeting with the site manager and several potential buyers around that time.'

'I just don't know what to think about Goldie's abduction...' Chloe said, breaking a crusty roll and spreading butter. 'The obvious answer is, someone heard I wasn't going to sell up, and is trying to ensure my business fails. But who?'

'I honestly don't know at this point but I can't hound people without any cause,' Finn told her, grinning.

Chloe sighed. A quick change of subject seemed in order. 'I know, and I'm sorry. You don't need extra hassle on top of the murder case. How is Sheetal? Jonas said she was going home to spend time with her parents.'

'She is. It is pretty terrifying to know that you possibly just escaped murder,' Finn said.

'Don't tell me anything if you can't. I mean, I'm not trying to pry.' Chloe was intrigued though. Petty, spiteful crimes against her property and herself were all very well, but it was good to know the murder seemed to be something that *wasn't* connected to her. 'I'm glad you've got Kaila, if it was her, I mean. It must be so awful for Matthew's family wondering what happened, and why...'

'Well, the press seem to have their own ideas, and they aren't always right.' Finn met her eyes and smiled. 'I can't tell you anything else, but let's say I hope you feel that you can rest easier in your bed, knowing that we have solved Matthew's murder case.'

Relieved, but not entirely convinced, Chloe nodded. 'Thank you. And you honestly think Melissa is all right?'

'We have to hope so. I have no evidence to suggest that she isn't, put it that way. Whatever the family dynamics between her brother and stepfather, I think it would be fair to say, she can take care of herself.'

'But I still have her painting,' Chloe reminded him, 'and she must think I still have her money too. And she knows that you know. Now I'm getting confused!'

She had brought the painting with her to show him before dinner. In the safety of his car, they had both checked the packaging and the painting for clues, and then Finn had locked it securely in the boot, saying he would see if the police could get any prints from it.

Their starters arrived, and Chloe tucked into delicious sushi rolls, served on pretty blue glass plates. It was lovely eating with Finn, who, in the short time they had known each other, never made her feel self-conscious. She had always enjoyed her food, but Mark's constant comments about her weight, her bad taste in wine, her lack of enthusiasm for whatever venue he had chosen, had put her off.

The sun had lost the intense heat of the day, but the evening warmth was lingering.

'So tell me about the Kite Festival,' she said, deliberately relaxing and taking another sip of wine, as the main courses arrived. She had chosen Bermuda style Rockfish, with toasted almond gremolata, and Finn was eating Bermudian fish chowder, which smelled heavenly. 'I think I remember going down to Horseshoe Beach to fly a home-made kite with Dre when I was a child, but it's a bit like a half memory. Something that could have been a dream.'

'It's part of the Easter celebrations. Usually there are around ten of us, friends, relatives... We grab a spot on the sand, lay down the blankets and enjoy the show. There's always plenty of food too. The kids have been making kites all week.'

'Did you say you have five nieces?'

'Yes. And two nephews. It will be a good way for you to get to know a few more people, tout for business.' He was grinning at her.

'Business? Do you mean for the stables?' She paused to take a sip of wine.

'Unless you're going to tell me that you have another budding business idea tucked under your wings somewhere?'

She laughed, then looked down at the pale-blue tablecloth, smoothing out the tiny creases with a finger. 'Of course not. The photoshoot has saved the stables for a while... Fiona sent an email with a contract proposal for Palm Bay Hotel, and it looks to be an excellent way forward. But we can't afford to lose any more bookings.'

'I thought your other ideas for the stables and horses were great – the art classes and the yoga on the beach after a ride... You can do whatever you want, Chloe, and it doesn't have to be just one thing.' He was smiling at her in the candlelight.

'You're right.' She could see the waiting staff hovering as more tables were filling up. 'Thank you so much for dinner too, it was wonderful.'

'No problem, I enjoyed it too. Now we need to go and collect your new dog, don't we?'

'Yes! If you're sure you have the time?' Chloe said, trying to read his expression.

'It's not a long drive and I'd like to see your new guard dog safely installed at the stables,' Finn told her.

Chloe laughed. 'You make her sound like a surveillance camera!'

After a short wrangle over payment (Finn insisted and she allowed him to pay on the premise that she would get their next meal) they wandered down the steps, out into the darkness.

Chloe felt the first squirming of awkwardness. It was too romantic. The candlelight, the setting... Although as Fiona had observed when they first met, in Bermuda you'd be hard pushed to find anywhere that wasn't romantic, she chided herself.

Their hands brushed as they walked, and she chattered on about her business plans to fill the silence.

There was one moment, when they reached the car, and he opened the door for her. She bent down to get in, gathering her long dress around her, and found their heads close together. Panicking, she quickly got in, and made a random remark about how she had to be up early and how kind it was of him to offer to pick up Hilda.

The drive to the rescue centre was slightly tense, with Chloe keenly aware of Finn's tall, solid presence next to her. She broke the silence with some chatter about how she hoped the dog would settle in okay.

Finn smiled at her. 'I should think she'll be very happy. Stop worrying.'

Helen was at the gate watching for them. She had brought Hilda out of the kennels and into her house ready. The dog was wildly excited, snuffling both Finn and Chloe with a very cold, wet nose. But she was well behaved and didn't jump up.

'She's a lovely dog and I'm sure she'll be very happy with you,' Helen said, handing her over, 'but if you have any problems or just want to chat something over then call me.'

'I will, and thank you.' Chloe was on her knees, the pretty dress pooling at her feet as she cuddled the delighted dog.

Spared any awkwardness by Hilda's bouncy presence in the car, Chloe thanked Finn again for a lovely evening and fled towards her house, hearing him depart down the driveway as she opened the front door.

Hilda seemed pleased with her new home, and after an initial exploration sank down happily on the rug in the living room, tongue lolling as she panted. Her bright brown eyes inquisitive and roving around the room.

As instructed, Chloe filled up the water bowl, and gave Hilda just a small handful of food to help settle her in. The dog ate quickly, tail waving constantly, and after a quick drink she consented to a walk around the garden with Chloe.

Chloe kept her on the lead, showing her the fence line but stopping short of the stables. The night garden was cool, fresh and fragrant with spring flowers. She steeled herself as her phone buzzed again, hoping it would be Finn, or Helen checking up on her. But it wasn't:

Be careful, Chloe. Trust nobody. Stay safe.

Had the tone of the message changed a little? This was certainly more of a warning. Chloe darted a worried gaze around the perimeter of her garden, walking to the gate, accompanied by Hilda. The yard was quiet, the gates locked and stable doors bolted. Goldie gave a low wicker, but the other horses were silent.

Later, with Hilda settled on her bed in the kitchen, Chloe decided the texts seemed to be concerned for her safety, warnings for her own protection, and therefore, could safely be considered unthreatening. No need to worry anyone else with them. She could deal with this. Murder and the like was a case for the police. Not this.

She dragged off the dress, pulled on her pyjamas, and

poured a glass of rum. Unable to think about sleep, Chloe determinedly turned on her computer and settled down to working on the Beachside Stables website. Work would take her thoughts away from the many worries wriggling around at the back of her mind.

The dog, having slipped unnoticed from her bed, padded across the room, resting a soft muzzle on her leg. Chloe fondled the soft ears, smiling as Hilda's tail wagged hopefully.

'You need to go back in your bed,' she told her eventually.

Hilda padded obediently back to her smart tweed bed, watching Chloe's movements with her head on her paws. Slightly worried that Hilda might feel abandoned, Chloe left her bedroom door open a crack, so the dog could see her.

It was just past one when Chloe woke, blinking blearily at her bedside clock. She lay still, closing her eyes again, when the sound came. It was a scraping noise, like something heavy was being dragged.

From her feet came a small growl, and she bolted upright, hands encountering soft fur and a wet nose. It seemed that Hilda had decided Chloe's bed was more comfortable than hers.

The dog growled again, ears pointed upwards, hackles rising, her eyes bright.

'What's wrong?' Chloe whispered to her, smoothing a shaking hand across her back. The dog ignored her, and continued the low rumble in her throat.

Fully awake, her heart thumping, Chloe pulled her dressing gown on and crept out of her bedroom. The moonlight flooded her house, making the rooms almost as clear as day. She paused and listened again. Hilda was still growling.

The noise was fainter. Was someone in the yard? Almost

without thinking, she found herself grabbing the big heavy torch, unlocking the door and walking quickly towards her horses, the black dog trotting at her side. No way was anyone hurting them again, and she was sick of this campaign. She would find out who was doing their very best to drive her away.

All at once, the anger that had driven her out left her standing in the middle of the moonlit yard. There was rustling of straw and the horses poked their noses over the half doors, watching her with interest.

But she wasn't looking at the animals, she was staring at the bare concrete of the yard. As ever it was swept clean by Antoine, but now there was an addition to the pale neatness.

Somebody had written in red paint:

GO AWAY

Really? The relief was so sharp she found herself laughing like a crazy woman. She had been all keyed up for... for a dead body or a missing horse, but this... Blinking tears from her eyes, taking deep breaths of the salty night air, she studied the graffiti carefully.

Next to the unimaginative wording was a daubed drawing of a hangman dangling from a noose. She remembered playing the game as a kid, but here, in the lonely depths of the night, it didn't seem so funny. Chloe stopped laughing and shivered.

23

A noise from behind made her jump, but it was only a large ginger cat, his eyes luminous and huge as he padded towards the muck-heap. Hilda eyed the cat but didn't chase him. Clearly the dog was used to cats and knew who had the upper hand.

Chloe stood and dithered for a moment longer. She couldn't hear anything else. The tack room and storage shed were locked and bolted. Her house! She had come out and left the door open in her haste, idiot that she was. In her pocket was her mobile phone. But again she hesitated to call the police. She was fed up with someone trying to scare her. She was a grown woman, a homeowner, a business owner, not a child. And there was the stables to consider. After the success of the photoshoot, the new hotel contract, she didn't need any bad press. Goldie's abduction had turned the press in her favour and she wanted to keep it that way.

She would deal with this herself. It had become a mantra. After all, she told the cat and dog firmly, it was just a bit of paint that would wash off in the morning. Annoyed to discover her hands were shaking, she snapped a few photos with her phone, just in case the police ever needed to know.

Once this was done, Chloe walked carefully back to her house, pointing her torch at shadows, and dark corners. Comforted by the dog's lack of interest, she watched her jog round the garden, snuffling for night creatures. Her hackles were down now, and if she wasn't bothered, whoever had disturbed them was clearly gone.

Back in the house, she checked every single inch for intruders, and finally went to sleep in an armchair, the torch and phone on her lap, Hilda at her feet.

The next morning she woke up stiff and exhausted to hear Antoine banging on her door. 'I'm fine and I know about the paint,' she told him sleepily, as she opened the door.

'Did you see who did it?' Antoine asked, brow crinkling with worry.

'No. I heard a noise, and went outside about one, but there was no sign of any visitors, just the writing,' she told him. 'Coffee? Oh this is Hilda by the way.' The little dog sniffed Antoine's fingers and wagged her tail. With her big black ears flopped sideways, and her wide grinning mouth she looked a little like a frog.

'She's... cute. Did she bark last night?' He came in and sat down, drumming his fingers on the table. 'And have you called the police?'

Chloe turned back to face him, a steaming mug in each hand. The heavenly smell of fresh coffee forced her brain to work properly. 'She woke me up growling, and when I went out she looked around the garden but whoever did it was clearly gone by then.' Chloe paused, thinking. 'And no to the police. I didn't call them and I'm not going to. Listen, I've been going over and over the whole thing, and I want to try a new approach. We aren't going to bother the police, because each time we do, the incident is logged, word gets out that something else has happened.'

'You want to keep it quiet so we keep the Palm Bay contract?'

'Exactly. And the other guesthouse ones that have come in off the back of Goldie's disappearance and reappearance. If the business is going to survive we can't afford any more trouble. So when you've finished your coffee, would you mind washing that paint off the yard, please?' She smiled. 'I'll muck out and do the water buckets. I think I'll try and bring Hilda with me, because Helen said the more she gets used to my usual routine the easier she'll settle in.'

'Wow, you are something else, Mrs C. But just promise me if you think there is any real danger, you'll call the police?'

'I promise. Now get moving, because we have a busy day. I've been redesigning our website and sorting out social media accounts. I want some nice photos of the horses and you in the yard,' Chloe told him.

'I thought you were going for a ride this morning?' He was halfway out the door, mug still in hand.

'I am, but business first. I'm multitasking,' she informed him, shooing him out, and shutting the door firmly on a gaggle of chickens who were clucking hopefully towards her. Hilda sniffed at the closed door, and then wandered over to her water bowl and drank noisily.

She checked the news and saw another few articles on Matthew's murder and Kaila's arrest. It was reassuring, somehow, to see it down in print.

Alone in the kitchen with her dog, Chloe felt a surge of confidence. She wouldn't allow herself to be bullied. She'd been weighed down with Matthew's murder and Melissa's odd behaviour, and it had clouded her judgement. Nothing that had been done to her was dangerous. Mildly threatening, but not enough to scare her out.

Chloe briskly ticked off the facts in her mind. Goldie had been stolen but unharmed. Practically unharmed, and that was the only major crime against Beachside Stables and Chloe herself.

As for the murder, and attempted murder, Kaila Montana was the perpetrator, and no doubt she would soon be charged. Reiterating the facts gave her the reassurance she needed.

There was still a niggling little unvoiced worry, that someone might be trying to put her out of business, but she felt safer knowing the murderer had been caught.

She would continue with her plans, let gossip spread about her future ideas, and about how well Beachside Stables was doing. Chloe picked up one of her home-made candles and held it to her nose, inhaling the sharp sweetness. Hilda settled at her feet with a heavy sigh, resting her square nose on her rather large front paws.

Chloe reached down to stroke the dog, before getting back to work. After yet another edit, taking a deep breath, she hit the publish button on her new website, reasoning that it was easy to add more photographs, and best to have something in place while she did so.

The home page was headed with a snap of all six horses looking out over their stable doors, and the contact page was neat and easy to navigate. Done. Chloe felt a fizz of excitement. The social media accounts were now set up too, just waiting for her to add updates and gorgeous photos.

The Kite Festival started tomorrow and she would go looking bloody gorgeous, distributing her business cards to all and sundry. If Finn hadn't wanted to kiss her last night, he certainly would when he saw her again.

This thought made her pause on her way to the shower. Did she *want* him to kiss her? Would it ruin their developing friendship? She certainly found him attractive, but she also loved the time they spent together, and wasn't sure it was worth risking a friendship. Still, there was no harm in being a bit more adventurous. She might even go for another swim tonight.

A large parcel arrived just as she was ready to go out to the yard. The candle-making equipment she had ordered online. Taking a few moments to unpack, she sorted the boxes of soy flakes, labels and jars until she reached the fragrances. All natural, because she hated the synthetic smell of air fresheners and cheap candles, and felt breathing in chemicals couldn't be healthy.

The pine was lovely, and there was salt, lavender, ylang-ylang and rose. Carefully picking the scents, she decided to make some for her neighbours, one for Antoine's girlfriend Louisa, one for Peter and his wife, and one for Finn. It was a good way of showing how much she appreciated their kindness and welcome, she thought.

She had been so engrossed in her tasks she hadn't noticed four chickens slip in at the open door. They were now sitting comfortably on her rug by the sofa, beady eyes taking in the industry in the kitchen, wings spread out in the warmth. Hilda was eyeing them guiltily but made no move towards the feathered intruders.

Chuntering to herself, Chloe shooed them out, grabbed an iced drink, and her phone and hurried down the garden path with Hilda trotting beside her on her smart leather lead.

By the time she got out to the yard, the concrete was back to its usual pristine state, and Antoine was saddling Star and Jupiter ready for a booking. Chloe had elected to ride gentle Goldie again.

'Okay, I'll take some photos for the website now, before the clients arrive if you don't mind?' Chloe said. 'Just look natural.'

Antoine looked stunning in the photos, as she had known he

would. He could easily pursue a modelling career, but when she mentioned it, he brushed the idea off, laughing.

'Louisa would kill me! She says I should stick with horses.'

'Well, you are brilliant with them. Does Louisa like horses?'

'Yeah, she rides really well, but what *she* really wants is to make lots of money. It's tough at the moment, which is why she's studying graphic design and working two jobs. I think she prefers working for the tourist board though.'

Chloe had seen pictures of Louisa, although they hadn't met yet, and she was very pretty, with curly brown hair, green eyes, and a determined set to her jaw. 'You're both still so young. There's no hurry to decide. Sometimes careers change. Look at me! I never thought, at fifty, that I'd own a riding stables.'

'It suits you, Mrs C, and so does Bermuda. When you first came here you were really quiet and sad, and now you seem happy.' He frowned and flushed. 'Sorry, I probably shouldn't have said that.'

'I'm glad you did,' Chloe assured him, 'and you're right, I'm happy now. I used to think fifty was like a full stop in my life, when I hit old age and there was nothing to look forward to. Now I see I was completely wrong, and I just needed to make some changes. Thanks to Dre, I came here to make them.' Thinking she might have said too much herself, Chloe glanced away a little awkwardly, but was relieved to see Antoine was amused.

'You remind me so much of Dre sometimes!'

'I'll take that as a compliment,' Chloe said, picking up a body brush and unbolting Goldie's door. She had already set out a space in the shade for Hilda, and she tied her lead to a long rope, giving the animal access to a big water bowl. 'I hope Hilda's going to be okay. I won't be gone long, and in time I'd like to train her to run alongside the horses.'

'She'll be fine. I'll keep an eye on her,' Antoine called from the next stable. 'We've got a booking later, but there's plenty of time for you to get your ride in.'

'Don't you ever ride out?' Chloe asked suddenly.

He shrugged, eyes on the dog, who was dozing peacefully in the shade. 'Not really. I might take Jupiter down the beach in the evenings sometimes but I'm happy enough looking after them. I had a bad fall showjumping at a competition a few years ago, right before I came to work here, and I guess I lost my nerve a bit.'

'Well any time you want to take a horse out, please do,' Chloe said gently. He was a lovely boy and she was very lucky to have such a good stable manager, she thought.

Deciding that the half doorway framed the yard beautifully, Chloe took out her phone again, and carried on snapping pictures, and a short video of Star and Jupiter dozing in the sunshine.

Goldie seemed to feel she was being neglected and reminded Chloe of her presence with a sharp nudge in the back.

'Sorry, sorry, I'll get you ready now,' Chloe told her, patting the sleek neck and brushing out the mare's white mane. But as she worked, her mind was still on the business, mulling over new ideas.

The setting of the yard, right on the edge of the trail to the beach, and the picturesque white-roofed building was so perfect and would surely help her to get more bookings if she could manage to convey its tranquil beauty through her photos and videos. 'Oh, Antoine,' she called across the yard, 'I need you to write a short piece on the horses, when you get a minute later. You know, age, height, cheeky personalities. Obviously we can mention Goldie being used in a photoshoot too.'

'An equine CV? Yup. Hey, do you want me to take Hilda for a little walk around the neighbourhood while you ride. I haven't had a dog since I was a kid.' He was smiling.

'Yes, please, if you don't mind? I'll clean Goldie's tack when I get back. I'll be about half an hour!'

Chloe waited until dog and boy had left, before she took Goldie over to the stone mounting block, and hauled herself into the saddle. Glad there were no spectators, she chose the higher trail, which wound above Tranquility House through the trees. Common sense told her there was no need to avoid the lower trail, but still that frisson of fear made her turn right.

Goldie plodded obediently along, occasionally shaking her mane when tiny flies landed on her golden neck. The screams of seabirds, the chirp of insects and the gentle thump of Goldie's hooves were a soothing accompaniment to Chloe's tangled thoughts.

Tranquility House was almost right next to this trail. Instead of the shadowy, tantalising glimpses she had caught before, Chloe found herself viewing a once grand house. Stone walls had been decorated with some vulture-type stone birds, which now lay crumbling in the undergrowth.

As usual, when confronted with a derelict building, Chloe felt a surge of excitement. If she had been younger and more aware of the possibilities, she might have done as Shay and Michelle were doing – breathing life and imagination back into the beautiful old structures.

Finn had said the police searched the building after Matthew's death, and there was evidence of trampled paths to and from the doors and windows. Chloe dismounted and tied Goldie's reins firmly to a twisted tree next to the wall. She gave her a pat, and a handful of feed from the bag in her pocket.

The mare sighed gustily and settled down to wait, lazily swishing her tail, and Chloe trod carefully up the path to the front door.

The proportions of the house were lovely; symmetrical with lots of windows. Shutters still hung crookedly from some of these. Most of the windows were boarded up, but several, probably used by the police, were accessible and hung open on broken catches, bare of glass and inviting.

Shay's pictures tempted her in. She gave a quick, wary glance at Goldie, but the horse seemed contented enough. Fallen masonry made a natural step up, and with a heave, Chloe was inside, breathing in dust, flinching away from cobweb-encrusted corners.

The rooms were still partly furnished, and she could immediately see the area where Shay and his girlfriend had set up a few pieces for their shots. The old sofa, with its elegant scrolled hand rests was carefully positioned beside a heavy table.

Moving to the kitchen, Chloe wiped her hot face. It was at the back of the house and the windows were all boarded up, making her feel claustrophobic. There was enough light to see from the cracks in the ceiling and the lines around the glass, where the boards didn't quite fit. As she turned to inspect the table, treading tentatively on the rotten boards, a sound made her jump.

It was a sharp click, as though somebody had shut a door, or dropped a latch on one of the windows, followed by a quick scuff of footsteps. In an instant the house went from pleasant eeriness to downright terrifying.

It was a moment before she realised what had happened. The kitchen door had been closed behind her. She was shut in the fetid darkness of a derelict house with an unknown person.

Trying to control her rising panic, Chloe held her breath, peering at the door. Had it swung shut on its own? Had she imagined the footsteps? There must be numerous animals and birds now living in the house... She slipped a hand into her pocket and dragged out her phone with a sweaty hand. Her breath now came in short, sharp gasps and the shadows seemed to lengthen towards her.

'*Stop it*,' she told herself sharply. Then, gathering courage. 'Is anyone there? Shay?'

Outside, she could hear the vines shifting against the roof in the light breeze. Sweat dripped down her nose. Okay, if somebody had followed her in, what would they do now? Was she just imagining things?

There was no other way out of the kitchen. The boards at the windows looked pretty secure and a quick glance told her there were no heavy implements or furniture she could use to batter them with.

She looked at her phone. No signal.

It would have to be the door. Cautiously, she edged towards it, then took a deep breath and shoved at it. It swung open easily enough, and as it did so she saw a broken latch dangling from the framework. It was rusty and fragile. Gaining confidence, she dodged quickly around the furniture to her exit point, scrambling unhindered from the glassless window.

Blinking in the sunlit jungle, she focused on the spot where she had left Goldie. With a definite feeling of disbelief she saw that the mare had vanished.

Chloe ran back out of the tangled garden, onto the trail and saw with relief the horse was grazing on a patch of grass about ten yards away, her golden coat dappled by the tree canopy, long white tail swishing lazily.

Dropping to a walk and approaching carefully, Chloe picked up the reins and tugged the mare's head up. Goldie, mouth full of grass, looked at her reproachfully, but she didn't seem bothered. The reins were unbroken.

'So,' Chloe addressed the horse, 'did you untie the knot yourself and I imagined someone in the house, or did someone set you free and come inside to try and scare me?'

Her phone buzzed as the signal returned, and she pulled it from her pocket, relieved, hands still shaking.

Keep away from Melissa. She is dangerous.

Really? For heaven's sake! It was time to get on with the ride, so Chloe shoved the phone away, determinedly swung back into the saddle and continued until she reached the road. Goldie was keen to canter on the way home. As there wasn't anyone to witness her being feeble (she felt), and holding on to the saddle, Chloe let her, arriving back at the stables unscathed, with aching muscles and a sense of satisfaction.

She untacked and chattered nonsense to the horse as she rubbed her down, still thinking about the possibility that someone had been in the house. In the bright sunlit yard, with the animals around her, and the sea murmuring below the cliff, the ghosts had faded and she was very ready to believe she had just imagined the incident.

The messages on her phone must be from a crazy person. How could Melissa be dangerous? Trouble was she had now given her mobile number to so many people, not to mention it was up on the website along with Antoine's for bookings. She frowned at the possible mistake. Maybe she should get a business phone and keep her personal number private.

'You're back sooner than I thought!' Antoine walked back into the yard with the dog trotting happily next to him on her long lead.

'Was Hilda okay?' Chloe asked quickly, bending down and making a fuss of her dog. Hilda bounced happily around, licking her bare hands.

'Yeah, she was fine. Shall I tie her back up until you're done?'

'Please.' She refilled Goldie's water bucket, checked Hilda had drunk some water and prepared to head back inside. She closed the garden gate with a sharp click and unclipped Hilda's lead.

The dog trotted happily round the garden, snuffling at the chickens, who seemed to be digging up plants in Chloe's flower beds.

'Hilda!' Chloe called, and was pleased when the dog bounced towards her on her short, stout legs, ears flapping in the breeze. She cast a quick glance back at the stables at the noise of a vehicle on the driveway.

Antoine went out to greet the taxi that was now pulling up outside the yard. A large man and two slender teenage girls emerged. The girls immediately went up to the horses, petting them and talking eagerly.

By lunchtime, she'd fed Hilda, made a sandwich for herself, added several posts to all the social media feeds, and fired off emails to all of their current clients thanking them for their custom.

Next up was emailing all the photographers on the island offering Goldie as an equine model.

Ailsa popped over at three, practically bursting with excitement, followed by her usual avian entourage, who were screeching away at the cockerel in the far hedge. 'Chloe, have you seen they've actually charged Kaila Montana?'

24

'No. Have they really?' Chloe asked, putting a tin of flapjacks on the table, and flicking the switch on the kettle. 'I did see something in the news this morning about it...'

Ailsa and Hilda collided in the doorway and Chloe hastily called the dog off. 'Sorry, I forgot you two hadn't met! This is Hilda, she's super friendly.'

'Nice. I thought you said a Staffie cross?' Ailsa inquired, reaching down, smiling at the dog, who promptly rolled onto her back, tail still wagging. 'She looks like a right mixture. Maybe some terrier in there somewhere too!'

'Probably lots of things, but yes, she is great and I'm very happy with her,' Chloe said. She debated whether to tell Ailsa about the disturbance in the night, but decided against it. Her neighbour had enough on her mind, and Chloe still felt awkward after her suspicions about Jordan. The more she thought about it, the more she felt he *was* the only person who could have taken the painting and the money.

Ailsa waved the inky sheets of *The Royal Gazette*. 'Anyway, as I was saying, there's an exclusive right here. It says she was jealous of Matthew's success, they had a row, and she killed him.

There was DNA evidence on the trail where his body was dumped, apparently. Not to mention she was involved in dealing drugs, and not just historically either.'

Chloe frowned. 'So that's good. Not the drugs thing, but I mean that it's solved then.' But her earlier relief was tempered by another thought. 'You just mentioned the trail though... How on earth did she get his body down there? He wasn't a small man, was he?'

Ailsa stuck her nose back in the paper, popping her reading glasses back onto the bridge of her nose. 'They were walking along the trail when she killed him. It also says she denies the charges against her, *and* that items belonging to her were found at the scene.'

'Sounds pretty conclusive.' Chloe still felt edgy. 'Can I have a quick look?' Hadn't Josonne mentioned a 911 call to BFR just before Jonas had called in the murder? Had someone else suspected Kaila was going to harm Matthew and wanted to get some first responders down to the scene?

Ailsa passed the paper over and propped her chin on her hand. 'I brought you an extra box of eggs, too.'

'Thank you, you are sweet! I gave Antoine the last of mine this morning. He's going to give them to his mum.' Chloe realised she had been expecting this latest revelation to tie up all the loose ends, but Melissa wasn't mentioned at all in the article. On the other hand, Finn clearly knew exactly what he was doing, and the police had been very good to her, so she really shouldn't doubt them. Should she?

'Did you get your locks changed all right?' her neighbour enquired.

'Yes, thanks, Benji was very efficient.'

She nodded. 'He's a good lad, not like some tearaways I could mention.'

'Is Jordan still giving your daughter a hard time? I thought you said he'd got back into his cricket?' Chloe asked tentatively.

'I don't know... Cheryl said he was out all night again, and he didn't get the job in the sports shop.' Ailsa screwed up her face. 'He's young, though, so perhaps it'll sort itself out.' She didn't sound hopeful.

'I was thinking of visiting a couple of the other stables on the island.' Chloe changed the subject as they sipped their drinks. 'Just for a friendly chat. Do you think they'd mind?' She stretched out a foot and gently rubbed Hilda's tummy. The dog grinned, still upside down, legs splayed, displaying perfect white teeth. Chloe giggled, remembering Antoine's previous comment. 'She does look a bit like a frog.'

'I wouldn't say frog, but she's obviously got character.' Ailsa laughed at the dog and Chloe's indulgence. 'Anyway, back to your question, I would say it depends on who you visit.' her neighbour suggested cautiously, picking up a handmade candle and holding it gingerly to her nose. 'This is nice. Smells of the sea. One of yours, I suppose?'

'Yes, it is, and you can take one if you like... I know Dre and Ellis Jack had a long-standing feud but I think he might talk to me. He did volunteer information when Goldie was stolen, which was kind. Not that we know who took her yet.'

'He did?' Ailsa looked sceptical. 'If I were you I'd leave Green Ridge Stables alone.'

'Oh. Well perhaps the Daileys at Cliff End then?'

'They haven't been doing so well either, from what I hear, but I'm sure Sarah would be up for a natter.' Ailsa approved the choice.

Annoyed that her previous euphoria of a job well done seemed to have disappeared, leaving a mess of loose ends trailing like untied shoelaces, Chloe got back to work after her neighbour left.

Back to the laptop, she edited the rest of the photographs she had taken this morning and loaded them onto the website, gave the wording another tweak and emailed the photographer from the shoot to remind him of his kind offer to send some of the Palm Bay pictures over.

By now, a headache nudged at her neck and jaw, and the sunshine beckoned. Stretching her arms above her head, she had a sudden longing to be out in the sea, allowing the waves to wash her worries away.

Not wanting to tempt fate and put too much into Hilda's first few days, Chloe gave her a dog biscuit and set her down on her tweed bed. 'You stay here, darling, and I won't be long.'

Hilda looked sulky, but tucked into her biscuit as Chloe went into the bedroom.

Changing quickly into her swimsuit, she collected a towel and went down to the beach. Braver now, she swam out further, and then along the beach, past several hidden coves and rock formations. A shoal of fish, their scales silvered by the sunlight, swam along with her, and she even ducked her head under for a quick look.

It was a huge step, and she had to tread water afterwards and wipe her salty eyes, but she had done it. She thought she might buy a snorkel set so she could investigate further.

Rejuvenated by the sea and sunshine, she went back to the house, showered and changed, before taking Hilda for a quick run up to the paddocks. Practising calling her back, still attached to the long lead, Chloe felt the little dog had settled in so well she would soon be able to take her everywhere without a lead.

Inside, she refilled the water bowl and called Jonas at the gallery.

'Chloe! How nice. Have you called to set a date for our dinner?'

She'd forgotten he'd asked her out on the beach where they had found Goldie. 'Um... That would be lovely, Jonas, but I'm a bit busy this week. The stables need quite a lot of attention and relaunching the business is taking up more time than I'd thought.'

'Of course,' he said.

There was an awkward pause. She hoped she hadn't offended him. 'Actually, Jonas, you said that Melissa was back, and I'd love to have a quick chat with her. About the possible commission.'

'She's out at a meeting with my stepfather, but I can get her to give you a call. They should be back by four...'

'That's great, thank you.'

'Chloe, why don't you bring some of your flyers to the gallery? We don't have any photographs at the moment and Fiona was saying that the photographer from your shoot was keen to display a few.'

'Was he? That would be wonderful and Goldie was such a beautiful model.' Well, she *had* been thinking along the same lines regarding the flyers, Chloe told herself, but she also thought of Emma and the community shop and made a frustrated face in the mirror opposite. She was thankful Jonas couldn't see her squirming. 'Are you sure? That would be very kind.'

'Bring a box in, and we'll pop them on the counter. You know, one of my clients was in buying a wedding gift for her son yesterday. He's getting married in Hamilton next month. Perhaps you could do wedding vouchers for your trail rides too?'

He was being so helpful, Chloe instantly felt guilty for having suspected him of anything. 'I'd have to check my contract with Fiona, but it's a wonderful idea!'

'Are you going to the Kite Festival this weekend?'

'Yes, I...' Should she say she was going with Finn?

'I'll look forward to seeing you there, then. Melissa and Arron will be coming and we'll get a few bottles and a hamper. It's tradition.'

'Your stepfather is staying on the island for a while, then?'

She could hear the tension in his voice. 'Yes, for another couple of weeks, before he goes to Madrid. Normally, as I said, he leaves Melissa and I to run various parts of the business, but he seems very taken with Bermuda just now.'

'I suppose with the Skylight Foundation here, he wants to support the community?' Chloe suggested.

Jonas made a noise that sounded like a half laugh, half snort. 'He has charities and foundations coming out of his ears, and all over the world. I don't think this one means any more to him than any other. Sorry, I shouldn't have said that. Things are just... rather tense at the moment.'

'No problem, I understand. I'll see you tomorrow at the festival and thank you so much for your offer about the flyers.'

Chloe rang off and stared out of the window. In the faint reflection, her face was tanned and healthy, but her eyes were worried.

25

Hilda's bark woke her up. The little dog had cosied up on Chloe's bed again and looked at her with such sad, pleading eyes she had given in and let her stay.

Now, blinking around the darkened room, trying to identify the feeling of danger, Chloe reached out for Hilda. But the dog had headed for the front door and was barking, rushing back and forth between Chloe's bedroom and the exit to the outside.

Her phone rang and she fumbled for it, dropping it off her bedside table, leaving it on the floor as she ran to the window, feeling the cool air from the draft around the sill. It was mixed with something. Tendrils were drifting across the room now, soft and menacing, stroking her face, making her nose twitch. Smoke. Fully awake, and aware. There wasn't any fire in the house, she could see that very quickly, which meant it was outside. The stables!

Tugging on tracksuit bottoms with shaking hands, she picked her phone up and dialled 911. The horses were whinnying in fear, and panic clogged her voice as she gave her address to the operator. Hilda was still barking, spinning around by the front door like a frenzied creature. Slamming the phone down, Chloe wrenched open the door and ran outside into the thick darkness with the dog right beside her.

The gate to the stables was open, but the yard gate, which led onto the trail was still shut. Momentarily indecisive, she froze. Where could she take the horses that would be safe? Smoke was billowing thickest near the tack room, and the crackle of orange flames could be seen at ground level.

Already neighbours were shouting, running to help. She tore a nail on the latch as she swung open the gate to the small paddock, and ran to shoot the bolts on the doors.

The flames were reaching greedily towards the stables now, fanned by the Atlantic breeze, but Chloe guessed she had woken pretty much as soon as it was started, judging by the fact it was still small and fairly contained.

There was no time for halters, and through the smoke she was aware of others helping, grabbing manes and noses, running the animals to the safety of the paddocks. The goats and chickens followed, hustled by shouting helpers, until the yard was clear.

She yelled that she had called the fire service and turned on the hose, dragged it across the yard towards the tack room. Two men were filling buckets from the trough, forming a human chain. Looking round in another brief burst of panic, Chloe was relieved to see Hilda, a little black shadow amongst darker shadows, faithfully tailing her owner.

The sparks rained down on the surrounding area as Chloe aimed her jet of water at the base of the flames. She had no idea if she was doing the right thing, but there was no way she was going to watch her livelihood burn down.

More people joined the fight, with more buckets. The yard was slippery with water and grime, and Chloe was half choking from the acrid smoke. She wiped her sweaty face with her forearm and grimly concentrated on the task in hand.

Torches spotlit the scene and the golden heart of the fire burnt brightly.

The noise and heat made conversation impossible, but fairly soon it became obvious that they were winning. Even before the blue flashing lights and sirens grew louder, vehicles jolting up her driveway, the flames were spluttering defiantly into a thick smoky mess.

Chloe relinquished the hose to a neighbour, and went straight up to check on the animals. By the time she returned from the paddock, Ailsa had staggered through the hedge, pushing aside Chloe's makeshift barrier, struggling to tie her pink quilted dressing gown, but determined not to miss any gossip.

'What happened?' Josonne asked Chloe, as the firefighters spread out. Some checking for any further fires around the yard or house, and others cooling the heart of the fire, salvaging anything that they could, and piling it into an untidy heap on the other side of the stables.

'My dog woke me up, and then I smelt smoke.' Chloe could see Finn getting out of his car. 'All the horses are okay. Whoever started it must have only just scarpered, because when I got out here it was just starting to spread.'

'Thank God you woke up,' Josonne told her, and Finn joined them, concern in his eyes.

Finn added, 'This could have been very bad, Chloe. Did you see anyone?'

She shook her head. 'No... I was sort of hoping that things had died down.' Chloe reached down to fondle the dog's velvet ears. 'Thank God I got Hilda. She was the one who heard, or I guess smelt what was going on. If I woke up any later it might have spread to the stables.' She couldn't bear to think of her precious horses trapped and terrified, so hastily swung her thoughts back to the perpetrator. Who was doing this? Jonas and the developers? Jordan's name had to be up there with the suspects, but could she do that to Ailsa? What would her neighbour's grandson have to gain by ruining her livelihood?

'Chloe,' Finn said gently, 'what are you thinking? Did you see anyone?'

'No! I honestly didn't. But during the last week I've been doing a lot to promote the business. You know, saying how great we were doing, touting for new bookings. Perhaps whoever did this didn't like that?'

'You certainly rattled someone's cage, but that was a pretty dangerous way of doing it,' Finn said, in concern.

Chloe wiped sweat and grime off her face, and squared her shoulders. 'I didn't do it on purpose! I was trying to save the business. I honestly can't understand who would have any motive for destroying my home and stables apart from the developers. But I won't let anyone drive me out. Doesn't matter if I can't prove who is doing this, I won't let them win,' she said passionately.

Suddenly she remembered the call on her phone, right after Hilda had started barking. On pretext of checking a message she flicked the screen to recent calls. An unknown number registered a call, just as she had thought. No voicemail. Another warning?

Finn grinned at her, but his eyes were serious, probing. 'Come back to us, Chloe. What are you thinking?'

'Sorry, distracted by a text. I am fine, honestly. And like I said, business will go on as usual.'

'The warrior spirit is strong. But it could also get you in serious trouble. Let's go inside and talk,' Finn suggested.

Josonne, who was surveying the yard, asked suddenly, 'And have you rung Antoine?'

'No. He'll be asleep.'

'He won't. Word spreads fast. By now somebody will have

woken him up and told him about the fire. Wouldn't surprise me if he was on his way over. He loves those horses, doesn't he?'

'Oh God, you're right. I don't want him to worry. I'll text him now,' Chloe promised.

As they reached the door of the house, Ailsa was waiting in the shadows, eyes red-rimmed and tired. 'I suppose you'll want the tea made? Hallo, Hilda!' She leant down and petted the dog.

'Ailsa, you shouldn't have come over. I can make the tea. Are you all right?' Chloe asked, concerned by the fatigue in her neighbour's face, the lines of worry that wrinkled her forehead.

'I'm fine. Just wanted to check all the horses were safe. I was hardly going to lie in bed with an inferno next door, was I?' Ailsa retorted, with a spark of her usual spirit.

'We're all fine. It's all over now, so you're welcome to head home and go back to bed. Or come in for a hot drink if you prefer?'

The older woman shook her head firmly. 'I'm fine and I'm coming in.' Any awkwardness that might have lain between the two of them after the dinner at The Ocean Club was rapidly dissolved by Ailsa's presence. Finn went through the usual questions for his report on the fire, another officer taking notes, deferring to his superior but occasionally slipping in other questions, or asking for clarification on an answer.

Chloe answered everything carefully, sipping her tea, conscious now of her dirty tracksuit bottoms and baggy, torn, white T-shirt. Her hair had come loose from its night-time plait and she pushed tendrils back from her sweaty face. Exhaustion made her stumble over her words, and her headache was back. Hilda sat firmly at her feet as she boiled the kettle and reached mugs out of the cupboard, wet nose just touching Chloe's bare ankle. Her presence was extremely comforting.

While they were talking, Ailsa drank her own tea, poked around Chloe's kitchen, discovered cake in the tin, and made another four cups for Josonne and his team. Only when she had dumped all this on a tray, did she turn back to the table.

'I'll put those on a tray and take them out,' Chloe said, standing up, but Ailsa put out a hand.

'Wait a bit, I've got something to say to both of you.'

Finn and Chloe exchanged surprised glances.

'Yes, something important to say.' She sat down, slowly and carefully, linking her hands together and putting them firmly on the table in front of her. 'I've given this a lot of thought, but I know whose side I'm on.'

'Go on,' Chloe said gently.

'I know who's been trying to run you out of business. It's been me.'

26

Ignoring Chloe's gasp and Finn's quick exclamation she went on. 'It's true, but maybe not how you think.'

She sighed, suddenly looking sad as well as tired. 'It's time this came out. Too many years and too many lies. You know of Ellis Jack?'

'Yes. He and Dre had some long-standing feud, didn't they?' Chloe said, staring wide-eyed at Ailsa. Never in a million years would she have suspected her. But the niggling little voice told her, perhaps even though she claims responsibility it might still be her grandson... She quickly tuned back into what Ailsa was telling them.

'...She accused him of neglecting his animals. Mud sticks and it took him a long time to get rid of the reputation. He lost a load of money after that. His agent dropped him and he couldn't tour. He was in debt up to his eyeballs. But it was more than that. His farm is only leased, and Dre owned her land and buildings outright. He wanted what she had, so when she died, and left the place to you, he told me to help get rid of you.' Ailsa was staring at the table, unable to meet Chloe's eyes as her words came rushing out.

'But why would you help him? I thought you liked Dre?' Finn said.

'A long time ago, Ellis did me a favour, and now he wants it paid back,' Ailsa said reluctantly.

'Can you tell us what the favour was?'

'I don't think I can at the moment. It was... personal. But I can tell you he agreed to turn a blind eye to something important. He did it because he and I...' – she flushed and played with her teaspoon – 'He and I had an affair many years ago. After we were both married. Neither of our partners found out, and it blew itself out fairly quickly. I'm not proud of it.'

'So he turned a blind eye to something because he was... fond of you?' Finn suggested.

'Something like that.' She sighed again. 'But then a couple of years ago, after the thing with Dre, he was struggling financially and he started asking me for money. My husband left me a bit when he passed away, and the house, and Cheryl makes a lot. He said I owed him. I didn't do much, just put around a bit of gossip that Beachside Stables wasn't doing well. Ellis' girlfriend, Kelly was at the gallery the night you landed the Palm Bay Hotel contract and photoshoot. She told him, and he spun that story about his lad being sacked and going missing so you'd keep him up to date on what was happening.'

'He took Goldie, then?' Chloe queried, anger in her voice.

Ailsa shook her head. 'He got someone else to take Goldie and lead her down to the Railway Trail. He met them and took her away. I thought that was it, and it was finally over.'

'Someone else? He was blackmailing you,' Chloe said coldly, shocked to the core that her friend could have been involved in all this.

The other woman nodded. 'He's changed as he's got older. Bitter as anything now, and just before Dre died his landlord gave him a year's notice on his stables. She wants to turn it into guesthouses. Ellis said if you sold, and I gave him enough to buy you out, we'd forget about the favour – we'd be quits. I didn't see any way of saying no, but then I met you, and liked you. You were a bit lost and I know you aren't blood relatives, but you're a lot like Dre in so many ways.'

'Did Ellis threaten you?' Finn asked gently.

She hesitated, then nodded very slowly. 'Yes. He kept saying that he was only asking for me to pay my dues. But eventually I told him I wasn't going to help drive you out. There's been too much water under the bridge.'

'And he hit you?'

'Yes. He came over that day, and he wasn't pleased. He's always had a temper. When I came out of hospital and heard about Goldie, I knew it was him. I rang him and shouted at him to give her back. But now the fire, he's getting desperate, and I'm scared he might hurt somebody.'

'Are you happy to make a statement?' Finn asked.

Chloe was still trying to come to terms with the fact that Ellis Jack had been behind the hate campaign. Not Jonas, or even the boy, Jordan. The hurt cut deep, and it came to her that the reason she felt so betrayed was because she thought she had escaped all this. Childishly, she had felt like she had strayed into a parallel world of paradise and sunshine, and now her illusions were shattered. 'Do you or Ellis have any ties to Jonas and Melissa Aliente?'

'Them again! No, of course not.' Ailsa was watching her beadily now, regaining her spirits slightly, now the confession was over with. 'You've got a right bee in your bonnet about that pair, haven't you? But no, their business is nothing to do with ours. That murdered artist wasn't anything to do with Ellis either, but you already know that. He was pleased, though, because it was so close to your place. He said it was fate's way of telling you to get off the island.'

Chloe stood up, and grabbed the tray, before noticing the tea was cold. 'Thank you for telling us, Ailsa.' She tried to keep her voice steady and cool, fighting hard with her emotions. It wasn't Ailsa's fault. She had been blackmailed, and she hadn't realised the consequences of what she was doing... But she still knew what was happening. Tears were bright and stinging behind her eyes and she busied herself with clearing empty mugs, hiding her hurt.

'It was the right thing to do.' The other woman nodded, watching her with something that might have been sorrow.

'Okay, I'll get moving, Chloe. Ailsa, I'll send someone over in the morning to take a proper statement, and don't worry, we'll be over at Ellis' place by first light,' Finn said briskly.

After Chloe had remade the tea, taken it out to the appreciative fire service, and helped Ailsa home, it was 2am. Back in her own house, she sank down onto the sofa, still filthy, and pulled a blanket over her. Sleep was immediate.

Knowing that Antoine would be over as soon as he woke up, she had left the front door unlocked, and the coffee mugs out. Now that she knew Ellis would be arrested this morning, she felt sure he wouldn't try another attack so soon after the fire, and anyway, Hilda had curled her warm furry body into the small of Chloe's back, like a canine hot water bottle.

Sure enough, her stable manager bounded through the door at half past five, making the dog bark and bombarding her with questions.

'You make the coffee, I'll tell you what happened,' she muttered sleepily.

After two mugs, she fed Hilda and let her out into the garden. She began to feel slightly more human, and was able to give Antoine a brief summary of the night, including Ailsa's confession.

Antoine was shocked. 'Who would have thought Ellis was

behind it? He's always come across as such a straight guy, but I kind of remember the scandal when he was accused of animal cruelty. I almost went to work for him, you know. It was him or Dre, but Dre was giving me a shot at being manager and he just wanted another stable lad.'

'It was Dre, wasn't it, who reported him for the cruelty?' Chloe put in, pulling her hoody around her shoulders against the cool morning air as Hilda rushed back inside. 'That was when all this started.'

'I can't believe he was blackmailing Ailsa,' Antoine said.

'I know!' But although Chloe had given Antoine an abbreviated version of the truth, it was the missing pieces that still worried her. What was the favour behind the blackmail? And was it possible Ellis could have stolen her package and made off with the money? According to Ailsa he needed the money from her to buy Chloe's house and land, so it wasn't just a case of frightening her into selling.

'At least we know who was behind it. Now we can get on with building up the business,' Antoine said cheerfully.

'Yes. You're right, but the first thing I need is a shower and another cup of coffee,' Chloe told him, 'especially as I should think it'll take a few weeks to get everything sorted out. The tack room is a pile of ashes. We'll have to store saddles and bridles in the house for safety until we get it rebuilt.'

Antoine nodded. 'Once the insurance pays up we can get someone in. What about tack in the meantime?'

Chloe shrugged. 'Well, Ellis Jack won't be needing his for a while, will he? Or perhaps I can pick some up cheap, second-hand... I don't know. Cancel the booking for today and tomorrow and I promise I'll have something sorted by then.'

'Yes, boss!'

Chloe was still mulling over the missing pieces of her puzzle when Antoine left to sort out the horses, and she went for a hot shower. As she washed the soot out of her hair, it came to her.

She was certain now, Jordan must have taken the package, and then removed the money, but returned the painting. He would have had access to the key, and nobody would have suspected Jordan if they saw him hanging around Ailsa's house. He was a familiar face. And now, finally, after Ailsa's confession, she felt she could confront her neighbour without any ill feeling.

Resolving to pay Ailsa another visit after the police had taken their statements, Chloe, dressed, but with her wet hair bundled up in a towel, padded off in search of toast and more coffee. Hilda looked so beseeching, with her big brown eyes and mournful frog-like expression, that Chloe gave her a piece of toast. 'Just this once, mind.'

Hilda took the prize over to her bed, popped it between her front paws, and crunched it with evident pleasure.

But when Chloe, gathering her courage, popped next door a few hours later, Ailsa was out and her door locked. Even the chickens had departed to Martha's garden two doors over. The confrontation would have to wait.

27

Having dithered over taking Hilda to the Kite Festival, Chloe finally decided that she would. The dog bounced around the yard as she mucked out, running after an orange ball Antoine had bought her.

'She's settling in really well!' he said, smiling at the panting dog. 'I can always look after her if you need to go out.'

'Thanks, Antoine.' Chloe wheeled the barrow over to the muck-heap, dodging chickens as she went. 'But you've got competition from Ailsa, who has also fallen for her amphibian-like charms.'

'I'll have to be second on the list then, I wouldn't mess with Ailsa and her chickens.' He laughed. 'Hey, didn't you say you needed to be ready by ten thirty. It's nearly quarter past already.'

Chloe dumped the last water bucket under the tap and called to Hilda. 'Done. See you later!'

Finn picked her up bang on ten thirty, and laughed at her bulging shopping bags.

'Well, you said everyone brought food, so I've got a selection from the market.' Chloe smiled at him. 'Mostly healthy stuff like crisps and cake.'

'I'm sure that will be a perfect contribution. Hallo, Hilda, and no, there isn't any food for you in here,' Finn told her, opening the boot. 'By the way, I've brought your picture back. No other prints apart from Melissa's, and it has never been listed as stolen, or even appeared in any of Matthew's collections.'

'So what do I do with it?'

'I'd hang on to it as Melissa asked you, and wait for her to collect it. I know she denied all knowledge of the painting and the money when I asked her, but if you can let her know you still have it safe...'

'What about the money?'

'No leads I'm afraid.'

'I can't believe we still don't know what's really going on!' Chloe said in frustration.

'Hey, it's meant to be a holiday today. Time out and time off. Let's see what happens,' Finn said.

'Okay. I just need to hide the painting though. Looks like I might be stuck with it for a while.'

He waited in the car as she ran back towards the house, but paused at the door. Antoine was at the top of the paddock, picking up droppings now, so there was nobody in the yard. Although the tack room was in ruins, the storage shed was a pretty good, secure hiding place. Chloe unlocked the heavy padlock, slipped the package between two boxes, and locked the door again behind her.

Glancing quickly around, she popped the keys in her bag and went back to Finn's car.

~

The Kite Festival was being held on Horseshoe Beach on Good Friday, another stunningly beautiful sweep of bay where the creamy pink sand met the turquoise sea in a foamy kiss.

'Wow!' Chloe stepped out of the car, straight into the crowds and music. She glanced anxiously at Hilda, slightly worried she had made a mistake in bringing her along, but the dog was standing calmly next to her, wagging her tail. Above them, on the headland, multicoloured kites of all sizes were already flying, tugging at their ropes in the strong breeze. 'I didn't realise there would be so many people!'

Ailsa was still missing by the evening, so Chloe had called Cheryl, who said her mother was staying with her for a couple of nights. She had been guarded, but friendly enough, and when Ailsa came on the line, she assured Chloe she was fine, just a little shaken up by her confession. They would all see her at the Kite Festival, she told her. Cheryl and Jordan would be with her.

Finn was now calling out greetings to friends, unloading a picnic hamper from the boot. 'Yes, it's a proper celebration. Local legend says a Sunday school teacher was trying to teach his students about Christ's ascension and used a kite to demonstrate. And that led to the Good Friday celebration we know today.'

'Ailsa's daughter and her grandchildren are coming later. She went to stay with them last night,' Chloe said, helping with the towels and bags.

'Is she still feeling guilty?' Finn enquired. 'Because Ellis was taking advantage of their shared history, blackmailing her. It isn't busting any protocol to tell you that he won't say what the favour was either. It shows how strong she is that she managed to confront him and then turn it around by telling us.'

'I said as much.' Chloe had already decided to get Jordan on his own and interrogate him today. There simply hadn't been time to tackle her neighbour about it, and if she was honest with herself, she shrank from causing any more tension between them.

The more she thought about Jordan, the more it made sense. And the favour? It could even be something to do with Ailsa's grandchildren? The twins had been tearaways and in trouble with the law. Maybe Ellis had witnessed some of their antisocial behaviour, and kept quiet for Ailsa. It was unlikely that Alfie would have been awarded a scholarship to the UK with a criminal record, wasn't it?

'Ellis will be far too busy answering the charges against him to think about any retaliation. It's all over now. We can enjoy the day.' Finn started walking across the car park, joining the throng of revellers as they surged towards the beach. 'Are you coming?'

She blinked, abandoned her whirling thoughts, and followed him through the crowd, Hilda sniffing the air, walking carefully on the sand at the end of her lead. There was plenty of good-natured jostling for the best picnic spots, and Finn threw their blanket down further along the beach, away from a makeshift stage, and the fishcake competition.

There was a decent amount of shade from an overhanging rock, providing a cooler space for Hilda to lie down. Chloe unpacked her water bowl and filled it to the brim.

Children were shrieking and running up and down the water's edge, colourful kites streaming behind them. Tourists were snapping selfies next to the sheltered little cove nicknamed 'Baby Beach', because of its shallow depth, encircled by a protective barrier of rocks.

Several people came over to greet Chloe, to admire Hilda, and Finn introduced her to many more. Somehow, meeting new faces on the beach in the glorious sunshine, with sand beneath her toes, was far easier than the formal party at the gallery.

People seemed to know who she was now, asking about her horses, about Antoine, and how she was settling in.

Jonas wasn't around, but about an hour after they set up on the sand, Melissa arrived with Arron.

Chloe scrambled up. 'Melissa!' She brushed sand off her dress and smiled at the girl, scanning her face, hoping her voice hadn't betrayed any emotion. 'How are you?'

'Hi, Chloe. I'm fine, thanks. Very busy at the New York gallery. Jonas mentioned you have a friend who wants to discuss a bespoke piece?' Melissa had reverted to the cool, glossy exterior Chloe had first seen at the gallery. Her grey eyes were hidden by sunglasses, and her cream, linen summer dress was fitted and obviously expensive.

Oh damn. Chloe had forgotten to email Alexa back when she asked about contact details. 'Yes. Perhaps you'd like to pop over sometime and we can discuss it?'

Arron, who was opening a picnic hamper, red-faced and sweaty with his grey hair sticking up in peaks, looked up. 'Or you are always welcome in the gallery, Chloe. If your friend decides against Melissa's work I can show you some of our up-and-coming talent. Oh, is that your dog? Isn't she cute!'

He held out a big hand and Hilda sniffed him politely, staying in the shade of the rock, all four legs stretched out, tail flapping gently on the picnic blanket.

Melissa's expression didn't change, nor did she mention Hilda, but Chloe could feel the flinty gaze fixed on her from behind the tinted glass. 'Of course. Alexa was very taken with Melissa's work, though, and once she has made up her mind there is usually no stopping her. Melissa, why don't you give me your mobile number and we can set up a meeting?'

There was no way she could refuse without seeming rude, and Chloe really couldn't see for the life of her why she would want to. After a pause Melissa reeled off her number and Chloe carefully added it to her own phone.

'I'm so sorry about everything that happened... Kaila's arrest must have come as a terrible shock,' Chloe said to Arron.

He was also wearing sunglasses, so she couldn't see his eyes, but his lips smiled, showing excellent white teeth. He wiped his forehead with the edge of a towel. 'It was a shock, yes, and I am horrified that there should have been such bitterness amongst my artistic community. But thankfully the Bermuda Police Service were able to bring the perpetrator to justice' – he nodded at Finn – 'we are very lucky to have such good criminal investigators in Bermuda.'

'How lovely to see you, Arron, and Melissa,' Finn said, his voice smooth, quick brown eyes missing nothing of the awkward exchange.

Melissa acknowledged the pleasantry, accepted a glass of champagne from her stepfather and then, as he murmured something to her, smiled at Finn and Chloe. 'We must catch up later. Arron wants me to meet someone.'

Arron smiled again. 'Sorry, won't be long. Just a bit of business to take care of.' He stumbled slightly in the sand as he moved away.

As they walked away, neither Chloe nor Finn missed the fact that Melissa shrugged away from Arron as he put a gentle hand on her shoulder. As before, when his stepson reacted in exactly the same manner, Chloe saw him drop the hand, his own shoulders drooping slightly.

28

Chloe went back to arranging the picnic food on paper plates. Tipping crisps into a plastic bowl, she glanced up at Finn. 'That was strange. I mean, I sort of feel sorry for Arron. His stepchildren seem to hate him.'

He grinned lazily down at her. 'Mrs Canton is back on the case.' His expression changed. 'I know you've been worried about her all along, and I understand why. But family dynamics aren't a police matter. And we've solved the murder case now. This could just be a simple matter of family disagreements.'

'I know, and I do see. There's just something still bothering me about Melissa. She never admitted she'd given me the package, so is she going to leave it with me, and pretend it never existed, or will she tell me what happened at some point? She had that bruise, Finn. Somebody had hit her, and she was terrified.'

'I know...' His expression was thoughtful. 'There is no solid evidence to tie her to any of Matthew's or Kaila's illicit dealings with drugs in the States. She may have bought or even sold some pills for Matthew, and perhaps still owe money... I don't know. This is pure speculation, unless she asks us for help.'

'She doesn't seem to be the type to ask for help,' Chloe said dryly, and smiled when he laughed. 'Yes, I can see why that's funny. I'll still keep an eye on her. And I want her to have the painting back.'

He picked up a slice of watermelon. 'Why don't we wait and see if she reaches out to you now she's back on the island?'

'I suppose' – Chloe narrowed her eyes against the sunlight, taking in the party atmosphere – 'she might even come back for a chat.' She bent down and gave Hilda a crisp, checking she wasn't too hot in the shade. But her coat was cool, and her nose still wet. There were a few other dogs on the beach and she supposed she might be fussing unnecessarily.

'If you can get her to ask for help, then we can do something, but until then, my hands are tied.' He poured her a glass of water and passed it across the blanket, before taking out a box of cupcakes.

Chloe accepted the water, sipping slowly, still thinking. 'I'll work on it. I know I'm nosy, but I feel... I don't know... like she needs help.' She thought this sounded a bit stupid and hastily changed the subject. 'Hilda has her beady eyes on those luscious-looking pink cupcakes.'

Finn removed the box from the dog's reach, ignoring her reproachful glance. 'She'll be fine here for a minute and we can keep an eye on her. Come and watch the sandcastle competition!'

Chloe and Finn joined the audience, clapping as various sand sculptures and multi-turreted castles were judged and winners announced, enjoying the live music and the buzz of chatter. But her eyes were searching the crowds for Melissa.

'Chloe!' This time it was Ailsa, with her daughter and Jordan dragging baskets and a picnic blanket. 'Hallo, Finn. Hallo, Hilda, darling!'

'She's sulking because Finn wouldn't give her a cupcake,'

Chloe told her, laughing. She greeted Cheryl and Jordan. The boy seemed slightly sulky too, his wide mouth turned down, shoulders drooping, dark hair tumbling into his eyes. He kept his eyes lowered and mumbled 'hallo' in response to his grandmother's prompt.

'Nice to meet you properly,' Chloe said, as they settled side by side, squeezing into a space next to the rocks.

Cheryl was tall and pretty, with long curly hair tied back in a floral scarf, and a wide smile. 'I'm so sorry about everything. Mum told me what happened. How are you coping after the fire?'

'Nearly cleared up already. Antoine is a brilliant worker. He managed to get some tack on loan from a friend of Louisa's and it will be business as usual from tomorrow.'

'I'm so glad,' Ailsa put in. Her bruises had faded into her tan, but she put up a hand and touched them self-consciously. 'I'm also glad Ellis won't be able to hurt anyone else.'

'Or blackmail them,' Cheryl said, frowning, turning back to her mother. 'I can't believe you didn't *tell* me!' Clearly she had no problem with bringing everything out into the open, and Ailsa gave a martyred sigh.

Finn started pouring drinks, passing Chloe a Dark 'n' Stormy straight from the tin. 'I have added ice flakes from the box, but I'm short on glasses.'

'It's lovely, thank you,' Chloe told him.

Kites fluttered as the breeze picked up, pulling hard against their restraining strings, and more families arrived. Tanned teens were dancing to the live band, younger children paddling in the sea, and a group of men were playing cards in a sheltered corner by the rocks.

Ailsa, on the pretext of taking Hilda for a walk, was now up by the washrooms, chatting to a group of friends. Hilda, still on the lead, was leaping around with two terriers and a hairy, cream-coloured dog.

After they had eaten, Chloe saw Jordan slouch down the beach, brushing off a friendly greeting from another boy. Checking that her companions were still busy with various conversations, she followed him, weaving her way through the mass of people.

He kept close to the water's edge and went right to the end of the beach, where another curve of rocks divided the sand from the next cove. Pulling himself up onto a rock, he seemed engrossed in his phone.

'Jordan?'

He jumped violently, and scowled at her. But not before she'd seen a flash of panic in his eyes.

'Can I talk to you for a moment?'

He shrugged.

This child was responsible for recklessly taking someone's life, Chloe thought, but he just looked sad and very young. 'Did your grandmother tell you that someone broke into my house?'

'Yeah. She reckons it was probably Ellis, but he said no. I heard them talking on the phone when she came out of hospital.'

'Do you know anything about the break-in?'

He stared at her for a long moment, before he seemed to deflate. The arrogance faded from his expression and the childish helplessness was back.

'Why don't you tell me what happened to the money, Jordan?'

'Are you going to tell the inspector?'

'It depends on what you tell me. It was you, wasn't it?' Chloe said gently.

'Yeah. I saw that girl from the gallery, Melissa, come to your house in the night. I was staying with my gran because I had a row with my mum, and the scooter woke me up. The girl was carrying a package and I thought maybe you were into drugs too or something and she was doing a delivery. I'd heard a lot of rumours about her and the gallery so when I saw who it was I was interested. I stayed awake and saw her leave a couple of hours later, without the package.'

'So you decided to find out what was going on?'

He glanced down at the rock, tracing the lines with a fingertip. 'It wasn't just that. People said you must have a lot of money, to just come in and live here without working.'

Chloe laughed. 'I wish. I took redundancy from my job in London, which left me just enough to live on until I get the stables up and running.'

'I needed money.' For the first time he met her eyes. 'I was going to pay off Ellis Jack for Gran. I knew what was going on, and if he had the money, he just needed you out and he'd leave her alone.' He paused, still glaring right at her, fists clenched at his sides. 'I gave him the money, I stole the horse and I set the fire.'

Stunned by the half-expected revelations, Chloe leant against the rock herself. 'You did?'

He nodded. 'I had to get him off her back.'

'I understand that, but you could have just told the police, and they would have helped. So Ellis Jack has the money?'

'Yeah, all of it. You going to tell the police?'

'You could do it yourself?' Chloe suggested. 'I admire the fact you wanted to protect Ailsa, but the money isn't actually mine. It belongs to Melissa, so it would be good to get it back. I assume the money was to buy my house when I sold up?'

'He already had some stashed away that he managed to hide from the taxman, but he needed more. That was why this seemed like it was meant to be. He was seriously crazy, and I was afraid he'd lose it and kill my gran or something...'

29

Chloe watched the waves dashing lazily onto the beach. The noise of the festival seemed miles away. She would give him a minute, she thought, and if he disagreed she would hand him straight over to Finn.

'All right, I'll do it,' Jordan told her suddenly.

'You will?'

'Yeah. You're right. It isn't for me to be ashamed of, is it? It was him that started it all, and him that beat up Gran.'

Chloe said nothing as they walked back along the sand, dodging partygoers, but Jordan kept sneaking her little glances seemingly relieved to have got the weight of the confession off his back, if clearly worried about what would happen next.

She watched as he went straight over to his mum and grandmother, and started talking. Finn had once said he was clearly a good kid at heart, which under the circumstances was amazingly forgiving, but in this instance she would make sure he followed through on his promise.

Meanwhile, Chloe accepted another Rum Swizzle from Finn, and sat back on the blanket, stroking Hilda's soft ears.

'Ailsa gave her back, then? I thought she'd kidnapped her for the day.'

'She was worried about her getting too hot.' Finn grinned. 'And I think they've done the social rounds anyway.'

Chloe smiled, narrowed her eyes against the sun, and rummaged in her bag for sunglasses. The drinks were very strong, and she was already getting a bit dizzy. She made a mental note to stick to juice for a bit after this one.

'Oh look, my sisters are here,' Finn said, waving through a crowd of picnicking families at a group of newcomers. 'Tasha, Karren and Rita, this is Chloe.'

Chloe suddenly felt her social anxiety return under their assessing eyes, and she smiled quickly, gulping the last of her drink. 'Nice to meet you.' Her voice, to her own ears, sounded far too high-pitched, and she hastily cleared her throat.

Mary, who looked just like Finn, and was almost as tall, broke the ice. 'Great to meet you too. Finn has told us so much about you, and we were all close to Dre. She taught the kids to ride, you know. Is this your dog?'

Hilda, seemingly exhausted by all the attention, had flopped upside-down in her shady spot.

Karren and Rita were also so warm and friendly Chloe felt herself relaxing a little. She was soon asking about their children, their jobs and explaining her own business ideas.

'Finn said you make candles too? I'm such a sucker for anything like that,' Mary said.

'She's got a house full of embroidered cushions and scented candles already, but every time we shop, she buys something else.' Rita laughed, one eye on her two teenage girls, who were running in from the sea with bodyboards.

'Hey, I only buy things I need,' Mary told her, with a twinkle in her amber eyes.

'Like the onion doorstop last week?' Karren suggested, grinning.

'Don't ask,' Finn advised Chloe, laughing at his younger siblings.

They chatted some more about the Stone Gallery and Kaila, before Chloe spotted Melissa at one of the pop-up bars near the entrance to the beach. She excused herself quickly and went after her quarry, threading her way around sandcastles, parasols and buckets.

The girl paid for two cans of Coke and turned back to the beach.

'Melissa!' Chloe was slightly breathless, but determined to get this sorted out.

A quick flash of panic shadowed across Melissa's face, but her eyes were still hidden by the expensive sunglasses. 'Sorry, Chloe, can we talk later? I need to get these drinks back.'

A few metres away, Chloe caught sight of Arron beckoning his stepdaughter, with Jonas beside him in a panama hat. She dropped her voice, blocking Melissa's way. 'Sorry if I seem nosy, but you did leave me with a bit of a mystery, and I've been worried about you.'

'No need,' Melissa told her, but her voice wobbled slightly. 'It's nothing I can't handle.'

'Okay, but you can come to me if you do need help.'

She wavered. 'You told the police about my painting.'

'I *had* to.' Chloe explained about the theft. 'But that's all sorted now. I've got the painting back. I don't know what will happen about the money, but I would guess if Ellis Jack wanted it to buy my place, he still has it. It will be returned.'

'I...' Melissa dithered, scuffing a sandal in the white sand. One of the cans of Coke slipped out of her hand and she and Chloe knocked heads as they both bent to retrieve it. 'I need them both, really, the money and the painting, but...' She glanced over at her stepfather, who had started walking towards them. 'I'll ring you. But not from my mobile, from the gallery, okay?'

'Chloe! Is Melissa buying you a drink? Let me get it for you!' Arron reached them and took the cans from Melissa's hands.

'No, thank you very much, I was just... coming back to join the party.' Chloe waved vaguely towards the long, low building which housed the washrooms. 'And I bumped into Melissa.'

'Do join us for a little while. Jonas mentioned that he wanted to see you.' Arron was still trying hard, the genial party host, and shepherded them both towards a little group of elegant festivalgoers.

Chloe, with sandy feet and windswept, salty hair, decided to escape from these immaculate women as soon as she could. Silk dresses and a few floral playsuits fluttered in the sea breeze, and their hair and make-up was immaculate.

Jonas, cool and poised, passed her a champagne flute, and she took it, sipping for the sake of politeness. She really must stop or she was going to be drunk. They talked about the gallery, the island, the festival, and the brightly fluttering kites. It was painful and Chloe soon felt she had observed social niceties for long enough, excusing herself on Hilda's account.

Walking back, she took off her sandals and splashed along the shoreline, letting the clear water cool her feet. Throughout the conversation Arron had watched his stepchildren, smiling too much, hanging around like a hopeful outsider. When Melissa, all false chatter and glamour, told one of the elegant women that her inspiration to paint came from the sea, Arron smiled indulgently, and opened his mouth to contribute.

But she quickly flipped the conversation on to another banal subject, her voice brittle and the hand that smoothed her long dark hair was a little shaky.

Even so, it was as Finn had observed, a tense family

dynamic. At least Melissa *had* seemed relieved by the news of the money and her painting, and she *had* said she would call.

'Where have you been? We thought you'd got lost!' Ailsa was sitting in a deckchair, wriggling her toes in the sand, Hilda now lying underneath the chair.

'Oh just chatting to a few people,' Chloe told her. 'Is Jordan talking to Finn?'

'He is,' Cheryl said. 'Thank you for giving him a push, love. He's told us all about it. He said you wouldn't press any charges about the money he stole from you?' Her voice was hopeful, and Chloe hastened to reassure her.

'No. I'm just glad it's all sorted out, and Ellis Jack can answer for his crimes. Jordan shouldn't have taken the money, but he did it for his grandmother so...'

'I'm still grounding him,' Cheryl said decisively. 'And if his dad gets out of the office for long enough, we're going to England to see Alfie play in some county games next month. That should wake Jordan up a bit.'

'I always said he could be just as good if he set his mind to it,' Ailsa put in. She had a plastic cup on the sand next to her and she was carefully sewing a little needlework picture as she enjoyed the sun.

Chloe leant over and smiled when she saw the outline of a flock of chickens appearing from the clever needlework. 'You know, if Jordan wants to come and help out at the stables, he's very welcome.' She hoped Antoine wouldn't mind. 'I can't afford another member of staff at the moment but he could do some mucking out and things.'

Cheryl's face lit up. 'That would be kind. And he can work for nothing and start repaying his debt. It'll be character-building.'

Chloe grinned. 'Well, mucking out six horses is certainly good for the muscles!' She decided she liked Cheryl a lot.

As the sun started to sink towards the sea, bathing the waves and beach in a beautiful blush pink, people started to pack up, gathering children and picnics. The music went up a notch and several buskers had joined the group of teens at the water's edge.

'Shall we make a move?' Finn asked Chloe, and she nodded.

But as they loaded the car, popping Hilda in amongst the basket and blankets, she caught sight of Arron driving carefully out of the car park. Beside him, Melissa sat stony-faced, hands knotted in her lap, shoulders tense, not responding to Chloe's wave. Something was very wrong.

30

It was late when Finn dropped her off, and he drove away quickly in response to a call from work, mouthing that he would call her.

The house seemed very silent and Chloe ignored a twinge of unease as she made some toast and scrambled eggs for dinner. Checking her phone for missed calls, she was disappointed to find Melissa hadn't taken the chance to get in touch. By the time darkness fell she was still wired and worrying.

Her mobile rang, making her jump. It was Finn.

'Chloe, I just thought you should know that Ellis Jack committed suicide this evening. Nobody else was involved and he left a note confessing to trying to drive you out. He admits he was responsible for the various acts against you, but he doesn't mention anyone else.'

There was stunned silence.

'Wow. Oh God, Finn that's awful. I feel responsible somehow.' Chloe put a hand out and leant against the table, heart pounding. It was true, at that moment she felt nothing but guilt for setting this in motion.

'Well you aren't. I'm sorry but I thought you would rather hear it from me.'

'Are you going to tell Ailsa?'

'Yes. I'm sending someone over to her daughter's house now.'

~

Drained by the news of another death, Chloe decided to do a last check of the yard and then go to bed. With Hilda trotting beside her, she walked swiftly down to the stable yard. The horses watched with interest as she carefully unlocked the storage shed. No damage and no lurking watchers tonight, but she glanced over her shoulder, feeling the hairs on the back of her neck rise.

The torch she had brought from the house was small and light. She used the beam to find the space between the boxes, and knelt in the dust. Chloe wriggled her fingers underneath the cardboard, and tugged out the package. Hilda, delighted at this unexpected outing, ran around sniffing for rats.

The package was undisturbed. Quickly, carefully, she unwrapped the plastic covering, running a gentle finger across the painting. All was as it should be. The only thing to do was to wait until the owner returned to claim it. A bird called high and shrill outside and she fumbled, dropping her torch. It fell with a little crack on the concrete flooring, leaving her in darkness.

Should she leave it here? Or hide it somewhere else? Melissa would come back for it, she was sure after their conversation on the beach. Perhaps even tonight?

Slipping out of the storage shed, she made a circuit of the yard, checking bolts and padlocks. The chickens, safe in their coop, murmured sleepily, but the horses were alert, tracking her progress with large dark eyes, nostrils slightly flared.

Hilda stopped in her wanderings and growled, hackles

rising.

'What's wrong?' Chloe whispered, her breath quickening, trying to see into the shadows.

The sea whispered soothingly in the distance, but her heart was thumping hard with fear. In the deeper darkness, by the gate to the trail, a movement made her gasp and Hilda leapt forward, barking.

'Hallo, Chloe. I hope you don't mind an impromptu visit. Please don't be scared,' Jonas said softly.

Swallowing down curse words, Chloe moved backwards, slowly, carefully, until she came up against Goldie's stable door. He followed her, cat-footed amongst the shadows, trying to fend off Hilda, who was jumping stiff-legged around Chloe, barking and growling.

Unusually, he was wearing trainers and a jogging suit, his hair messy and sweat gleaming on his face. 'I need your help.'

Chloe felt Goldie's warm breath on her shoulder, and stretched a hand up to cup the soft muzzle. It was comforting, familiar. This was her own place and she wasn't going to be bullied. 'Okay, Hilda, it's all right.' She reached down and slipped her fingers under the dog's collar, patting her head. The barks subsided, but her furry body trembled with growls. 'We could go into the house?' she suggested, annoyed to find her voice came out a tone too harsh.

'No. Down here is probably safer. Melissa sent me.'

'*What*? What the hell is going on, Jonas?' Anger was pushing through her fear, making her stronger. Had he seen her go to the shed and inspect the package?

'Did Melissa ever say anything to you, in confidence?' His expression was pleading.

'No?' She was cautious. Perhaps she had misjudged him.

'No... Chloe, there are things you don't know, but I really believe that she is in danger.'

'So go to the police.'

'I can't. That would make things worse.' He came closer, reaching out to touch her arm. 'I'm trying to help her, really I am. That's why she sent me tonight. To get the painting.'

She shrank back. 'Tell me what's really going on. Why didn't she call me to let me know?'

Distress clouded his eyes. He looked far from the sleek and well-groomed, charming businessman she had come to know. Now he seemed older, more vulnerable. 'Okay, but you need to believe I love my sister and I don't want to see her hurt. Melissa is very strong-willed.' He moved away slightly as Hilda growled again. 'She fell in love with Matthew Georgias, and... when he was murdered she was devastated. She said she wanted to find out who killed him.'

'She didn't know Kaila killed him?'

'Of course not! How could she? But I'm afraid that now she has discovered the real murderer.'

'*What*?' Chloe's head was spinning, and she couldn't work out whether it was excess alcohol from the festival or sheer confusion over this whole conversation. 'Jonas, we all *know* who did it now. The police have already charged Kaila Montana with the murder. She killed Matthew and she tried to kill Sheetal to see off the competition.'

Jonas dismissed this with a wave of his hand. 'I saw Melissa after the Kite Festival, and she was scared. When Arron is in Bermuda he stays with us in the duplex, but he went into the office to answer a call. Melissa came and found me. She kept talking about Matthew's death, and she was getting more and more upset. Eventually she went out, left the apartment and told me she needed to do something. I've tried her phone numerous times since then and she hasn't answered.'

'What's Melissa's relationship with Arron like?' Chloe asked.

'He is... very controlling. I told you he likes to interfere with the business at all levels. He considers Melissa and I to be part of his extensive list of possessions.' Jonas scowled. 'It can be hard, but mostly we get on with the work and keep our heads down. In Bermuda we've had more freedom.'

'Why don't you leave, start your own business somewhere else?' Chloe said.

Jonas laughed. 'Arron Stone is everywhere. If we tried to start anywhere in the art world he would crush us like bugs. He holds the purse strings, and we would have no money to start again.'

'So do something else,' Chloe said impatiently. She was trying to equate Jonas' descriptions of his stepfather with the bumbling, try-too-hard man she had become used to seeing.

He shook his head. 'I can't.'

'Melissa could.'

'She'd never leave without me.' Something like panic touched his eyes. 'I need to take the painting now.'

'The police still have it. How do I know you're telling the truth?' Chloe pulled out her phone. 'Perhaps I should just call the police?'

His hand closed over hers, warm and firm, preventing her from further action. 'No. It will do more harm than good. I came to you because I trust you, and you aren't a part of any of this. I need your help. For Melissa's sake, and for my own.' His words practically mirrored his sister's when she had stood, pleading with Chloe. 'This needs to end now. If I can get the painting to Melissa, then I just need one more thing from you.'

She hesitated, her hand still in his. Physical contact seemed to come as naturally as breathing to Jonas, and now he held her fingers gently, pleading with his eyes. Finn had told her the police couldn't help unless a crime had been committed, or unless Melissa asked for help. But now Jonas was asking for help, and he seemed so genuine. Should she trust him?

Chloe sighed. 'What do you want me to do?'

31

After Jonas' late-night visit Chloe lay awake for a long time, thinking about what he had said. Loose ends needed to be tied up, but was she stupid to put herself in danger?

In the end, she hadn't given him the painting, sticking to her story and instead trying Melissa's mobile, which was switched off. The obvious conclusion was that they were preparing to run away together, despite Jonas' denials and apparent fear of his controlling stepfather. Chloe thought that maybe when Matthew was alive all three were preparing to run. That would explain why they needed that cash and the painting to live on. No bank cards would leave no paper trail. Was Arron really at the heart of this, or were the siblings trying to turn him into some kind of scapegoat for a drugs plot gone awry?

But Melissa now knew the cash had been stolen so they must have some more. If Kaila killed her ex-boyfriend, had she discovered he was going to run off with Melissa? Surely that would mean she had free rein to take his spot at the gallery, and no need to kill him. Jealousy? Chloe's head felt like it was going to explode with all the different theories that last night had thrown up.

Jonas had indicated Kaila didn't kill Matthew. That had definitely been the gist of the garbled conversation. But she also thought she now knew who did.

By dawn, Hilda was fast asleep on her tweed bed, and Chloe had a plan of action. She couldn't involve Finn. He had already found his murderer and if Melissa was wrong it could create all kinds of trouble for him, and for her. No, she would sort it out herself.

She dropped her dog with Ailsa, who gave her a hard look, but asked no more questions than normal.

'I think I just need a morning off,' Chloe explained carefully.

Ailsa nodded, fussed over Hilda and took two scones from a tin, wrapping them in cling film. She held them out to Chloe, who winced away. 'What's wrong?'

'Sorry, Ailsa, but I'm a bit phobic about cling film. I'm really sorry and I know it's weird, it just makes me feel all cold and clammy...'

Ailsa laughed. 'You're scared of sandwich wrapping? Girl, you are something else.' But she rewrapped her gift in a paper bag and pushed it into Chloe's hands. 'Off you go and have a bit of time to yourself.'

'Thanks, Ailsa.' Chloe smiled gratefully, shamefaced at having revealed her rather odd phobia.

After feeding and mucking out quickly, she left a note tacked to Goldie's door telling Antoine she had decided to go out for the day. It was the only way she could think of not bumping into anyone and not being tempted to tell Finn about Jonas' visit. Or her reluctant agreement to help him and his sister.

She got the first bus that came and studied her maps. Something challenging, something that would completely distract her from tonight... Her finger paused on the map. Perfect.

The Blue Hole was buried deep in Tom Moore's Jungle. She

remembered visiting the trails as a child, peering at the still waters of the hole in trepidation. Now, social media was full of pictures showing backpackers leaping into the depths. It was a challenge, and it would keep her out all day.

She got the bus to the stop opposite the jungle trail, thanked the driver and hoisted her small rucksack onto her shoulders. The sun was already warming the dusty trail, and she was grateful for the shady trees as she plunged deeper into the jungle.

It was a beautiful place, and Chloe was early enough to miss the crowds. Following her map, she trudged carefully through the vines and twisted trunks to The Hole.

There was a new wooden walkway and viewing platform, along with a sign asking people not to swim in the waters. Chloe watched the still blueness, vanishing into dark rocky caves on two sides, and the jungle ravine on the other two. Bubbles drifted across the water as some fish or other creature swam underneath.

Chloe stripped down to her swimsuit, leaving her belongings underneath the viewing platform. The sharp rocks and coral made her wince, as they bruised her bare feet. But she slipped down to the water without major incident.

It was unexpectedly freezing, and she could see dark shapes that might have been fish. Without any further thought, she pushed off. The icy water made her gasp, and she swam quickly out to the very centre, treading water and spluttering. The sun heated the bare skin on her shoulders, but she was shivering, goosebumps dotting her arms. For a second she thought she caught a glimpse of movement on the left bank, but as a bird flew up, she relaxed.

It was incredible. The eerie solitude, and the natural beauty of the place made her almost feel like crying. She swam slowly around the perimeter, inspecting beautiful plants, tendrils and leaves seeming to dip tentative fingers into the oily blue depths.

The caves went a little way into the cliff and dripped with stalactites. On her way back to the platform, Chloe took a deep breath for courage, and ducked under, swimming strongly, eyes open. A shoal of multicoloured fish shimmied away from her, but a larger, languid, grey specimen merely stared at her as it passed. The weed fronds near the bottom stroked her legs, and some tiny yellow fish darted around in a patch of sunlight.

Surfacing, she took deep breaths of the warm air, relishing the sun's rays on her head. '*I did it!*'

She found she was laughing as she swam back, and hastily towelled down. By the time she had changed and strolled back up through the jungle, the tourists were starting to arrive, and the vines rang with children's laughter. At every corner people were snapping pictures, exclaiming over the views.

It was beautiful, and she had had it all to herself. All the same, Chloe thought, she would certainly heed the signs in future, about not swimming in the natural water holes. This had been a one-time thing, a challenge accepted and completed. She had taken care not to wear any sunscreen because she knew of the dangers to the precious biodiversity in this area.

She checked her phone when she got back to the road, and saw a missed call from Finn, and a text from her 'unknown caller':

Stay safe, Chloe, and stay away from the gallery.

Shoving the phone back into her bag, she set off up the hill for a late brunch at The Swizzle Inn. She hoped to stay safe but she certainly wasn't going to stay away from the gallery. Although the texts seemed more and more to mean her no harm, she would be glad to discover who was sending them...

Had there been someone tailing her today, watching the house on the night of the fire? A guardian angel or someone more sinister?

Chloe sat for a long time at her roadside table, sating her hunger on fishcakes, chips and mango juice, and just resisting the urge to order a Rum Swizzle. After yesterday's binge at the picnic, she needed to keep a clear head today.

The impulse to escape and to challenge herself that had sent her down to catch the early bus, had been a good one. Tired now, she decided to catch the next bus, which would go back to Hamilton as a matter of course. Having sent the artwork through via email, she could pick up her flyers, have a wander around, maybe reacquaint herself with Front Street, even see if the old apartment she had shared with Dre as a child was still there. A quick cup of coffee at any of the abundant cafes and she could go home safe in the knowledge she was ready for tonight.

32

_____

The Dockyard was full of shadows.

Patches of grey, and a deeper darkness around the taller buildings that made Chloe's heart beat faster. A cruise ship sat squat and enormous, lights glittering like a sinister sea creature.

'Are you sure you've got the right time? I can't see any lights on in the shopping mall...' Peter said. 'Look, I'll get a bit closer. That'll save us carrying the box so far.'

Chloe was very aware that although the box was fairly large, it was quite a pathetic excuse for her gallery visit so late at night. 'Thanks, Peter. I... I would have dropped them off earlier but they weren't ready for me.'

He said nothing, but reversed the taxi neatly into an empty space opposite the mall, and helped Chloe unload the box of flyers. It was the cover she and Jonas had agreed on. Her stomach was full of fluttering nerves, as underneath the box was the package containing _The Painted Lady_. Hilda, settled for the evening with a bone, had watched in disgust as Chloe went out and left her again.

'Jonas said he'd come out and meet us,' Chloe told the taxi

driver, as they headed for the side door. 'He was going to leave the door unlocked...' Her voice trailed off as they approached the building. She remembered his voice, soft and urgent in the darkness:

'*Meet me at the gallery at half nine. You were going to bring your flyers down anyway. Do it tomorrow night instead of in daylight. Get Peter to drive you over, just as you would if we were really working late, ready for the next exhibition. Melissa and I will meet you in the gallery. We'll tell you everything. There is no reason for anyone else to be there, but if they are, just explain that you're setting up ready for the event.*'

Security lights flickered on, illuminating the path directly in front. The side door was made of glass and metal. Chloe put her box down and pushed it gently.

The door opened smoothly into darkness.

'Jonas? Melissa? It's me, Chloe!' she called. But her voice echoed through the empty mall, and their footsteps seemed far too sharp for the silence. 'It's odd the gallery lights are off. He said he'd be working until at least ten, getting ready for tomorrow.'

They advanced towards the gallery and Chloe heard a quick intake of breath from Peter. The glass doors were smashed, as though somebody had thrown a heavy object against them.

'Hallo? Is anybody there?' Peter called.

They stopped, surveying the damage, their shoes crunching on scattered glass.

'Did you say Jonas and his sister would be here?' Peter asked, his voice tense.

'Something must have happened to him. Do they have security at Dockyard?' Chloe found she was shaking.

'Yes. There's an office on the other side of the marina, next to where the cruise ships dock.'

'Can you go and get them? I'll wait just outside the side door.

Leave all this stuff. It doesn't matter. Something's badly wrong,' Chloe said, trying to keep her voice steady.

'Will you be all right?'

'Yes. Whatever happened there's nobody here now. And if I yelled, you'd still hear me from over there.' She pointed towards the cruise ship.

Peter nodded and set off at a brisk walk, skirting the water. His shadow vanished into other shadows, and Chloe turned back to the gallery, shivering with fear.

Moving quickly, she retraced their steps. '*Melissa*? Are you there?'

There was no answer, but feeling braver at the sound of her own voice, she clicked the main lights on. The interior of the gallery showed no signs of damage. Paintings still hung in their places, and a stack of boxes sat against the counter.

She walked over, noting the various artworks that were clearly in the process of being unwrapped. These must be the sculptures Jonas had been talking about.

A laptop charging lead sat on top of the counter. Chloe made her way into the office. It was neat and tidy. The labels for tomorrow in coloured piles. A bundle of flyers advertising the event. But there was no laptop. What had Jonas often said? He carried it everywhere. Surely he would have been referring to files as he worked.

The desktop computer was switched off. As she moved back towards the door, ready for Peter's return, she saw the blood.

It wasn't much, just a smear, as though someone had flung a hand out, but shocking against the pristine white wall. Chloe spun around. Had she been wrong about Melissa? She had been so sure she was innocent, but what if she and Jonas were both guilty and she was being lured into a trap? Her pulse quickened and her breathing became shorter, sharper, hurting her chest. She had gone blindly into this, trusting her instincts, trusting her intuition, but what if her trust was misplaced?

As her confidence faltered, Mark's words came back to her. *'How can you possibly change career now? It's far too late. Best get some cats and knitting...'*

But she, Chloe, was stronger than Mark had ever known. The magic of her swim in The Blue Hole came back to her, the memory flowing freely, sending a flash of confidence and strength into her veins.

She walked slowly back to the glass entrance doors, treading carefully on the balls of her feet, tense and ready to fight or flee.

Instead of turning right to the side door, she turned left. A glimmer of light showed another fire exit, right at the end of the mall. On the floor, black in the sliver of light, was another smear of blood. Larger this time, and pooling thickly on the concrete tiles.

33

'Oh God... *Melissa? Jonas?*' Her voice came out in a sob of fear.

She suddenly heard Jonas' voice in her head, once again remembering their conversation in the shadows. He had seemed edgy, scared, and she had been distracted from his actual words, focusing on Melissa:

'*Sometimes for larger deliveries, I use the fire exit at the back. Security don't like it, but it's the only way to get the larger, heavier pieces in here.*'

Chloe glanced back, sickened by the blood. She should wait for the security guards, for Peter, but a tiny noise drew her attention back to the fire exit. But then she heard it. A moan, followed by a low grunt of pain.

'*Jonas?*' Before she could think, she was moving quickly. The door opened easily when she pressed the bar, and a pile of boxes was sat outside. There was a van, with the back open, and the tailgate down.

Bewildered, she glanced around, seeing nothing but shadows.

'*Chloe?*'

He was lying further along the wall, his face contorted with pain, arms outstretched as though he had been trying to crawl away.

'Oh my God, are you okay? What happened to you?' She knelt beside him, scrabbling for tissues to blot his cuts, giving up and taking off her shirt.

The wound to his forehead was still bleeding, sluggishly, and she held the soft fabric to this, applying firm pressure.

His mouth was swollen and bruised, but he managed to speak, slowly and painfully. 'Chloe, you need to go after him. He's got Melissa and he's leaving now. You need to stop him...' He paused, wincing and clutching his ribs. 'That bastard. He'll kill her...'

'*Who*? Who are you talking about?' Chloe was looking wildly around. 'Where has he gone?'

'Arron, of course. He found out we were planning to leave tonight. God knows how.' Jonas was gasping in pain, writhing on the ground. 'I tried to follow but they hit me with something and knocked me out.'

'Arron? Where has he gone?'

'Chloe, please, please get the police. He went towards Snorkel Beach. He's got two of his bodyguards with him... You can see...' His voice trailed off as he passed once again into unconsciousness.

As he did so Chloe heard a scream, high and clear, carrying across the night air. Again, she responded without thinking. Instead of calling the police, gripped her torch, and ran through the moonlit darkness in the direction of Snorkel Beach.

In the daylight, the beach was a family attraction. A shallow cove sheltered by the high wall of Dockyard. In the evening it became a bar and club where teenagers and cruise-ship passengers partied the night away.

But the venue was closed for maintenance tonight, with a

red sign warning tourists to keep away across the entrance. The beach was in darkness now, populated only with shadows. Chloe tried to see what was happening; peering, trembling, into the blackness. She could hear muted voices, splashes, followed by a male voice raised in anger. She slipped through the barrier, and skirted carefully around the main wooden building.

A boat was moored off the beach, with a smaller, inflatable craft now being unloaded onto it. Another scream made the hairs on the back of her arms and neck rise, and she found she was shaking.

Melissa. Chloe sent one desperate glance back up the beach, but could see nothing. It was up to her. She edged along the wall and kicked off her shoes, before easing slowly into the sea. Seaweed on the rocks was treacherously slippery, and she held her breath as the cold water reached up to her chest.

Keeping in the shadows on the wall, she swam out to the point where her cover stopped, as the wall curved away to the west. She blinked salty water from her eyes, breath coming in little gasps.

Final preparations seemed to be being made on board the larger boat, and now she was closer, Chloe could see the outlines of figures. At least four men, and a figure slumped on the deck near the railings, hands tied behind their back. Melissa? And was Arron down below deck?

She hardly hesitated, and so focused on her mission that there was no time for fear as she struck out into the waves. Chloe swam smoothly and swiftly to the right of the boat, keeping out the way of the few lights that decorated the rigging. She was vague on boats, but this one looked sleek and powerful. It also had, she saw as she swam closer, a ladder that dropped down from the deck to the sea. A pleasure craft then or was this a special adaptation to allow goods to be passed up more easily?

The men had finished their task. Two went below deck, and

the two others stepped back into the inflatable. The sharp buzz of an engine roared briefly and it shot away, coasting over the breakers, heading out to sea.

Now Chloe was close enough to the vessel to haul herself up the ladder. She was shivering and her muscles screamed with exertion. A cautious look over the top revealed the slumped figure was indeed Melissa. The men were still busy below deck, talking in lowered voices.

'*Melissa!*'

Chloe padded over and touched her shoulder. The girl jumped, turning terrified eyes towards her. Her hands were bound behind her back, but her legs were free. A piece of silver tape served as a gag.

Chloe fumbled for a moment with what appeared to be plastic ties holding Melissa's hands in place. But they were too strong to break. Instead, she ripped the tape off her mouth and spoke quickly in her ear, 'Can you swim? We need to get over the side now.'

'Yes,' Melissa breathed. 'You might need to help me, but I can use my legs. Is it just you? Have you seen Jonas? Is he all right?'

'Yes, and he's hurt but okay. Come on.' Chloe pulled her to her feet, and urged her towards the ladder. Too late, she realised there was no way the girl could climb with no hands. 'I'll have to push you overboard, but I'll be right next to you. Look, we'll go through this gap in the rails...'

'Do it.'

'Okay, one, two, three, *jump!*' Chloe grabbed Melissa's shoulder, hanging on to her shirt as they both leapt off the boat.

The noise of a double splash brought the men up on deck and Chloe heard yells of anger. But she was too busy hauling Melissa away from the boat to give them any attention.

'*Melissa*? What the hell are you doing?' The man added to his companion, 'Turn the lights on and get her back.'

He clearly didn't realise Melissa had a companion in the water. Chloe swam harder, shoulder muscles screaming in pain, towing the girl behind her. Melissa was kicking her legs, occasionally ducking her whole upper body underwater to make it easier for Chloe to pull her along by her bound hands. They were both gasping for breath, straining to get away from the vessel.

But escape wasn't going to be easy. The noise of an engine starting ripped through the night, just as the two women reached the outermost curve of the wall. Two powerful floodlights illuminated the water, casting this way and that, like cat's eyes searching for prey.

'Stay near the wall, and when I say, duck under again,' Chloe managed to shout.

Melissa nodded, and as the light swung towards them the boat began to move.

'*Now!*'

Chloe held her breath for as long as she could, but the unfamiliar exertion of the night had taken a toll on her body, and she burst out of the waves too quickly. The white glare was unforgiving, and she thought she heard a shout of triumph, followed by another splash.

'Damian is coming after us!' Melissa shouted over the noise of the vessel.

The boat turned swiftly and easily towards the trapped women, washing up frothy waves and bashing both of them against the rocks that lay under the wall. Pinned in the floodlight, they were sitting ducks for the bodyguard, who was slicing through the water with a powerful front crawl.

'Two of you!' he said, clearly surprised. He reached them and made a grab for Melissa.

Chloe shoved him hard in the chest, lashing out with bare feet underwater. For a second he was caught off balance, and she was able to pull Melissa away, spreading her arms wide to shield her. 'Leave her alone! The police are coming...' God, she hoped Peter had found the security guard, and that they had called the police. In her haste to follow Melissa, she hadn't rung them as Jonas had asked.

Arron was hanging over the side of the boat, and seeing the cowering women, laughed. 'Chloe, the nosy art lover. Who would have thought? What are you doing down there?'

She shouted, 'I've already seen Jonas. He told me everything. The police are coming, so go if you must, but leave Melissa alone.'

'Damian, bring them both in. It will be nice for my daughter to have a bit of female company on her long trip. For me too... Come on, man, they are two pathetic women, surely you can deal with them.'

'Damian, please,' Melissa gasped out, 'just let us go! The police really are coming.'

The big man seemed to hesitate, but in that second Chloe saw lights and figures on the beach, and felt her heart leap. '*Help!* We're over here,' she yelled.

The large boat and its floodlights had effectively illuminated the scene and uniformed officers were already launching their own inflatable, and some were wading into the sea.

Damian, panicking, began to swim back to the craft. But it seemed that Arron was cutting his losses as he gunned the boat and began to gain speed.

'He's getting away!' Chloe shouted, as she and Melissa staggered into the shallows to meet their rescuers.

A man leant down from the inflatable and offered a hand. 'Don't worry, he won't get far.'

She took his hand and was hauled dripping onto the boat,

just as other vessels, blue lights flashing, could be seen zipping across the water.

'See?'

She turned back, checking Melissa was also safe, and registered that the man was Finn. 'It was Arron. Melissa and Jonas were trying to get away from him and he...' It all came out in a rush and her chattering teeth were no help at all.

The silver foil blanket that someone slipped around her shoulders was very welcome as the chill sea breeze cut through her soaked dress.

'It's okay, we know. Well, most of it anyway. We saw Jonas on the way down.'

'You know more than I do, then,' Chloe muttered, still shaking.

'Is Jonas really all right? My stepfather said he would get Damian to beat him up because he had double-crossed him,' Melissa put in. She held her hands out in front now, wincing as she rubbed her wrists. 'We were trying to leave him. Chloe, I'm sorry for dragging you into this but it seemed like our last chance.'

'Jonas will be fine. He's on his way to hospital,' Finn told her reassuringly.

The boat began to move slowly back to the beach, and when they got out Chloe found her legs were shaky. Finn slipped a hand under her elbow to steady her.

'Chloe came to rescue me.' Melissa managed a smile, although, as the light shone on her face, her rescuers could see numerous bruises, and a long cut across her forehead. 'He always said he wouldn't kill me, but this time... He was so mad...'

34

Back in Dockyard, amidst the flashing lights, Melissa sat huddled under her foil blanket next to Chloe. 'He found out about me and Matthew, and he didn't like it. He never liked me to have close friends or boyfriends unless he had something on them, some kind of blackmail he could use against them. He always said friends and lovers have to be useful or there is no point in them.'

'Did you plan to run away with Matthew? Sorry, I'm still struggling to keep up,' Chloe said gently.

'Arron has always been very controlling. Ever since our father died he has used us in the business. He doesn't just run legitimate galleries selling artwork, he has all kinds of dirty deals going on. Gradually, as we got older, we realised we were part of it.' Her grey eyes filled with tears. 'He has always been violent too. With my mother, with us. She realised far too late what kind of a man he was, but she never had the strength to leave, even when we begged her.'

'Oh, Melissa, I'm sorry...' Chloe said softly.

She ran her tongue over her sore lips, and shrugged. 'He sat us down when I was eighteen and showed us that we had already been part of his stolen art rackets, his drug deals, and money-muling. Of course, we had no idea, because until then it had just been business. If he asked us to pick up a package from the New York gallery and take it to a collector in Sau Paulo then we did, no questions asked. But we were delivering stolen goods, dirty money, all kinds of things. He wouldn't ever have let us go.'

'You and Jonas were essential to his dirty business. What happened with Matthew?' Chloe asked. 'Was it because he found out about the stolen art and the real business?'

Melissa took a deep breath, gratefully accepting the hot cup of coffee Peter pushed into her hands. 'Not entirely. The package I gave to you is the original *Painted Lady*. Matt painted a smaller version before he did the larger copy. He wanted me to have it because...'

'Because it's you!' Chloe exclaimed, suddenly seeing the distorted female body in the scarlet sea, the grey eyes and perfect red lips. 'You were his muse?'

'Yes.' She gave a sad, secret smile. 'I loved him. We met in New York, dated secretly while he was still seeing Kaila. He broke it off with her for me, and she went mad. She was dealing drugs and tried to get him into the whole scene. He was kind of on the edge until I persuaded him it was a bad idea. But Kaila didn't kill him. Or poison Sheetal.'

'Dear God,' Chloe said.

'The money and the painting were for us to run away together. He was going to give everything up for me. We would still paint, but not to sell. We loved each other.' She wiped away a tear. 'Jonas was going to come too. We would never leave each other with Arron.'

'But wasn't Matthew already rich? His work was selling, and *The Painted Lady*, the large version must have made him enough that he could have whisked you away anywhere he wanted,' Chloe said, confused.

'No. My stepfather held all the money, and paid it in instalments. Matt never would sign with an agent, which was a mistake. Once Arron found out about me dating Matt, he told him he could only have it if we split up.'

'Emma at the shop said you had a fight with Matthew the night he was killed.'

Melissa nodded. 'We staged it, hoping enough people would see and think we had broken up. By then, we were ready. Matt had bought plane tickets, arranged everything, but my stepfather is so strong and powerful... He knows everyone and can go everywhere. That night he asked me if it was true we were leaving him, that Matt and I were still lovers. I lied and told him I wasn't but he hit me...'

'It's okay, go on.' Chloe wrapped an arm comfortingly around her trembling body.

'My phone kept ringing, because Jonas and Matt must have got worried when I didn't show up at the meeting point. We had a place to stay and then we were catching the first flight out in the morning.'

'How did Arron find out you were going?'

'He tapped our phones and had cameras all over the duplex. He said we were ungrateful... Matt walked in as he hit me, and went mad. He said if Arron didn't let us leave and then left us alone, he would tell the police about the stolen art, about the money, the abuse, everything.'

'So Arron was trapped.'

'He had his bodyguards with him but they weren't in the room when we were arguing. I think Arron saw at that point he couldn't control Matt as he controlled everyone else and he didn't know what else to do. I didn't even know he carried a knife...' Melissa was staring into the distance now, her voice a monotone as she recounted the horrors of that night. One pale hand slipped up and rubbed her bruised forehead. '...He lunged at Matt and got him in the chest, again and again. I was screaming and someone hit me from behind. I think perhaps it was Frankie... When I woke up it was dark, they had all gone, and there was blood everywhere.'

'And he came back after he dumped Matthew's body?'

'Yes, they all did. Damian and Frankie helped him. They cleared everything up, and Arron told me if I opened my mouth Jonas would be as good as dead. I was... I couldn't think straight, and I was half crazy about Matt's death. I couldn't cope with Jonas being killed too. He insisted we were both back at work that day, the day you came to visit.'

'You were certainly both very cool,' Chloe said, looking back at the slightly awkward conversation.

'We are used to behaving as though nothing has happened after Arron gets in one of his rages. Even murder... but we knew we would still run. That's why I brought the painting and money to you for safekeeping that night. Jonas distracted Arron and I slipped out. I was back before it was light.' She half smiled. 'I hardly slept in your spare bed after all your kindness. I just lay awake thinking about how we could still get away, and yet somehow let the police know Arron had killed Matthew.'

Finn, approached from the shadows with a grim look on his face. 'We've got him. The coastguards were able to intercept his craft and board it. We also extracted a man from the water.'

'Damian,' Chloe said, with a shiver that had nothing to do with her soaked clothing. 'I think there was another man on board too?'

'Luke, Frankie and Elijah as well. They drive the boat and run errands. They'll be long gone by now. They took the inflatable.' Melissa stared at Chloe, pursing her lips. 'It carries loads of equipment and spare fuel.'

'When you feel up to it, I need to take a statement from you,

Melissa, but let's get you checked out in hospital first, shall we?' Finn suggested.

She nodded, and he offered a hand to Chloe and gently pulled her up from the crate she was sitting on. 'I can't believe you swam out to rescue Melissa yourself. Why didn't you wait for Peter and the security guards? He was beside himself with worry when we got here. He said he came back, found Jonas unconscious, you gone and called 911 straight away.'

'I know, and I do feel bad. It was pretty stupid.' Chloe glanced down at the girl, who smiled up at her. 'I heard Melissa scream and just ran. There wasn't any time to think.'

Finn squeezed her hand. His own was large and warm, and his dark eyes fixed on her face. 'Well I think you're very brave, Chloe. Maybe leave the dangerous stuff to us in the future, though... I assume there will be a future?' he added anxiously. 'This hasn't put you off staying on the island?'

Chloe rubbed her bruises, breathed in the salty air and returned his smile. 'No, I'm pretty happy here, actually. I would never have been chasing down murderers, or even starting my own business back in London. Bermuda clearly brings out the best in me' – she clapped a hand to her mouth – 'Oh God, I must get back to Hilda!'

Chloe slept late after her night-time escapades, and woke with bruises and a sore head. Calling Finn right away, as promised, he sounded pleased to hear from her.

'You know what I can't figure out? Why did you think Kaila had killed Matthew?' Chloe asked. 'The papers said something about DNA and drug deals.'

Finn sighed down the phone. 'Arron led us right up the garden path on that one. He hired some professionals to leave

DNA evidence at the scene, to go through her whole life, leaving little clues for us to follow. It was easy enough, because she has made some bad life choices. The drug dealing was a prime example.'

'I see...' Chloe was still trying to take it all in.

'And finally, they made an attempt on Sheetal's life to ensure the heat was off Matthew's murder. It was a very good effort, and I can honestly say Kaila might have gone down for this if Melissa and Jonas hadn't planned to do a last-minute runner, and it hadn't all gone pear-shaped.'

'I think Melissa was telling the truth when she said once they got away she would have somehow told the police about Arron,' Chloe said thoughtfully. 'But you never seemed totally happy with Kaila as the perpetrator?'

'It was that obvious was it?' Finn laughed. 'I'm going to have to be careful what I say around you, aren't I?'

'I guess you are.' Chloe smiled into the phone.

35

At home in her sunlit kitchen, bruises fading, Chloe pulled up the news pages again.

Melissa and Jonas were both out of hospital and had been in touch to say they hoped to stay and run the gallery once all the legal wrangling was over, which apparently could take years. Melissa had been in tears on the phone, thanking Chloe for her kindness, and at that moment, Chloe realised how much the girl, and probably her brother too, had been keeping behind closed doors, beneath icy exteriors. It was horrifying that a murder had finally led them to safety.

Chloe sighed, and made herself another mug of coffee. She did hope it would work out for them. Before she shut down the computer, on impulse, she googled another name.

It seemed a little macabre, and she felt faintly guilty for even looking as she read the accounts of Finn's wife's death. But something had been niggling away in the back of her mind. She paused after the first page, frowning at the paragraphs.

It had been there all the time. A scooter had sent Ellie's car careering off the road. The driver, Jordan, had served time in a rehabilitation centre. The final account she discovered, was longer, with more detail. It stated the only witness to the crash had been a Mr Ellis Jack, of Green Ridge Stables. Mr Jack was quoted as saying:

> 'I was a way behind Mrs Harlow's car, but I saw the scooter coming on the wrong side of the road. The driver had a helmet on so I didn't see his face. By the time I'd stopped the car and run to the edge, I was in a right state, but I remember the scooter had stopped on the other side of the road. The driver was just sitting there, and I just took it for granted he would come and help. But when I remembered to look again, he was gone.'

But what if there had been two people on the scooter? Two teenage boys who had thought it might be fun to steal a scooter and drive at speed along the dangerous road. If Ellis Jack had been a witness, protecting Alfie for Ailsa's sake, but lied in his statement, it would be a perfect motive for blackmail.

She checked the dates. One of the boys might have been celebrating winning a sports scholarship, and when the crash happened they switched places – Alfie running off and Jordan staying to face the tragedy they had created. Ellis backing up the story. Jordan had taken the blame. Ellis must have seen both boys on the scooter.

It was guesswork, but it fitted. Chloe sat back, reading and rereading as the story unfolded in her head. She closed her eyes, horrified by the enormity of the deception. 'You wanted to know,' she chided herself. She had wanted all her puzzle pieces fitting neatly together, but that wasn't life, was it? Life was ragged edges and missing parts, and she had forced her way to the truth.

Her face was wet with tears, and she scrubbed them crossly away.

~

'You're right,' Ailsa said, tears in her eyes when Chloe gently confronted her.

'So Ellis lied for them?'

'He knew Alfie had just got the sports scholarship, knew how much it meant to me. He would have lost it because of one awful mistake. Jordan could easily have been driving. They were terrible when they were together, used to egg each other on. Ellis came to see me when it was over and told me what really happened, but he promised he wouldn't say another word.'

'He killed himself for another reason too then, to protect the secret he threatened to reveal?'

'Yes.' She looked up, her own lashes damp. 'I'd like to think he had retained a little bit of the old Ellis, and it wasn't just a case of if he couldn't have what he wanted, that was the end. But we'll never know.'

Chloe wandered to the edge of the garden, taking in the sea and sky, her heart pounding. 'Does Finn know?'

'He guessed. After Ellis shot himself he came over to Cheryl's and we talked. He's a good man, and sees no reason to tear everything apart again.'

It had been both twins on the scooter, both of their faults, but Alfie had come so far since the accident, and Jordan seemed to have atoned for his faults. And it had been an accident. It wouldn't bring Finn's wife back, it would hurt Cheryl and destroy Alfie's career if she didn't keep the secret. 'I suppose that's what it comes down to. That it won't bring Ellie back, I mean.'

'That's right.'

Chloe stared at her. 'Ailsa, did you happen to send me any text messages recently?'

Ailsa looked away, flicking a fly from the air around her face. 'Text? No, I make phone calls, me.'

Chloe smiled to herself, watching her neighbour's averted profile, and swept her hair back from her face, plaiting it quickly, decisively.

When she glanced up, Ailsa met her eyes. The Longtails twisted and dived in the wide blueness above, and the sea whispered softly below them. 'What are you going to do now, Chloe?'

'I'm going for a ride,' she said crisply. 'Oh watch out, I can see that cockerel coming after your hens again!'

36

Chloe went back to her own house, changed into her pink shirt and jeans, called Hilda and headed for the yard.

Antoine was cleaning tack. 'Bookings are up again. We're jam-packed for the next month. The farrier's coming on Tuesday and a mate of mine is coming tomorrow to start work on the new building.'

'That's great news. Have I got time to take Goldie out for a quick ride?'

He glanced at his watch, surprised. 'Sure. I'm taking Star and Jupiter for the next one anyway. Go for it. Do you want me to tack up?'

'No thanks, I can easily do it myself, and you're busy,' Chloe said briskly.

Antoine wandered over as she whistled to the dog, who was exploring the muck-heap. 'It's just a case of getting your confidence back,' he told her cheerfully. 'The more you ride, the easier it'll get.'

The sun was bright in the sky, the sea a smooth turquoise, and the salty spring air touched Chloe's lips and face with gentle fingers. Hilda trotted happily next to the horse, occasionally diving into the undergrowth after imagined monsters, but always scurrying back to her mistress when Chloe whistled.

The high season was coming, and she was in Bermuda. And she was happy. The thought came as a shock. Happy and confident. Dre's last gift to her had been her best.

Gently, she tugged a rein and Goldie plodded towards the beach trail. The trees overhead made a dusty canopy, full of shadows, but as they passed the place where Matthew's body had lain, the trail was clear.

There were no ghosts today. Chloe rode on, down towards the pink-and white-sand, and the frothy waves.

THE END

AFTERWORD

CHLOE'S BERMUDA

Bermuda is definitely an island to fall in love with, and if you are planning a visit, you can follow in Chloe's footsteps and enjoy some of her favourite places. As this novel is a work of fiction, some places mentioned are imagined, but where possible, genuine destinations have been used:

Horseshoe Bay

This is a magnificent sweep of sand, and one of the most popular beaches on Bermuda. There are a couple of concessions – a cafe, toilets, showers, shop and the parking is plentiful. If you walk along the bay, away from the main beach, you can explore the picturesque coves beyond, like **Chaplin Bay**.

The Ocean Club

Chloe and Finn enjoyed dinner at this lovely restaurant in Southampton Parish, which is owned by the Fairmont Hotel. The menu is fish-based, the venue is right on the beach, and you can eat outside on the veranda and watch the sun go down.

Horse riding

Beachside Stables, the equestrian personalities and establishments in this series are entirely fictional, but if you fancy some riding on the island, try **Watson Performance and Trail Horses,** in **Warwick Parish.** Mike Watson is a professional horseman and offers lessons and trail rides on beautiful quarter horses.

St Catherine's Fort

Chloe and Finn spent the day in and around **St George's** and **St Catherine's Fort** and beach and they are around a 5km hike from the town. If you can drag yourself away from the beauty and history of the town, including **The Unfinished Church** on Government Hill Road, the fort and beach are well worth a visit. Break your hike at **Tobacco Bay Beach** for a drink in the cafe, before continuing uphill. This beach is also one of the best for snorkelling, with its beautiful, clear, shallow waters. Snorkel gear can be rented from the kiosks on the beach so you don't need to lug everything around if you are hiking further up the hill. The towering limestone rock formations are a haven for marine life and you might spot blue parrotfish, angelfish and grouper.

There is also an excellent bus service for those less mobile.

The Royal Naval Dockyard

Dockyard is easily worth a day of exploration. Although the community shop run by Emma is fictitious, there is a local produce store, and other shops nestled amongst the former military buildings where you can pick up rum cakes, souvenirs and essentials.

The imposing grey stone buildings are fascinating and a trip up to the **Commissioner's House** and the **Museum** is highly recommended.

The Clocktower Mall

Although the **Stone Gallery** is an author creation, **Clocktower Mall** does indeed contain some wonderful galleries, clothing stores, jewellery makers and crafters. After chatting to the busy creatives you will definitely want to stop off at the **Haagen Dazs Bar** and sample some luscious ice cream.

Snorkel Beach

Chloe pulls off a dramatic rescue on **Snorkel Beach**, which is located within the walls of Dockyard. The small beach has a safe, shallow area for children in the daytime and a lively music and bar scene in the balmy evenings.

The Swizzle Inn

Bermuda has two national drinks; Firstly, the 'Dark 'n' Stormy', which is made with Gosling's Black Seal rum, ginger beer, and a twist of lime. Its origins trace back to WWi when sailors discovered adding a splash of local Gosling's rum to ginger beer made a tasty drink. Secondly, the 'Rum Swizzle', a punch, was said to be invented at **The Swizzle Inn** in 1932. Patrons are said to, 'swagger in and stagger out', so you have been warned!

The original **Swizzle Inn** is Bermuda's oldest pub. Situated in Hamilton Parish on Bailey's Bay and great for families.

Sister pub **The Swizzle (South Shore)** is in Warwick Parish on South Shore Road. There is a bus stop opposite the pub. Chloe drops in for a bite to eat after her hike around **Tom Moore's Jungle**.

Both pubs have an excellent, varied food menu too.

Bonefish Bar and Grill

Chloe has lunch here when she visits the Royal Naval Dockyard for the first time. Excellent indoor/outdoor dining, waterfront views, and perfect for a sandwich and cold drink in the day or something more in the evening. Can be very busy when cruise ships are docked, but this applies to the whole area.

Fishcakes

When Chloe first arrives on Bermuda, her neighbour, Ailsa, gives her some home-made fishcakes. There are a great many different recipes for codfish cakes, and these are traditionally served as a Sunday breakfast dish. These became a popular dish when traders in the 18th century used to trade salt (made by evaporating seawater) for codfish from the incoming fishermen. For a luscious, indulgent breakfast try codfish cakes, and Portuguese doughnuts.

Tom Moore's Jungle/The Blue Hole

Chloe sneaks off for the day, challenging herself to an adventure and ends up here. The jungle is in Hamilton Parish and the bus stops right across the road from where the trail starts. The going can be a little rough, but the jungle isn't huge (approx twelve acres) and you reach *The Blue Hole* after about fifteen minutes hiking. The signage isn't great but the paths are all well trodden.

The views from the coastal path are stunning, and you can dip into the sea for a swim if you don't mind the sharp rocks. There are a lot of caves in the jungle and they are fascinating. Signage asks that you don't swim in these beautiful natural rock formations, but you can go right underground to take pictures. Just watch your head as the roofs are often low!

The Blue Hole is nothing short of amazing, which is why I wanted Chloe to experience it at a time when she was rediscovering herself. The water is ice cold and vivid turquoise.

One the other side of the jungle is *Tom Moore's Tavern*, perfect for a drink and snack, or if you return the other way, *The*

Swizzle Inn is just half a mile up the road, and is where Chloe stopped to refuel.

Getting around Bermuda

Chloe uses the bus for most of her trips and the public transport system is economic and efficient. Taxis are expensive.

For more information on Bermuda visit: www.gotobermuda.com

ACKNOWLEDGEMENTS

Huge thank you to British Airways, for rostering me Bermuda flights all those years ago, and thus allowing the original inspiration for this book to take shape. I am lucky to have travelled to so many wonderful destinations as cabin crew, but Bermuda retains a special place in my heart.

Much thanks to my wonderful agent, Lina Langlee, for believing in this book, and my writing in general, and to the fabulous team at Bloodhound Books for publishing the Chloe Canton Mysteries.

Thanks also due to the epic team of bloggers, readers and reviewers – I write for you, and read every single one of your reviews and messages.

Daisy x

A NOTE FROM THE PUBLISHER

Thank you for reading this book. If you enjoyed it please do consider leaving a review on Amazon to help others find it too.

We hate typos. All of our books have been rigorously edited and proofread, but sometimes mistakes do slip through. If you have spotted a typo, please do let us know and we can get it amended within hours.

info@bloodhoundbooks.com

LOVE CRIME, THRILLER AND MYSTERY BOOKS?

Join our mailing list to hear about our latest
releases and receive exclusive offers.

Sign up today to be the first to hear about new releases and exclusive offers, including free and discounted ebooks!

SIGN UP

Why not like us or follow us on social media to stay up to date with the latest news from your favourite authors?

YOU WILL ALSO ENJOY:

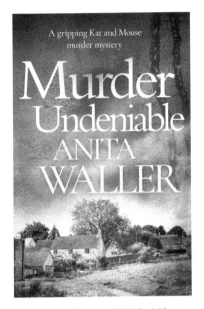

Anita Waller's Murder Undeniable

BUY NOW